The War has begun! MVFOL

A band of desperate heroes will risk all to unite a world on the brink of destruction. From them will arise one of the greatest heroes Ansalon has ever known, a leader to forge the forces of good into a mighty weapon against the darkness.

But the forces of the Dark Queen are moving, conquering or destroying all who oppose them. Their march will take them across the free lands of Ansalon . . .

To the Gates of Palanthas.

CHRONICLES

By Margaret Weis & Tracy Hickman

A Rumor of Dragons

Night of the Dragons

The Nightmare Lands

To the Gates of Palanthas

Hope's Flame
(January 2004)

A dawn of Dragons
(March 2004)

CHRONICLES

PART
4

TO THE
GATES
OF
PALANTHAS

MARGARET WEIS & TRACY HICKMAN

COVER ART
Glen Angus

INTERIOR ART
Vinod Rams

MIRROR
STONE

TO THE GATES OF PALANTHAS

©2003 Wizards of the Coast, Inc.

Distributed in the United States by Holtzbrinck Publishing. Distributed in Canada by Fenn Ltd.

Distributed to the hobby, toy, and comic trade in the United States and Canada by regional distributors.

Distributed worldwide by Wizards of the Coast, Inc. and regional distributors.

Printed in the U.S.A.

Cover art by Glen Angus
Cartography by Dennis Kauth
First Printing: October 2003
Library of Congress Catalog Card Number: 2003100844

9 8 7 6 5 4 3

US ISBN: 0-7869-3096-9
UK ISBN: 0-7869-3097-7
620-86040-001-EN

U.S., CANADA,	EUROPEAN HEADQUARTERS
ASIA, PACIFIC, & LATIN AMERICA	Wizards of the Coast, Belgium
Wizards of the Coast, Inc.	T. Hosfveld 6d
P.O. Box 707	1702 Groot-Bijgaarden
Renton, WA 98057-0707	Belgium
+1-800-324-6496	+322 457 3350

Visit our web site at **www.mirrorstonebooks.com**

To my parents, Dr. and Mrs. Harold R. Hickman, who
taught me what true honor is.
—Tracy Raye Hickman

To my parents, Frances and George Weis, who gave me a
gift more precious than life—the love of books.
—Margaret Weis

We gratefully acknowledge the help of the authors of
the Advanced Dungeons & Dragons® Dragonlance®
roleplaying adventure game modules:

Douglas Niles, *Dragons of Ice*; Jeff Grubb,
Dragons of Light; and Laura Hickman, co-author,
Dragons of War.

Finally, to Michael: *Est Sularus oth Mithas.*

continent of ansalon

1 palanthas
2 high clerist tower
3 kalaman
4 gooshome
5 neraka
6 sanction
7 flotsam
8 solace
9 thorbardin
10 tarsis

blood sea
of istar

gooolund

noromaar

estwilde

khur

ballfor

silvanesti

solamna

new
sea

northern
ergoth

southern
ergoth

qualinesti

plains of dust

ice wall

sirrion
sea

Table of Contents

The story of the companions' journey to Ice Wall Castle and their defeat of the evil Dragon Highlord, Feal-thas, became legend among the Ice Barbarians who inhabit that desolate land. It is still told by the village cleric on long winter nights when heroic deeds are remembered and songs are sung.

Song of the Ice Reaver

I am the one who brought them back.
I am Raggart I am telling you this.
Snow upon snow cancels the signals of ice
Over the snow the sun bleeds whiteness
In cold light forever unbearable.
And if I do not tell you this
The snow descends on the deeds of heroes
And their strength in my singing
Lies down in a core of frost rising no more
No more as the lost breath crumbles.

Seven they were from the hot lands
(I am the one who brought them back)
Four swordsmen sworn in the North
The elf-woman Laurana
The dwarf from the floes of stone
The kender small-boned as a hawk.
Riding three blades they came to the tunnel
To the throat of the only castle.

Down among Thanoi the old guardians
Where their swordsmen carved hot air
Finding tendon finding bone

As the tunnels melted red.
Down upon minotaur upon ice bear
And the swords whistled again
Bright on the corner of madness
The tunnel knee-high in arms
In claws in unspeakable things
As the swordsmen descended
Bright steam freezing behind them.

Then to the chambers at the castle heart
Where Feal-thas awaited lord of dragons and wolves
Armored in white that is nothing
That covers the ice as the sun bleeds whiteness.
And he called on the wolves the baby-stealers
Who suckled on murder in the lairs of ancestors.
Around the heroes a circle of knives of craving
As the wolves stalked in their master's eye.

And Aran the first to break the circle
Hot wind at the throat of Feal-thas
Brought down and unraveled
In the reel of the hunt perfected.
Brian the next when the sword of the wolf lord
Sent him seeking the warm lands.
All stood frozen in the wheel of razors
All stood frozen except for Laurana.
Blind in a hot light flashing the crown of the mind
Where death melts in a diving sun
She takes up the Ice Reaver
And over the boil of wolves over the slaughter
Bearing a blade of ice bearing darkness
She opened the throat of the wolf lord
And the wolves fell silent as the head collapsed.

The rest is short in the telling.
Destroying the eggs the violent get of the dragons
A tunnel of scales and ordure
Followed into the terrible larder
Followed further followed to treasure.
There the orb danced blue danced white
Swelled like a heart in its endless beating
(They let me hold it I brought them back).
Out from the tunnel blood on blood under the ice
Bearing their own incredible burden
The young knights silent and tattered
They came five now only
The kender last small pockets bulging.
I am Raggart I am telling you this.
I am the one who brought them back.

TO THE GATES OF PALANTHAS

DARK JOURNEY.

1

Behind them, the snow rumbled and toppled over the side of the mountain. Cascading down in white sheets, blocking and choking the pass, it obliterated their presence. The echoes of Gilthanas's magical thunder still resounded in the air, or perhaps it was the booming of the rocks as they bounded down the slopes. They could not be certain.

The companions, led by Silvara, traveled the trails east slowly and cautiously, walking where it was rocky, avoiding the snowy patches if at all possible. They walked through each other's footsteps so that the pursuing elves would never know for certain how many were in their party. They were so careful, in fact, that Laurana grew worried.

"Remember, we want them to find *us*," she said to Silvara as they crept across the top of a rocky defile.

"Do not be upset. They will have no trouble finding us," answered Silvara.

"What makes you so certain?" Laurana started to ask, then she slipped and fell to her hands and knees. Gilthanas helped her stand. Grimacing with pain, she stared at Silvara in silence. None of them, including Theros, trusted the sudden change that had come over the Wilder elf since their parting with the knights. But they had no choice except to follow her.

"Because they know our destination," Silvara answered. "You were clever to think I left a sign to them in the cave. I did. Fortunately, you did not find it. Below those sticks you so kindly scattered for me I had drawn a crude map. When they find it, they will think I drew it to show you our destination. You made it look most realistic, Laurana." Her voice was defiant until she met Gilthanas's eyes.

The elflord turned away from her, his face grave. Silvara faltered. Her voice became pleading. "I did it for a reason, a good reason. I knew then, when I saw the tracks, we would have to split up. You must believe me!"

"What about the dragon orb? What were you doing with it?" Laurana demanded.

"N-nothing," Silvara stammered. "You must trust me!"

"I don't see why," Laurana returned coldly.

"I have done you no harm—" Silvara began.

"Unless you have sent the knights and the dragon orb into a deathtrap!" Laurana cried.

"No!" Silvara wrung her hands. "I haven't! Believe me. They will be safe. That has been my plan all along. Nothing must happen to the dragon orb. Above all, it must not fall into the hands of the elves. That is why I sent it away. That is why I helped you escape!" She glanced around, seeming to sniff the air like an animal. "Come! We have lingered too long."

"If we go with you at all!" Gilthanas said harshly. "What do you know about the dragon orb?"

"Don't ask me!" Silvara's voice was suddenly deep and filled with sadness. Her blue eyes stared into Gilthanas's with such love that he could not bear to face her. He shook his head, avoiding her gaze. Silvara caught hold of his arm.

"Please, *shalori*, beloved, trust me! Remember what we talked about, at the pool. You said you had to do these things—defy your people, become an outcast, because of what you believed in your heart. I said that I understood, that I had to do the same. Didn't you believe me?"

Gilthanas stood a moment, his head bowed. "I believed you," he said softly. Reaching out, he pulled her to him, kissing her silver hair. "We'll go with you. Come on, Laurana." Arms around each other, the two trudged off through the snow.

Laurana looked blankly at the others. They avoided her eyes. Then Theros came up to her.

"I've lived in this world nearly fifty years, young woman," he said gently. "Not long to you elves, I know. But we humans live those years, we don't just let them drift by. And I'll tell you this—that girl loves your brother as truly as I've ever seen woman love man. And he loves her. Such love cannot come to evil. For the sake of their love alone, I'd follow them into a dragon's den."

The smith walked after the two.

"For the sake of my cold feet, I'd follow them into a dragon's den, if he'd warm my toes!" Flint stamped on the ground. "Come on, let's go." Grabbing the kender, he dragged Tas along after the blacksmith.

Laurana remained standing, alone. That she would follow was settled. She had no choice. She wanted to trust Theros's words. One time, she would have believed the world ran that way. But now she knew much she had believed in was false. Why not love?

All she could see in her mind were the swirling colors of the dragon orb.

The companions traveled east, into the gloom of gathering night. Descending from the high mountain pass, they found the air easier to breathe. The frozen rocks gave way to scraggly pines, then the forests closed in around them once more. Silvara confidently led them at last into a fog-shrouded valley.

The Wilder elf no longer seemed to care about covering their tracks. All that concerned her now was speed. She pushed the group on, as if racing the sun across the sky. When night fell, they sank into the tree-rimmed darkness, too tired even to eat. But Silvara allowed them only a few hours of restless, aching sleep. When the moons rose, the silver and the red, nearing their fullness now, she urged the companions on.

When anyone questioned, wearily, why they hurried, she only answered, "They are near. They are very near."

Each assumed she meant the elves, though Laurana had long ago lost the feeling of dark shapes trailing them.

Dawn broke, but the light was filtered through fog so thick Tasslehoff thought he might grab a handful and store it in one of his pouches. The companions walked close together, even holding hands to avoid being separated. The air grew warmer. They shed their wet and heavy cloaks as they stumbled along a trail that seemed to materialize beneath their feet, out of the fog. Silvara walked before them. The faint light shining from her silver hair was their only guide.

Finally the ground grew level at their feet, the trees cleared, and they walked on smooth grass, brown with winter. Although none of them could see more than a few feet in the gray fog, they had the impression they were in a wide clearing.

"This is Foghaven Vale," Silvara replied in answer to their questions. "Long years ago, before the Cataclysm, it was one of the most beautiful places upon Krynn . . . so my people say."

"It might still be beautiful," Flint grumbled, "if we could see it through this confounded mist."

"No," said Silvara sadly. "Like much else in this world, the beauty of Foghaven has vanished. Once the fortress of Foghaven floated above the mist as if floating on a cloud. The rising sun colored the mists pink in the morning, burned them off at midday so that the soaring spires of the fortress could be seen for miles. In the evening, the fog returned to cover the fortress like a blanket. By night, the silver and the red moons shone on the mists with a shimmering light. Pilgrims came, from all parts of Krynn—" Silvara stopped abruptly. "We will make camp here tonight."

"What pilgrims?" Laurana asked, letting her pack fall.

Silvara shrugged. "I do not know," she said, averting her face. "It is only a legend of my people. Perhaps it is not even true. Certainly no one comes here now."

She's lying, thought Laurana, but she said nothing. She was too tired to care. And even Silvara's low, gentle voice seemed unnaturally loud and jarring in the eerie stillness. The companions spread their blankets in silence. They ate in silence, too, nibbling without appetite on the dried fruit in their packs. Even the kender was subdued. The fog was oppressive, weighing them down. The only thing they could hear was a steady drip, drip, drip of water plopping onto the mat of dead leaves on the forest floor below.

"Sleep now," said Silvara softly, spreading her blanket near Gilthanas's, "for when the silver moon has neared its zenith, we must leave."

"What difference will that make?" The kender yawned. "We can't see it anyway."

"Nonetheless, we must go. I will wake you."

"When we return from Sancrist—after the Council of Whitestone—we can be married," Gilthanas said softly to Silvara as they lay together, wrapped in his blanket.

The girl stirred in his arms. He felt her soft hair rub against his cheek. But she did not answer.

"Don't worry about my father," Gilthanas said, smiling, stroking the beautiful hair that shone even in the darkness. "He'll be stern and grim for a while, but I am the younger brother, no one cares what becomes of me. Porthios will rant and rave and carry on. But we'll ignore him. We don't have to live with my people. I'm not sure how I'd fit in with yours, but I could learn. I'm a good shot with a bow. And I'd like our children to grow up in the wilderness, free and happy . . . what . . . Silvara, why—you're crying!"

Gilthanas held her close as she buried her face in his shoulder, sobbing bitterly. "There, there," he whispered soothingly, smiling in the darkness. Women were such funny creatures. He wondered what he'd said. "Hush, Silvara," he murmured. "It will be all right." And Gilthanas fell asleep, dreaming of silver-haired children running in the green woods.

"It is time. We must leave."

Laurana felt a hand on her shoulder, shaking her. Startled, she woke from a vague, frightening dream that she could not remember to find the Wilder elf kneeling above her.

"I'll wake the others," Silvara said, and disappeared.

Feeling more tired than if she hadn't slept, Laurana packed her things by reflex and stood waiting, shivering, in the darkness. Next to her, she heard the dwarf groan. The damp air was making his joints ache painfully. This journey had been hard on Flint, Laurana realized. He was, after all, what—almost one hundred and fifty years old? A respectable age for a dwarf. His face had lost some of its color during his illness on the voyage. His lips, barely visible beneath the beard, had a bluish tinge, and occasionally he pressed his hand against his chest. But he always stoutly insisted he was fine and kept up with them on the trail.

"All set!" cried Tas. His shrill voice echoed weirdly in the fog, and he had the distinct feeling he'd disturbed something. "I'm sorry," he said, cringing. "Gee," he muttered to Flint, "it's like being in a temple."

"Just shut up and start moving!" the dwarf snapped.

A torch flared. The companions started at the sudden, blinding light that Silvara held.

"We must have light," she said before any could protest. "Do not fear. The vale we are in is sealed shut. Long ago, there were two entrances: one led to human lands where the knights had their outpost, the other led east into the lands of the ogres. Both passes were lost during the Cataclysm. We need have no fear. I have led you by a way known only to myself."

"And to your people," Laurana reminded her sharply.

"Yes—my people . . ." Silvara said, and Laurana was surprised to see the girl grow pale.

"Where are you taking us?" Laurana insisted.

"You will see. We will be there within the hour."

The companions glanced at each other, then all of them looked at Laurana.

Damn them! she thought. "Don't look to me for answers!" she said angrily. "What do you want to do? Stay out here, lost in the fog—"

"I won't betray you!" Silvara murmured despondently. "Please, just trust me a little further."

"Go ahead," said Laurana tiredly. "We'll follow."

The fog seemed to close around them more thickly, until all that kept the darkness at bay was the light of Silvara's torch.

No one had any idea of the direction they traveled. The landscape did not change. They walked through tall grass. There were no trees.

Occasionally a large boulder loomed out of the darkness, but that was all. Of night birds or animals, there was no sign. There was a sense of urgency that increased as they walked until all of them felt it, and they hurried their steps, keeping ever within the light of the torch.

Then, suddenly, without warning, Silvara stopped.

"We are here," she said, and she held the torch aloft. The torch's light pierced the fog. They could all see a shadowy something beyond. At first, it was so ghostly materializing out of the fog that the companions could not recognize it.

Silvara drew closer. They followed her, curious, fearful.

Then the silence of the night was broken by bubbling sounds like water boiling in a giant kettle. The fog grew denser, the air was warm and stifling.

"Hot springs!" said Theros in sudden understanding. "Of course, that explains the constant fog. And this dark shape—"

"The bridge which leads across them," Silvara replied, shining the torchlight upon what they could see was a glistening stone bridge spanning the water boiling in the streams below them, filling the night air with its warm, billowing fog.

"We're supposed to cross that!" Flint exclaimed, staring at the black, boiling water in horror. "We're supposed to cross—"

"It is called the Bridge of Passage," said Silvara.

The dwarf's only answer was a strangled gulp.

The Bridge of Passage was a long, smooth arch of pure white marble. Along its sides—carved in vivid relief—long columns of knights walked symbolically across the bubbling streams. The span was so high that they could not see the top through the swirling mists. And it was old, so old that Flint, reverently touching the worn rock with his hand, could not recognize the craftsmanship. It was not dwarven, not elven, not human. Who had done such marvelous work?

Then he noticed there were no hand-rails, nothing but the marble span itself, slick and glistening with the mist rising constantly from the bubbling springs beneath.

"We cannot cross that," said Laurana, her voice trembling. "And now we are trapped—"

"We *can* cross," Silvara said. "For we have been summoned."

"Summoned?" Laurana repeated in exasperation. "By what? Where?"

"Wait," commanded Silvara.

They waited. There was nothing left for them to do. Each stood staring around in the torchlight, but they saw only the mist rising from the streams, heard only the gurgling water.

"It is the time of Solinari," Silvara said suddenly, and—swinging her arm—she hurled her torch into the water.

Darkness swallowed them. Involuntarily, they crept closer together. Silvara seemed to have vanished with the light. Gilthanas called for her, but she did not answer.

Then the mist turned to shimmering silver. They could see once more, and now they could see Silvara, a dark, shadowy outline against the silvery mist. She stood at the foot of the bridge, staring up into the sky. Slowly she raised her hands, and slowly the mists parted. Looking up, the companions saw the mists separate like long, graceful fingers to reveal the silver moon, full and brilliant in the starry sky.

Silvara spoke strange words, and the moonlight poured down upon her, bathing her in its light. The moon's light shone upon the bubbling waters, making them come alive, dancing with silver. It shone upon the marble bridge, giving life to the knights who spent eternity crossing the stream.

But it was not these beautiful sights that caused the companions to clasp each other with shaking hands or to hold each other closely. The moon's light on the water did not cause Flint to repeat the name of Reorx in the most reverent prayer he ever uttered, or cause Laurana to lean her head against her brother's shoulder, her eyes dimmed with sudden tears, or cause Gilthanas to hold her tightly, overwhelmed by a feeling of fear and awe and reverence.

Soaring high above them, so tall its head might have torn a moon from the sky, was the figure of a dragon, carved out of a mountain of rock, shining silver in the moonlight.

"Where are we?" Laurana asked in a hushed voice. "What is this place?"

"When you cross the Bridge of Passage, you will stand before the Monument of the Silver Dragon," answered Silvara softly. "It guards the Tomb of Huma, Knight of Solamnia."

THE TOMB OF HUMA.

2

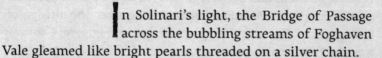

In Solinari's light, the Bridge of Passage across the bubbling streams of Foghaven Vale gleamed like bright pearls threaded on a silver chain.

"Do not fear," Silvara said again. "The crossing is difficult only for those who seek to enter the Tomb for evil purposes."

But the companions remained unconvinced. Fearfully they climbed the few stairs leading them up to bridge itself. Then, hesitantly, they stepped upon the marble arch that rose before them, glistening wet with the steam from the springs. Silvara crossed first, walking lightly and with ease. The rest followed her more cautiously, keeping to the very center of the marble span.

Across from them, on the other side of the bridge, loomed the Monument of the Dragon. Even though they knew they must watch their footing, their eyes seemed constantly drawn up to it. Many times, they were forced to stop and stare in awe, while below them the hot springs boiled and steamed.

"Why—I bet that water's so hot you could cook meat in it!" Tasslehoff said. Lying flat on his stomach, he peered over the edge of the highest part of the arched bridge.

"I'll b-bet it c-could c-cook you," stuttered the terrified dwarf, crawling across on his hands and knees.

"Look, Flint! Watch. I've got this piece of meat in my pack. I'll get a string and we'll lower it in the water—"

"Get moving!" Flint roared. Tas sighed and closed his pouch.

"You're no fun to take anywhere," he complained, and he slid down the other side of the span on the seat of his pants.

But for the rest of the companions, it was a terrifying journey, and all of them sighed in heartfelt relief when they came down off the marble bridge onto the ground below.

None of them had spoken to Silvara as they crossed, their minds being too occupied with getting over the Bridge of Passage alive. But when they reached the other side, Laurana was the first to ask questions.

"Why have you brought us here?"

"Do you not trust me yet?" Silvara asked sadly.

Laurana hesitated. Her gaze went once again to the huge stone dragon, whose head was crowned with stars. The stone mouth was open in a silent cry, and the stone eyes stared fiercely. The stone wings were carved out of the sides of the mountain. A stone claw stretched forth, as massive as the trunks of a hundred vallenwood trees.

"You send the dragon orb away, then bring us to a monument dedicated to a dragon!" Laurana said after a moment, her voice quivering. "What am I to think? And you bring us to this place you *call* Huma's Tomb. We do not even know if Huma lived, or if he was legend. What is to prove this is his resting place? Is his body within?"

"N-no," Silvara faltered. "His body disappeared, as did—"

"As did what?"

"As did the lance he carried, the Dragonlance he used to destroy the Dragon of All Colors and of None." Silvara sighed and lowered her head. "Come inside," she begged, "and rest for the night. In the morning, all will be made clear, I promise."

"I don't think—" Laurana began.

"We're going inside!" Gilthanas said firmly. "You're behaving like a spoiled child, Laurana! Why would Silvara lead us into danger? Surely, if there was a dragon living here, everyone on Ergoth would know it! It could have destroyed everyone on the island long ago. I sense no evil about this place, only a great and ancient peace. And it's a perfect hiding place! Soon the elves will receive word that the orb has reached Sancrist safely. They'll quit searching, and we can leave. Isn't that right, Silvara? Isn't that why you brought us here?"

"Yes," Silvara said softly. "Th-that was my plan. Now, come, come quickly, while the silver moon still shines. For only then can we enter."

Gilthanas, his hand holding Silvara's hand, walked into the shimmering silver fog. Tas skipped ahead of them, his pouches bouncing. Flint and Theros followed more slowly, Laurana more slowly still. Her fears were not eased by Gilthanas's glib explanation, nor by Silvara's reluctant agreement. But there was no place else to go and—as she admitted—she was intensely curious.

The grass on the other side of the bridge was smooth and flat with the steamy clouds of moisture, but the ground began to rise as they approached the body of the dragon carved out of the cliff. Suddenly Tasslehoff's voice floated back to them from the mist where he had run far ahead of the group.

"Raistlin!" they heard him cry in a strangled voice. "He's turned into a giant!"

"The kender's gone mad," Flint said with gloomy satisfaction. "I always knew it—"

Running forward, the companions found Tas jumping up and down and pointing. They stood by his side, panting for breath.

"By the beard of Reorx," gasped Flint in awe. "It *is* Raistlin!"

Looming out of the swirling mist, rising nine feet in the air, stood a stone statue carved in a perfect likeness of the young mage. Accurate in every detail, it even captured his cynical, bitter expression and the carven eyes with their hourglass pupils.

"And there's Caramon!" Tas cried.

A few feet away stood another statue, this time shaped like the mage's warrior twin.

"And Tanis . . . " Laurana whispered fearfully. "What evil magic is this?"

"Not evil," Silvara said, "unless you bring evil to this place. In that case, you would see the faces of your worst enemies within the stone statues. The horror and fear they generate would not allow you to pass. But you see only your friends, and so you may pass safely."

"I wouldn't exactly count Raistlin among my friends," muttered Flint.

"Nor I," Laurana said. Shivering, she walked hesitantly past the cold image of the mage. The mage's obsidian robes gleamed black in the moons' light. Laurana remembered vividly the nightmare of Silvanesti, and she shuddered as she entered what she saw now was a ring of stone statues—each of them bearing a striking, almost frightening resemblance to her friends. Within that silent ring of stone stood a small temple.

The simple rectangular building thrust up into the fog from an octagonal base of shining steps. It, too, was made of obsidian, and the black structure glistened wet with the perpetual fog. Each feature stood as if it had been carved only days before; no sign of wear marred the sharp, clean lines of the carving. Its knights, each bearing the dragonlance, still charged huge monsters. Dragons screamed silently in frozen death, pierced by the long, delicate shafts.

"Inside this temple, they placed Huma's body," Silvara said softly as she led them up the stairs.

Cold bronze doors swung open on silent hinges to Silvara's touch. The companions stood uncertainly on the stairs that encircled the columned temple. But, as Gilthanas had said, they could sense no evil coming from this place. Laurana remembered vividly the Tomb of the Royal Guard in the Sla-Mori and the terror generated by the undead guards left to keep eternal watch over their dead king, Kith-Kanan. In this temple, however, she felt only sorrow and loss, tempered by the knowledge of a great victory—a battle won at terrible cost, but bringing with it eternal peace and sweet restfulness.

Laurana felt her burden ease, her heart become lighter. Her own sorrow and loss seemed diminished here. She was reminded of her own victories and triumphs. One by one, all the companions entered the tomb. The bronze doors swung shut behind them, leaving them in total darkness.

Then light flared. Silvara held a torch in her hand, apparently taken from the wall. Laurana wondered briefly how she had managed to light it. But the trivial question left her mind as she stood gazing around the tomb in awe.

It was empty except for a bier carved out of obsidian, which stood in the center of the room. Chiseled images of knights supported the bier, but the body of the knight that was supposed to have rested upon it was gone. An ancient shield lay at the foot, and a sword, similar to Sturm's, lay near the shield. The companions gazed at these artifacts in silence. It seemed a desecration to the sorrowful serenity of the place to speak, and none touched them, not even Tasslehoff.

"I wish Sturm could be here," murmured Laurana, looking around, tears coming to her eyes. "This *must* be Huma's resting place . . . yet—"

She couldn't explain the growing sense of uneasiness that was creeping over her. Not fear, it was more like the sensation she had felt upon entering the vale—a sense of urgency.

Silvara lit more torches along the wall, and the companions walked past the bier, gazing around the tomb curiously. It was not large. The bier stood in the center and stone benches lined the walls, presumably for the mourners to rest upon while paying their respects. At the far end stood a small stone altar. Carved in its surface were the symbols of the orders of the Knights, the crown, the rose, the kingfisher. Dried rose petals and herbs lay scattered on the top, their fragrance still lingering sweetly in the air after hundreds of years. Below the altar, sunk into the stone floor, was a large iron plate.

As Laurana stared curiously at this plate, Theros came over to stand beside her.

"What do you suppose this is?" she wondered. "A well?"

"Let's see," grunted the smith. Bending over, he lifted the ring on top of the plate in his huge, silver hand and pulled. At first nothing happened. Theros placed both hands on the ring and heaved with all his strength. The iron plate gave a great groan and slid across the floor with a scraping, squeaking sound that set their teeth on edge.

"What have you done?" Silvara, who had been standing near the tomb regarding it sadly, whirled to face them.

Theros stood up in astonishment at the shrill sound of her voice. Laurana involuntarily backed away from the gaping hole in the floor. Both of them stared at Silvara.

"Do not go near that!" Silvara warned, her voice shaking. "Stand clear! It is dangerous!"

"How do you know?" Laurana said coolly, recovering herself. "No one's come here for hundreds of years. Or have they?"

"No!" Silvara said, biting her lip. "I—I know from the . . . legends of my people . . ."

Ignoring the girl, Laurana stepped to the edge of the hole and peered inside. It was dark. Even holding the torch Flint brought her from the wall, she could see nothing down there. A faint musty odor drifted from the hole, but that was all.

"I don't think it's a well," said Tas, crowding to see.

"Stay away from it! Please!" Silvara begged.

"She's right, little thief!" Theros grabbed Tas and pulled him away from the hole. "If you fell in there, you might tumble through to the other side of the world."

"Really?" asked Tasslehoff breathlessly. "Would I really fall through to the other side, Theros? I wonder what it would be like? Would there be people there? Like us?"

"Not like kenders hopefully!" Flint grumbled. "Or they'd all be dead of idiocy by now. Besides, everyone knows that the world rests on the Anvil of Reorx. Those falling to the other side are caught between his hammer blows and the world still being forged. People on the other side indeed!" He snorted as he watched Theros unsuccessfully try to replace the plate. Tasslehoff was still staring at it curiously. Finally Theros was forced to give up, but he glared at the kender until Tas heaved a sigh and wandered away to the stone bier to stare with longing eyes at the shield and sword.

Flint tugged Laurana's sleeve.

"What is it?" she asked absently, her thoughts elsewhere.

"I know stonework," the dwarf said softly, "and there's something strange about all this." He paused, glancing to see if Laurana might laugh. But she was paying serious attention to him. "The tomb and the statues built outside are the work of men. It is old. . . ."

"Old enough to be Huma's tomb?" Laurana interrupted.

"Every bit of it." The dwarf nodded emphatically. "But yon great beast outside"—he gestured in the direction of the huge stone dragon—"was never built by the hands of man or elf or dwarf."

Laurana blinked, uncomprehending.

"And it is older still," the dwarf said, his voice growing husky. "So old it makes this"—he waved his hand at the tomb—"modern."

Laurana began to understand. Flint, seeing her eyes widen, nodded slowly and solemnly.

"No hand of any being that walks upon Krynn with two legs carved the side out of that cliff," he said.

"It must have been a creature with awesome strength," Laurana murmured. "A huge creature—"

"With wings—"

"With wings," Laurana murmured.

Suddenly she stopped talking, her blood chilled in fear as she heard words being chanted, words she recognized as the strange, spidery language of magic.

"No!" Turning, she lifted her hand instinctively to ward off the spell, knowing as she did so that it was futile.

Silvara stood beside the altar, crumbling rose petals in her hand, chanting softly.

Laurana fought the enchanted drowsiness that crept over her. She fell to her knees, cursing herself for a fool, clinging to the stone bench for support. But it did no good. Lifting her sleep-glazed eyes, she saw Theros topple over and Gilthanas slump to the ground. Beside her, the dwarf was snoring even before his head hit the bench.

Laurana heard a clattering sound, the sound of a shield crashing to the floor, then the air was filled with the fragrance of roses.

The kender's startling discovery.

3

Tasslehoff heard Silvara chanting. Recognizing the words of a magic spell, he reacted instinctively, grabbed hold of the shield that lay on the bier, and pulled. The heavy shield fell on top of him, striking the floor with a ringing clang, flattening the kender. The shield covered Tas completely.

He lay still beneath it until he heard Silvara finish her chant. Even then, he waited a few moments to see if he was going to turn into a frog or go up in flames or something interesting like that. He didn't—rather to his disappointment. He couldn't even hear Silvara. Finally, growing bored lying in the darkness on the cold stone floor, Tas crept out from beneath the heavy shield with the silence of a falling feather.

All his friends were asleep! So that was the spell she cast. But where was Silvara? Gone somewhere to get a horrible monster to come back and devour them?

Cautiously, Tas raised his head and peered over the bier. To his astonishment, he saw Silvara crouched on the floor, near the tomb entrance. As Tas watched, she rocked back and forth, making small, moaning sounds.

"How can I go through with it?" Tas heard her say to herself. "I've brought them here. Isn't that enough? No!" She shook her head in misery. "No, I've sent the orb away. They don't know how to use it. I must break the oath. It is as you said, sister—the choice is mine. But it is hard! I love him—"

Sobbing, muttering to herself like one possessed, Silvara buried her face in her knees. The tender-hearted kender had never seen such sorrow, and he longed to go comfort her. Then he realized what she was talking about didn't sound good. "Choice is a hard one, break the oath . . ."

No, Tas thought, I better find a way out of here before she realizes her spell didn't work on me.

But Silvara blocked the entrance to the tomb. He might try to sneak past her. . . . Tas shook his head. Too risky.

The hole! He brightened. He'd wanted to examine it more carefully anyway. He just hoped the lid was still off.

The kender tiptoed around the bier until he came to the altar. There was the hole, still gaping open. Theros lay beside it, sound asleep, his head pillowed upon his silver arm. Glancing back at Silvara, Tas sneaked silently to the edge.

It would certainly be a better place to hide than where he was now. There were no stairs, but he could see handholds on the wall. A deft kender—such as himself—should have no trouble at all climbing down. Perhaps it led outside. Suddenly Tas heard a noise behind him. Silvara sighing and stirring. . . .

Without another thought, Tas lowered himself silently into the hole and began his descent. The walls were slick with moisture and moss, the handholds were spaced far apart. Built for humans, he thought irritably. No one ever considered little people!

He was so preoccupied that he didn't notice the gems until he was practically on top of them.

"Reorx's beard!" he swore. (He was fond of this oath, having borrowed it from Flint.) Six beautiful jewels—each as big around as his hand—were spaced in a horizontal ring around the walls of the shaft. They were covered with moss, but Tas could tell at a glance how valuable they were.

"Now why would anyone put such wonderful jewels down here?" he asked aloud. "I'll bet it was some thief. If I can pry them loose, I'll return them to their rightful owner." His hand closed over a jewel.

A tremendous blast of wind filled the shaft, pulling the kender off the wall as easily as a winter gale rips a leaf off a tree. Falling, Tas looked back up, watching the light at the top of the shaft grow smaller and smaller. He wondered briefly just how big the Hammer of Reorx was, and then he stopped falling.

For a moment, the wind tumbled him end over end. Then it switched directions, blowing him sideways. I'm not going to the other side of the world after all, he thought sadly. Sighing, he sailed along through another tunnel. Then he suddenly felt himself start to rise! A great wind was wafting him up the shaft! It was an unusual sensation, quite exhilarating. Instinctively, he spread his arms to see if he could touch the sides of whatever it was he was in. As he spread his arms, he noticed that he rose faster, borne gently upward on swift currents of air.

Perhaps I'm dead, Tas thought. I'm dead and now I'm lighter than air. How can I tell? Putting his arms down, he felt frantically for his pouches. He wasn't certain, the kender had very vague ideas as to the afterlife—but he had a feeling they wouldn't let him take his things with him. No, everything was there. Tas breathed a sigh of relief that turned into a gulp when he discovered himself slowing down and even starting to fall!

What? he thought wildly, then realized he had pulled both his arms in close to his body. Hurriedly he thrust his arms out again and, sure enough, he began to rise. Convinced that he wasn't dead, he gave himself up to enjoying the flight.

Fluttering his hands, the kender rolled over on his back in midair, and stared up to see where he was going.

Ah, there was a light far above him, growing brighter and brighter. Now he could see that he was in a shaft, but it was much longer than the shaft he had tumbled down.

"Wait until Flint hears about this!" he said wistfully. Then he caught a glimpse of six jewels, like the ones he'd seen in the other shaft. The rushing wind began to lessen.

Just as he decided that he could really enjoy taking up flying as a way of life, Tas reached the top of the shaft. The air currents held him even with the stone floor of a torch-lit chamber. Tas waited a moment to see if he might start flying again, and he even flapped his arms a bit to help, but nothing happened. Apparently his flight had ended.

I might as well explore while I'm up here, the kender thought with a sigh. Jumping out of the air currents, he landed lightly on the stone floor, then began to look around.

Several torches flared on the walls, illuminating the chamber with a bright white radiance. This room was certainly much larger than the tomb! He was standing at the bottom of a great curving staircase. The huge flagstones of each step—as well as all the other stones in the room—were pure white, much different from the black stone of the tomb. The staircase curved to the right, leading up to what appeared to be another level of the chamber. Above him, he could see a railing overlooking the stairs, apparently there was some sort of balcony up there. Nearly breaking his neck trying to see, Tas thought he could make out swirls and splotches of bright colors shining in the torchlight from the opposite wall.

Who lit the torches, he wondered? What is this place? Part of Huma's tomb? Or did I fly up into the Dragon Mountain? Who lives here? Those torches didn't light themselves!

At that thought—just to be safe—Tas reached into his tunic and drew out his little knife. Holding it in his hand, he climbed the grand stairs and came out onto the balcony. It was a huge chamber, but he could see little of it in the flickering torchlight. Gigantic pillars supported the massive ceiling overhead. Another great staircase rose from this balcony level to yet another floor. Tas turned around, leaning against the railing to look at the walls behind him.

"Reorx's beard!" he said softly. "Look at *that!*"

That was a painting. A mural, to be more precise. It began opposite where Tas was standing, at the head of the stairs, and extended on around the balcony in foot after foot of shimmering color. The kender was not much interested in artwork, but he couldn't recall ever seeing anything quite so beautiful. Or had he? Somehow, it seemed familiar. Yes, the more he looked at it, the more he thought he'd seen it before.

Tas studied the painting, trying to remember. On the wall directly across from him was pictured a horrible scene of dragons of every color and description descending upon the land. Towns blazed in flames—like Tarsis—buildings crumbled, people were fleeing. It was a terrible sight, and the kender hurried past it.

He continued walking along the balcony, his eyes on the painting. He had just reached the central portion of the mural when he gasped.

"The Dragon Mountain! That's it—there, on the wall!" he whispered to himself and was startled to hear his whisper come echoing back to him. Glancing around hastily, he crept closer to the other edge of the balcony. Leaning over the rail, he stared closely at the painting. It indeed showed the Dragon Mountain, where he was now. Only this showed a view of the mountain as if some giant sword had chopped it completely in half vertically!

"How wonderful!" The map-loving kender sighed. "Of course," he said. "It is *a* map! And that's where I am! I've gone up into the mountain." He looked around the room in sudden realization. "I'm in the throat of the dragon. That's why this room is such a funny shape." He turned back to the map. "There's the painting on the wall and there's the balcony I'm standing on. And the pillars . . ." He turned completely around. "Yes, there's the grand staircase." He turned back. "It leads up into the head! And there's how I came up. Some sort of wind chamber. But who built this . . . and why?"

Tasslehoff continued on around the balcony, hoping to find a clue in the painting. On the right-hand side of the gallery, another battle was portrayed. But this one didn't fill him with horror. There were red dragons, and black, and blue, and white—breathing fire and ice—but fighting them were other dragons, dragons of silver and of gold. . . .

"I remember!" shouted Tasslehoff.

The kender began jumping up and down, yelling like a wild thing. "I remember! I remember! It was in Pax Tharkas. Fizban showed me. There are *good* dragons in the world. They'll help us fight the evil ones! We just have to find them. And there are the dragonlances!"

"Confound it!" snarled a voice below the kender. "Can't a person get some sleep? What is all this racket? You're making noise enough to wake the dead!"

Tasslehoff whirled around in alarm, his knife in his hand. He could have sworn he was alone up here. But no. Rising up off a stone bench that stood in a shadowy area out of the torchlight was a dark, robed figure. It shook itself, stretched, then got up and began to climb the stairs, moving swiftly toward the kender. Tas could not have gotten away, even if he had wanted to, and the kender found himself intensely curious about who was up here. He opened his mouth to ask this strange creature what it was and why it had chosen the throat of a Dragon Mountain to nap in, when the figure emerged into the light. It was an old man. It was—

Tasslehoff's knife clattered to the floor. The kender sagged back against the railing. For the first, last, and only time in his life, Tasslehoff Burrfoot was struck speechless.

"F-F-F . . ." Nothing came out of his throat, only a croak.

"Well, what is it? Speak up!" snapped the old man, looming over him. "You were making enough noise a minute ago. What's the matter? Something go down the wrong way?"

"F-F-F . . ." stuttered Tas weakly.

"Ah, poor boy. Afflicted, eh? Speech impediment. Sad, sad. Here—"The old man fumbled in his robes, opening numerous pouches while Tasslehoff stood trembling before him.

"There," the figure said. Drawing forth a coin, he put it in the kender's numb palm and closed his small, lifeless fingers over it. "Now, run along. Find a cleric . . ."

"Fizban!" Tasslehoff was finally able to gasp.

"Where?" The old man whirled around. Raising his staff, he peered fearfully into the darkness. Then something seemed to occur to him. Turning back around, he asked Tas in a loud whisper, "I say, are you sure you saw this Fizban? Isn't he dead?"

"I know *I* thought so . . . " Tas said miserably.

"Then he shouldn't be wandering around, scaring people!" the old man declared angrily. "I'll have a talk with him. Hey, you!" he began to shout.

Tas reached out a trembling hand and tugged at the old man's robe."I—I'm not sure, b-but I think *you're* Fizban."

"No, really?" the old man said, taken aback. "I was feeling a bit under the weather this morning, but I had no idea it was as bad as all that." His shoulders sagged. "So I'm dead. Done for. Bought the farm. Kicked the bucket." He staggered to a bench and plopped down. "Was it a nice funeral?" he asked. "Did lots of people come? Was there a twenty-one gun salute? I always wanted a twenty-one gun salute."

"I—uh,"Tas stammered, wondering what a gun was. "Well, it was . . . more of a . . . memorial service you might say. You see, we—uh—couldn't find your—how shall I put this?"

"Remains?" the old man said helpfully.

"Uh . . . remains."Tas flushed. "We looked, but there were all these chicken feathers . . . and a dark elf . . . and Tanis said we were lucky to have escaped alive. . . ."

"Chicken feathers!" said the old man indignantly. "What have chicken feathers got to do with my funeral?"

"We—uh—you and me and Sestun. Do you remember Sestun, the gully dwarf? Well, there was that great, huge chain in Pax Tharkas. And that big red dragon. We were hanging onto the chain and the dragon breathed fire on it and the chain broke and we were falling"—Tas was warming up to his story; it had become one of his favorites—"and I knew it was all over. We were going to die. There must have been a seventy-foot drop" (this increased every time Tas told the tale) "and you were beneath me and I heard you chanting a spell—"

"Yes, I'm quite a good magician, you know."

"Uh, right," Tas stammered, then continued hurriedly. "You chanted this spell, Featherfall or something like that. Anyway, you only said the first word, 'feather' and suddenly"—the kender spread his hands, a look of awe on his face as he remembered what happened then—"there were millions and millions and millions of chicken feathers. . . ."

"So what happened next?" the old man demanded, poking Tas.

"Oh, uh, that's where it gets a bit—uh—muddled," Tas said. "I heard a scream and a thump. Well, it was more like a splatter actually, and I f-f-figured the splatter was you."

"Me?" the old man shouted. "Splatter!" He glared at the kender furiously. "I never in my life *splattered!*"

"Then Sestun and I tumbled down into the chicken feathers, along with the chain. I looked—I really did." Tas's eyes filled with tears as he remembered his heartbroken search for the old man's body. "But there were too many feathers . . . and there was this terrible commotion outside where the dragons were fighting. Sestun and I made it to the door, and then we found Tanis, and I wanted to go back to look for you some more, but Tanis said no . . ."

"So you left me buried under a mound of chicken feathers?"

"It was an *awfully* nice memorial service," Tas faltered. "Goldmoon spoke, and Elistan. You didn't meet Elistan, but you remember Goldmoon, don't you? And Tanis?"

"Goldmoon . . ." the old man murmured. "Ah, yes. Pretty girl. Big, stern-looking chap in love with her."

"Riverwind!" said Tas in excitement. "And Raistlin?"

"Skinny fellow. Damn good magician," the old man said solemnly, "but he'll never amount to anything if he doesn't do something about that cough."

"You *are* Fizban!" Tas said. Jumping up gleefully, he threw his arms around the old man and hugged him tight.

"There, there," Fizban said, embarrassed, patting Tas on the back. "That's quite enough. You'll crumple my robes. Don't sniffle. Can't abide it. Need a hankie?"

"No, I've got one—"

"Now, that's better. Oh, I say, I believe that handkerchief's mine. Those are my initials, "

"Is it? You must have dropped it."

"I remember you now!" the old man said loudly. "You're Tassle—Tassle-something-or-other."

"Tasslehoff. Tasslehoff Burrfoot," the kender replied.

"And I'm—" The old man stopped. "What did you say the name was?"

"Fizban."

"Fizban. Yes . . ." The old man pondered a moment, then he shook his head. "I sure thought he was dead. . . ."

SILVARA'S SECRET.

4

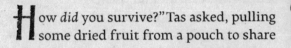

"How *did* you survive?" Tas asked, pulling some dried fruit from a pouch to share with Fizban.

The old man appeared wistful. "I really didn't think I did," he said apologetically. "I'm afraid I haven't the vaguest notion. But, come to think of it, I haven't been able to eat a chicken since. Now"—he stared at the kender shrewdly— "what are you doing here?"

"I came with some of my friends. The rest are wandering around somewhere, if they're still alive." He sniffed again.

"They are. Don't worry." Fizban patted him on the back.

"Do you think so?" Tas brightened. "Well, anyway, we're here with Silvara—"

"Silvara!" The old man leaped to his feet, his white hair flying out wildly. The vague look faded from his face.

"Where is she?" the old man demanded sternly. "And your friends, where are they?"

"D-downstairs," stammered Tas, startled at the old man's transformation. "Silvara cast a spell on them!"

"Ah, she did, did she?" the old man muttered. "We'll see

about that. Come on." He started off along the balcony, walking so rapidly, Tas had to run to keep up.

"Where'd you say they were?" the old man asked, stopping near the stairs. "Be specific," he snapped.

"Uh—the tomb! Huma's tomb! I think it's Huma's tomb. That's what Silvara said."

"Humpf. Well, at least we don't have to walk."

Descending the stairs to the hole in the floor Tas had come up through, the old man stepped out into its center. Tas, gulping a little, joined him, clutching at the old man's robes. They hung suspended over nothing but darkness, feeling cool air waft up around them.

"Down," the old man stated.

They began to rise, drifting toward the ceiling of the upper gallery. Tas felt the hair stand up on his head.

"I said *down!*" the old man shouted furiously, waving his staff menacingly at the hole below him.

There was a slurping sound and both of them were sucked into the hole so rapidly that Fizban's hat flew off. It's just like the hat he lost in the red dragon's lair, Tas thought. It was bent and shapeless, and apparently possessed of a mind of its own. Fizban made a wild grab for it, but missed. The hat, however, floated down after them, about fifty feet above.

Tasslehoff peered down, fascinated, and started to ask a question, but Fizban shushed him. Gripping his staff, the old mage began whispering to himself, making an odd sign in the air.

Laurana opened her eyes. She was lying on a cold stone bench, staring at a black, glistening ceiling. She had no idea where she was. Then memory returned. Silvara!

Sitting up swiftly, she flashed a glance around the room. Flint was groaning and rubbing his neck. Theros blinked and looked around, puzzled. Gilthanas, already on his feet, stood at the end of Huma's tomb, gazing down at something by the door. As Laurana walked over to him, he turned around. Putting his finger to his lips, he nodded in the direction of the doorway.

Silvara sat there, her head in her arms, sobbing bitterly.

Laurana hesitated, the angry words on her lips dying. This certainly wasn't what she had expected. What had she expected? she asked herself. Never to wake again, most likely. There had to be an explanation. She started forward.

"Silvara—" she began.

The girl leaped up, her tear-stained face white with fear.

"What are you doing awake? How did you free yourself from my spell?" she gasped, falling back against the wall.

"Never mind that!" Laurana answered, though she hadn't any idea how she had wakened. "Tell us—"

"It was *my* doing!" announced a deep voice. Laurana and the rest turned around to see a white-bearded old man in mouse-colored robes rise up solemnly out of the hole in the floor.

"Fizban!" whispered Laurana in disbelief.

There was a clunk and a thud. Flint toppled over in a dead faint. No one even looked at him. They simply stared at the old mage in awe. Then, with a shrill shriek, Silvara flung herself flat on the cold stone floor, shivering and whimpering softly.

Ignoring the stares of the others, Fizban walked across the floor of the tomb, past the bier, past the comatose dwarf, to come to Silvara. Behind him, Tasslehoff scrambled up out of the hole.

"Look who *I* found," the kender said proudly. "Fizban! And I flew, Laurana. I jumped into the hole and just flew straight up into the air. And there's a painting up there with gold dragons, and then Fizban sat up and yelled at me and— I must admit I felt really queer there for a while. My voice was gone and . . . what happened to Flint?"

"Hush, Tas," Laurana said weakly, her eyes on Fizban. Kneeling down, he shook the Wilder elfmaid.

"Silvara, what have you done?" Fizban asked sternly. Laurana thought then that perhaps she had made a mistake— this must be some other old man dressed in the old magician's clothes. This stern-faced, powerful man was certainly not the befuddled old mage she remembered. But no, she'd recognize that face anywhere, to say nothing of the hat!

Watching the two of them—Silvara and Fizban—before her, Laurana felt great and awesome power like silent thunder surging between the two. She had a terrible longing to run out of this place and keep running until she dropped with exhaustion. But she couldn't move. She could only stare.

"What have you done, Silvara?" Fizban demanded. "You have broken your oath!"

"No!" The girl moaned, writhing on the ground at the old mage's feet. "No, I haven't. Not yet—"

"You have walked the world in another body, meddling in the affairs of men. That alone would be sufficient. But you brought them here!"

Silvara's tear-stained face was twisted in anguish. Laurana felt her own tears sliding unchecked down her cheeks.

"All right then!" Silvara cried defiantly. "I broke my oath, or at least I intended to. I brought them here. I had to! I've seen the misery and the suffering. Besides"—her voice fell, her eyes stared far away—"they had an orb . . ."

"Yes," said Fizban softly. "A dragon orb. Taken from Ice Wall Castle. It fell into your possession. What have you done with it, Silvara? Where is it now?"

MARGARET WEIS & TRACY HICKMAN

"I sent it away . . ." Silvara said almost inaudibly.

Fizban seemed to age. His face grew weary. Sighing deeply, he leaned heavily upon his staff. "Where did you send it, Silvara? Where is the dragon orb now?"

"St-Sturm has it," Laurana interrupted fearfully. "He took it to Sancrist. What does this mean? Is Sturm in danger?"

"Who?" Fizban peered around over his shoulder. "Oh, hullo there, my dear." He beamed at her. "So nice to see you again. How's your father?"

"My father—" Laurana shook her head, confused. "Look, old man, never mind my father! Who—"

"And your brother." Fizban extended a hand to Gilthanas. "Good to see you, son. And you, sir." He bowed to an astonished Theros. "Silver arm? My, my"—he stole a look back at Silvara—"what a coincidence. Theros Ironfeld, isn't it? Heard a lot about you. And my name is . . ." The old magician paused, his brow furrowed.

"My name is . . ."

"Fizban," supplied Tasslehoff helpfully.

"Fizban." The old man nodded, smiling.

Laurana thought she saw the old magician cast a warning glance at Silvara. The girl lowered her head as if to acknowledge some silent, secret signal passed between them.

But before Laurana could sort out her whirling thoughts, Fizban turned back to her again. "And now, Laurana, you wonder who Silvara is? It is up to Silvara to tell you. For I must leave you now. I have a long journey ahead of me."

"Must I tell them?" Silvara asked softly. She was still on her knees and, as she spoke, her eyes went to Gilthanas. Fizban followed her gaze. Seeing the elflord's stricken face, his own face softened. Then he shook his head sadly.

Silvara raised her hands to him in a pleading gesture. Fizban walked over to her. Taking her hands, he raised her to her feet. She threw her arms around him, and he held her close.

"No, Silvara," he said, his voice kind and gentle, "you do not have to tell them. The choice is yours that was your sister's. You can make them forget they were ever here."

Suddenly the only color left in Silvara's face was the deep blue of her eyes. "But, that will mean—"

"Yes, Silvara," he said. "It is up to you." He kissed the girl on the forehead. "Farewell, Silvara."

Turning, he looked back at the rest. "Good-bye, good-bye. Nice seeing you again. I'm a bit miffed about the chicken feathers, but—no hard feelings." He waited impatiently a minute, glaring at Tasslehoff. "Are you coming? I haven't got all night!"

"Coming? With you?" Tas cried, dropping Flint's head back onto the stone floor with a thunk. The kender stood up. "Of course, let me get my pack . . ." Then he stopped, glancing down at the unconscious dwarf. "Flint—"

"He'll be fine," Fizban promised. "You won't be parted from your friends long. We'll see them"—he frowned, muttering to himself—"seven days, add three, carry the one, what's seven times four? Oh well, around Famine Time. That's when they'll hold the Council meeting. Now, come along. I've got work to do. Your friends are in good hands. Silvara will take care of them, won't you, my dear?" He turned to the Wilder elf.

"I will tell them," she promised sadly, eyes on Gilthanas.

The elflord was staring at her and at Fizban, his face pale, fear spreading through his soul.

Silvara sighed. "You are right. I broke the oath long ago. I must finish what I set out to do."

"As you think best." Fizban laid his hand upon Silvara's head, stroking her silver hair. Then he turned away.

"Will I be punished?" she asked, just as the old man stepped into the shadows.

Fizban stopped. Shaking his head, he looked back over his shoulder "Some would say you are being punished right now, Silvara," he said softly. "But what you do, you do out of love. As the choice was up to you, so is your punishment."

The old man stepped into the darkness. Tasslehoff ran after him, his pouches bouncing behind him. "Good-bye, Laurana! Good-bye, Theros! Take care of Flint!" In the silence that followed, Laurana could hear the old man's voice.

"What was that name again? Fizbut, Furball—"

"Fizban!" said Tas shrilly.

"Fizban . . . Fizban . . ." muttered the old man.

All eyes turned to Silvara.

She was calm now, at peace with herself. Although her face was filled with sorrow, it was not the tormented, bitter sorrow they had seen earlier. This was the sorrow of loss, the quiet, accepting sorrow of one who has nothing to regret. Silvara walked toward Gilthanas. She took hold of his hands and looked up into his face with so much love that Gilthanas felt blessed, even as he knew she was going to tell him good-bye.

"I am losing you, Silvara," he murmured in broken tones. "I see it in your eyes. But I don't know why! You love me—"

"I love you, elflord," Silvara said softly. "I loved you when I saw you lying injured upon the sand. When you looked up and smiled at me, I knew that the fate which had befallen my sister was to be mine, too." She sighed. "But it is a risk we take when we choose this form. For though we bring our strength into it, the form inflicts its weaknesses upon us. Or is it a weakness? To love . . ."

"Silvara, I don't understand!" Gilthanas cried.

"You will," she promised, her voice soft. Her head bowed.

Gilthanas took her in his arms, holding her. She buried her face in his chest. He kissed her beautiful silver hair, then clasped her with a sob.

Laurana turned away. This grief seemed too sacred for her eyes to intrude upon. Swallowing her own tears, she looked around and then remembered the dwarf. She took some water from his waterskin and sprinkled it on Flint's face.

His eyes fluttered, then opened. The dwarf stared up at Laurana for a moment and reached out a trembling hand.

"Fizban!" the dwarf whispered hoarsely.

"I know," Laurana said, wondering how the dwarf would take the news about Tas's leaving.

"Fizban's *dead!*" Flint gasped. "Tas said so! In a pile of chicken feathers!" The dwarf struggled to sit up. "Where is that rattle-brained kender?"

"He's gone, Flint," Laurana said. "He went with Fizban."

"Gone?" The dwarf looked around blankly. "You let him go? With that old man?"

"I'm afraid so—"

"You let him go with a dead old man?"

"I really didn't have much choice." Laurana smiled. "It was his decision. He'll be fine—"

"Where'd they go?" Flint stood and shouldered his pack.

"You can't go after them," Laurana said. "Please, Flint." She put her arm around the dwarf's shoulders. "I need you. You're Tanis's oldest friend, my advisor—"

"But he's gone without me," Flint said plaintively. "How could he leave? I didn't see him go."

"You fainted—"

"I did no such thing!" the dwarf roared.

"You—you were out cold," Laurana stammered.

"I never faint!" stated the dwarf indignantly. "It must have been a recurrence of that deadly disease I caught on board that boat—" Flint dropped his pack and slumped down beside it. "Idiot kender. Running off with a dead old man."

Theros came over to Laurana, drawing her to one side. "Who was that old man?" he asked curiously.

"It's a long story." Laurana sighed. "And I'm not certain I could answer that question anyway."

"He seems familiar." Theros frowned and shook his head. "But I can't remember where I've seen him before, though he puts me in mind of Solace and the Inn of the Last Home. And he knew me . . ."The blacksmith stared at his silver hand. "I felt a shock go through me when he looked at me, like lightning striking a tree." The big blacksmith shivered, then he glanced over at Silvara and Gilthanas. "And what of this?"

"I think we're finally about to find out," Laurana said.

"You were right," Theros said. "You didn't trust her—"

"But not for the right reasons," Laurana admitted guiltily.

With a small sigh, Silvara pushed herself away from Gilthanas's embrace. The elflord let her go reluctantly.

"Gilthanas," she said, drawing a shuddering breath, "take a torch off the wall and hold it up before me."

Gilthanas hesitated. Then, almost angrily, he followed her directions.

"Hold the torch there . . ." she instructed, guiding his hand so that the light blazed right before her. "Now—look at my shadow on the wall behind me," she said in trembling tones.

The tomb was silent, only the sputtering of the flaming torch made any sound. Silvara's shadow sprang into life on the cold stone wall behind her. The companions stared at it and—for an instant—none of them could say a word.

The shadow Silvara cast upon the wall was not the shadow of a young elfmaid.

It was the shadow of a dragon.

"*You're* a dragon!" Laurana said in shocked disbelief. She laid her hand on her sword, but Theros stopped her.

"No!" he said suddenly. "I remember. That old man—" He looked at his arm. "Now I remember. He used to come into the Inn of the Last Home! He was dressed differently. He wasn't a mage, but it was him! I'll swear it! He told stories to the children. Stories about good dragons. Gold dragons and—"

"Silver dragons," Silvara said, looking at Theros. "I am a silver dragon. My sister was the Silver Dragon who loved Huma and fought the final great battle with him—"

"No!" Gilthanas flung the torch to the ground. It lay flickering for a moment at his feet, then he stamped on it angrily, putting out its light. Silvara, watching him with sad eyes, reached out her hand to comfort him.

Gilthanas shrank from her touch, staring at her in horror. Silvara lowered her hand slowly. Sighing gently, she nodded. "I understand," she murmured. "I'm sorry."

Gilthanas began to shake, then doubled over in agony. Putting his strong arms around him, Theros led Gilthanas to a bench and covered him with his cloak.

"I'll be all right," Gilthanas mumbled. "Just leave me alone, let me think. This is madness! It's all a nightmare. A dragon!" He closed his eyes tightly as if he could blot out their sight forever. "A dragon . . ." he whispered brokenly. Theros patted him gently, then returned to the others.

"Where are the rest of the good dragons?" Theros asked. "The old man said there were many. Silver dragons, gold dragons—"

"There are many of us," Silvara answered reluctantly.

"Like the silver dragon we saw in Ice Wall!" Laurana said.

"It was a good dragon. If there are many of you, band together! Help us fight the evil dragons!"

"No!" Silvara cried fiercely. Her blue eyes flared, and Laurana fell back a pace before her anger.

"Why not?"

"I cannot tell you." Silvara's hands clenched nervously.

"It has something to do with that oath!" Laurana persisted. "Doesn't it? The oath you've broken. And the punishment you asked Fizban about—"

"I cannot tell you!" Silvara spoke in a low, passionate voice. "What I have done is bad enough. But I had to do something! I could no longer live in this world and see the suffering of innocent people! I thought perhaps I could help, so I took elven form, and I did what I could. I worked long, trying to get the elves to join together. I kept them from war, but matters were growing worse. Then you came, and I saw that we were in great peril, greater than any of us had ever imagined. For you brought with you—" Her voice faltered.

"The dragon orb!" Laurana said suddenly.

"Yes." Silvara's fists clenched in misery. "I knew then I had to make a decision. You had the orb, but you also had the lance. The lance and the orb coming to me! Both, together! It was a sign, I thought, but I didn't know what to do. I decided to bring the orb here and keep it safe forever. Then, as we traveled, I realized the knights would never allow it to remain here. There would be trouble. So, when I saw my chance, I sent it away." Her shoulders sagged. "That was apparently the wrong decision. But how was I to know?"

"Why?" Theros asked severely. "What does the orb do? Is it evil? Have you sent those knights to their doom?"

"Great evil," Silvara murmured. "Great good. Who can say? Even *I* do not understand the dragon orbs. They were forged long ago by the most powerful of magic-users."

"But the book Tas read said they could be used to control dragons!" Flint stated. "He read it with some kind of glasses. Glasses of true seeing, he called 'em. He said they don't lie—"

"No," said Silvara sadly. "That is true. It is too true, as I fear you friends may discover to their bitter regret."

The companions, fear closing around them, sat together in silence broken only by Gilthanas's choking sobs. The torches sent shadows dodging and dancing around the quiet tomb like undead spirits. Laurana remembered Huma and the Silver Dragon. She thought of that final, terrible battle— the skies filled with dragons, the land erupting in flame and in blood.

"Why have you brought us here, then?" Laurana asked Silvara quietly. "Why not just let us all take the orb away?"

"Can I tell them? Do I have the strength?" Silvara whispered to an unseen spirit.

She sat quietly for a long time, her face expressionless, her hands twisting in her lap. Her eyes closed, her head bowed, her lips moved. She covered her face with her hands and sat quite still. Then, shuddering, she made her decision.

Rising to her feet, Silvara walked over to Laurana's pack. Kneeling down, she slowly and carefully unwrapped the broken shaft of wood that the companions had carried such a long and weary distance. Silvara stood, her face once more filled with peace. But now there was also pride and strength. For the first time, Laurana began to believe this girl was something as powerful and magnificent as a dragon. Walking proudly, her silver hair glistening in the torchlight, Silvara walked over to stand before Theros Ironfeld.

"To Theros of the Silver Arm," she said, "I give the power to forge the dragonlance."

THE RED WIZARD AND HIS WONDERFUL ILLUSIONS!

5

Shadows crept across the dusty tables of the Pig and Whistle tavern. The sea breeze off the Bay of Balifor made a shrill whistling sound as it blew through the ill-fitting front windows, that distinctive whistle giving the inn the last part of its name. Any guesses as to how the tavern got the first part ended on sight of the innkeeper. A jovial, kind-hearted man, William Sweetwater had been cursed at birth (so town legend went) when a wandering pig overturned the baby's cradle, so frightening young William that the mark of the pig was forever imprinted on his face.

This unfortunate resemblance had certainly not impaired William's temper, however. A sailor by trade until he had retired to fulfill a lifelong ambition of keeping an inn, there was not a more respected or well-liked man in Port Balifor than William Sweetwater. No one laughed more heartily at pig jokes than did William. He could even grunt quite realistically and often did pig imitations for the amusement of his customers. (But no one ever—after the untimely death of Peg-Leg Al—called William by the name "Piggy.")

William rarely grunted for his customers these days. The atmosphere of the Pig and Whistle was dark and gloomy. The few old customers that came sat huddled together, talking in low voices. For Port Balifor was an occupied town—overrun by the armies of the highlords, whose ships had recently sailed into the Bay, disgorging troops of the hideous dragonmen.

The people of Port Balifor—mostly humans—felt extremely sorry for themselves. They had no knowledge of what was going on in the outside world, of course, or they would have counted their blessings. No dragons came to burn their town. The draconians generally left the citizens alone. The Dragon Highlords were not particularly interested in the eastern part of the Ansalon continent. The land was sparsely populated: a few poor, scattered communities of humans and Kendermore, the homeland of the kenders. A flight of dragons could have leveled the countryside, but the Dragon Highlords were concentrating their strength in the north and the west. As long as the ports remained opened, the Highlords had no need to devastate the lands of Balifor and Goodlund.

Although not many old customers came to the Pig and Whistle, business had improved for William Sweetwater. The draconian and goblin troops of the Highlord were well paid, and their one weakness was strong drink. But William had not opened his tavern for money. He loved the companionship of old friends and new. He did *not* enjoy the companionship of the Highlord's troops. When they came in, his old customers left. Therefore, William promptly raised his prices for draconians to three times higher than in any other inn in town. He also watered the ale. Consequently, his bar was nearly deserted except for a few old friends. This arrangement suited William fine.

He was talking to a few of these friends—sailors mostly, with brown, weathered skin and no teeth—on the evening that the strangers entered his tavern. William glared at them suspiciously for a moment, as did his friends. But, seeing road-weary travelers and not the Highlord's soldiers, he greeted them cordially and showed them to a table in the corner.

The strangers ordered ale all around—except for a red-robed man who ordered nothing but hot water. Then, after a subdued discussion centering around a worn leather purse and the number of coins therein, they asked William to bring them bread and cheese.

"They're not from these parts," William said to his friends in a low voice as he drew the ale from a special keg he kept beneath the bar (not the keg for draconians). "And poor as a sailor after a week ashore, if I make my guess."

"Refugees," said his friend, eyeing them speculatively.

"Odd mixture, though," added the other sailor. "Yon red-bearded fellow's a half-elf, if ever I saw one. And the big one's got weapons enough to take on the Highlord's whole army."

"I'll wager he's stuck a few of them with that sword, too," William grunted. "They're on the run from something, I'll bet. Look at the way that bearded fellow keeps his eyes on the door. Well, we can't help them fight the Highlord, but I'll see they don't want for anything." He went to serve them.

"Put your money away," William said gruffly, plunking down not only bread and cheese but also a tray full of cold meats as well. He shoved the coins away. "You're in trouble of some kind, that's plain as this pig's snout upon my face."

One of the women smiled at him. She was the most beautiful woman William had ever seen. Her silver-gold hair gleamed from beneath a fur hood, her blue eyes were like the

ocean on a calm day. When she smiled at him, William felt the warmth of fine brandy run through his body. But a stern-faced, dark-haired man next to her shoved the coins back to the innkeeper.

"We'll not accept charity," the tall, fur-cloaked man said.

"We won't?" asked the big man wistfully, staring at the smoked meat with longing eyes.

"Riverwind," the woman remonstrated, putting a gentle hand on his arm. The half-elf, too, seemed about to interpose when the red-robed man, who had ordered the hot water, reached out and picked up a coin from the table.

Balancing the coin on the back of his bony, metallic-colored hand, the man suddenly and effortlessly sent it dancing along his knuckles. William's eyes opened wide. His two friends at the bar came closer to see better. The coin flickered in and out of the red-robed man's fingers, spinning and jumping. It vanished high in the air, only to reappear above the mage's head in the form of six coins, spinning around his hood. With a gesture, he sent them to spin around William's head. The sailors watched in open-mouthed wonder.

"Take one for your trouble," said the mage in a whisper.

Hesitantly, William tried to grab the coins that whirled past his eyes, but his hand went right through them! Suddenly all six coins disappeared. One only remained now, resting in the palm of the red-robed mage.

"I give you this in payment," the mage said with a sly smile, "but be careful. It may burn a hole in your pocket."

William accepted the coin gingerly. Holding it between two fingers, he gazed at it suspiciously. Then the coin burst into flame! With a startled yelp, William dropped it to the floor, stomping on it with his foot. His two friends burst out laughing. Picking up the coin, William discovered it to be perfectly cold and undamaged.

"That's worth the meat!" the innkeeper said, grinning.

"And a night's lodgings," added his friend, the sailor, slapping down a handful of coins.

"I believe," said Raistlin softly, glancing around at the others, "that we have solved our problems."

Thus was born The Red Wizard and His Wonderful Illusions, a traveling road show that is still talked of today as far south as Port Balifor and as far north as the Ruins.

The very next night the red-robed mage began to perform his tricks to an admiring audience of William's friends. The word spread rapidly. After the mage had performed in the Pig and Whistle for about a week, Riverwind—at first opposed to the whole idea—was forced to admit that Raistlin's act seemed likely to solve not only their financial problems but other, more pressing problems as well.

The shortage of money was the most urgent. The companions might have been able to live off the land—even in the winter, both Riverwind and Tanis being skilled hunters. But they needed money to buy passage on a ship to take them to Sancrist. Once they had the money, they needed to be able to travel freely through enemy-occupied lands.

In his youth, Raistlin had often used his considerable talents at sleight of hand to earn bread for himself and his brother. Although this was frowned on by his master, who threatened to expel the young mage from his school, Raistlin had become quite successful. Now his growing powers in magic gave him a range not possible before. He literally kept his audiences spellbound with tricks and phantasms.

At Raistlin's command, white-winged ships sailed up and down the bar at the Pig and Whistle, birds flew out of soup tureens, while dragons peered through the windows, breathing fire upon the startled guests. In the grand finale, the mage—resplendent in red robes sewn by Tika—appeared to be totally consumed in raging flames, only to walk in through the front door moments later (to tumultuous applause) and calmly drink a glass of white wine to the health of the guests.

Within a week, the Pig and Whistle did more business than William had done in a year. Better still—as far as he was concerned—his friends were able to forget their troubles. Soon, however, unwanted guests began to arrive. At first, he had been angered by the appearance of draconians and goblins in the crowd, but Tanis placated him, and William grudgingly permitted them to watch.

Tanis was, in fact, pleased to see them. It worked out well from the half-elf's point of view and solved their second problem. If the Highlord's troops enjoyed the show and spread the word, the companions could travel the countryside unmolested.

It was their plan—after consulting with William—to make for Flotsam, a city north of Port Balifor, located on the Blood Sea of Istar. Here they hoped to find a ship. No one in Port Balifor would give them passage, William explained. All the local shipowners were in the employ of (or their vessels had been confiscated by) the Dragon Highlords. But Flotsam was a known haven for those more interested in money than politics.

The companions stayed at the Pig and Whistle for a month. William provided free room and board and even allowed them to keep all the money they made. Though Riverwind protested this generosity, William stated firmly that all he cared about was seeing his old customers come back.

During this time, Raistlin refined and enlarged his act which, at first consisted only of his illusions. But the mage tired rapidly, so Tika offered to dance and give him time to rest between acts. Raistlin was dubious, but Tika sewed a costume for herself that was so alluring Caramon was—at first—totally opposed to the scheme. But Tika only laughed at him. Her dancing was a success and increased the money they collected dramatically. Raistlin added her immediately to the act.

Finding the crowds enjoyed this diversion, the mage thought of others. Caramon—blushing furiously—was persuaded to perform feats of strength, the highlight coming when he lifted stout William over his head with one hand. Tanis amazed the crowd with his elven ability to "see" in the dark. But Raistlin was startled one day when Goldmoon came to him as he was counting the money from the previous night's performance.

"I would like to sing in the show tonight," she said.

Raistlin looked up at her incredulously. His eyes flicked to Riverwind. The tall Plainsman nodded reluctantly.

"You have a powerful voice," Raistlin said, sliding the money into a pouch and drawing the string tightly. "I remember quite well. The last song I heard you sing in the Inn of the Last Home touched off a riot that nearly got us killed."

Goldmoon flushed, remembering the fateful song that had introduced her to the group. Scowling, Riverwind laid his hand on her shoulder.

"Come away!" he said harshly, glaring at Raistlin. "I warned you—"

But Goldmoon shook her head stubbornly, lifting her chin in a familiar, imperious gesture. "I will sing," she said coolly, "and Riverwind will accompany me. I have written a song."

"Very well," the mage snapped, slipping the money pouch into his robes. "We will try it this evening."

The Pig and Whistle was crowded that night. It was a diverse audience—small children and their parents, sailors, draconians, goblins, and several kender, who caused everyone to keep an eye on his belongings. William and two helpers bustled about, serving drinks and food. Then the show began.

The crowd applauded Raistlin's spinning coins, laughed when an illusory pig danced upon the bar, and scrambled out of their chairs in terror when a giant troll thundered in through a window. Bowing, the mage left to rest. Tika came on.

The crowd, particularly the draconians, cheered Tika's dancing, banging their mugs on the table.

Then Goldmoon appeared before them, dressed in a gown of pale blue. Her silver-gold hair flowed over her shoulders like water shimmering in the moonlight. The crowd hushed instantly. Saying nothing, she sat down in a chair on the raised platform William had hastily constructed. So beautiful was she that not a murmur escaped the crowd. All waited expectantly.

Riverwind sat upon the floor at her feet. Putting a hand-carved flute to his lips, he began to play and, after a few moments, Goldmoon's voice blended with the flute. Her song was simple, the melody sweet and harmonious, yet haunting. But it was the words that caught Tanis's attention, causing him to exchange worried glances with Caramon. Raistlin, sitting next to him, grasped hold of Tanis's arm.

"I feared as much!" the mage hissed. "Another riot!"

"Perhaps not," Tanis said, watching. "Look at the audience."

Women leaned their heads onto their husband's shoulders, children were quiet and attentive. The draconians seemed spellbound, as a wild animal will sometimes be held by music. Only the goblins shuffled their flapping feet, seemingly bored but so in awe of the draconians that they dared not protest.

Goldmoon's song was of the ancient gods. She told how the gods had sent the Cataclysm to punish the Kingpriest of Istar and the people of Krynn for their pride. She sang of the terrors of that night and those that followed. She reminded them of how the people, believing themselves abandoned, had prayed to false gods. Then she gave them a message of hope: the gods had not abandoned them. The true gods were here, waiting only for someone to listen to them.

After her song ended, and the plaintive wailing of the flute died, most in the crowd shook their heads, seeming to wake from a pleasant dream. When asked what the song had been about, they couldn't say. The draconians shrugged and called for more ale. The goblins shouted for Tika to dance again. But, here and there, Tanis noticed a face still holding the wonder it had worn during the song. And he was not surprised to see a young, dark-skinned woman approach Goldmoon shyly.

"I ask your pardon for disturbing you, my lady," Tanis overheard the woman say, "but your song touched me deeply. I—I want to learn of the ancient gods, to learn their ways."

Goldmoon smiled. "Come to me tomorrow," she said, "and I shall teach you what I know."

And thus, slowly, word of the ancient gods began to spread. By the time they left Port Balifor, the dark-skinned woman, a soft-voiced young man, and several other people wore the blue medallion of Mishakal, Goddess of Healing. Secretly they went forth, bringing hope to the dark and troubled land.

By the end of the month, the companions were able to buy a wagon, horses to pull it, horses to ride, and supplies. What was left went toward purchase of ship's passage to Sancrist. They planned to add to their money by performing in the small farming communities between Port Balifor and Flotsam.

When the Red Wizard left Port Balifor shortly before the Yuletide season, his wagon was seen on its way by enthusiastic crowds. Packed with their costumes, supplies for two months, and a keg of ale (provided by William), the wagon was big enough for Raistlin to sleep and travel inside. It also held the multi-colored, striped tents in which the others would live.

Tanis glanced around at the strange sight they made, shaking his head. It seemed that—in the midst of everything else that had happened to them—this was the most bizarre. He looked at Raistlin sitting beside his brother, who drove the wagon. The mage's red-sequined robes blazed like flame in the bright winter sunlight. Shoulders hunched against the wind, Raistlin stared straight ahead, wrapped in a show of mystery that delighted the crowd. Caramon, dressed in a bearskin suit (a present of William's), had pulled the head of the bear over his own, making it look as though a bear drove the wagon. The children cheered as he growled at them in mock ferocity.

They were nearly out of town when a draconian commander stopped them. Tanis, his heart caught in his throat, rode forward, his hand pressed against his sword. But the commander only wanted to make certain they passed through Bloodwatch where draconian troops were located. The draconian had mentioned the show to a friend. The troops were looking forward to seeing it. Tanis, inwardly vowing not to set foot near the place, promised faithfully that they would certainly appear.

Finally they reached the city gates. Climbing down from their mounts, they bid farewell to their friend. William gave them each a hug, starting with Tika and ending with Tika. He was going to hug Raistlin, but the mage's golden eyes widened so alarmingly when William approached that the innkeeper backed away precipitously.

The companions climbed back onto their horses. Raistlin and Caramon returned to the wagon. The crowd cheered and urged them to return for the spring Harrowing celebration. The guards opened the gates, bidding them a safe journey, and the companions rode through. The gates shut behind them.

The wind blew chill. Gray clouds above them began to spit snow fitfully. The road, which they were assured was well traveled, stretched before them, bleak and empty. Raistlin began to shiver and cough. After awhile, he said he would ride inside the wagon. The rest pulled their hoods up over their heads and clutched their fur cloaks more closely about them.

Caramon, guiding the horses along the rutted, muddy road, appeared unusually thoughtful.

"You know, Tanis," he said solemnly above the jingling of the bells Tika had tied to the horses' manes, "I'm more thankful than I can tell that none of our friends saw this. Can you hear what Flint would say? That grumbling old dwarf would never let me live this down. And can you imagine Sturm!" The big man shook his head, the thought being beyond words.

Yes, Tanis sighed. I can imagine Sturm. Dear friend, I never realized how much I depended on you—your courage, your noble spirit. Are you alive, my friend? Did you reach Sancrist safely? Are you now the knight in body that you have always been in spirit? Will we meet again, or have we parted never to meet in this life—as Raistlin predicted?

The group rode on. The day grew darker, the storm wilder. Riverwind dropped back to ride beside Goldmoon. Tika tied her horse behind the wagon and crawled up to sit near Caramon. Inside the wagon, Raistlin slept.

Tanis rode alone, his head bowed, his thoughts far away.

THE KNIGHTS TRIALS.

6

"And—finally," said Derek in a low and measured voice, "I accuse Sturm Brightblade of cowardice in the face of the enemy."

A low murmur ran through the assemblage of knights gathered in the castle of Lord Gunthar. Three knights, seated at the massive black oak table in front of the assembly, leaned their heads together to confer in low tones.

Long ago, the three seated at this Knights Trials—as prescribed by the Measure—would have been the Grand Master, the High Clerist, and the High Justice. But at this time there was no Grand Master. There had not been a High Clerist since the time of the Cataclysm. And while the High Justice—Lord Alfred MarKenin—was present, his hold on that position was tenuous at best. Whoever became the new Grand Master had leave to replace him.

Despite these vacancies in the Head of the Order, the business of the Knights must continue. Though not strong enough to claim the coveted position of Grand Master, Lord Gunthar Uth Wistan was strong enough to act in that role. And so he sat here today, at the beginning of the Yuletide season, in judgment on this young squire, Sturm Brightblade. To his right sat Lord Alfred, to his left, young Lord Michael Jeoffrey, filling in as High Clerist.

Facing them, in the Great Hall of Castle Uth Wistan, were twenty other Knights of Solamnia who had been hastily gathered from all parts of Sancrist to sit as witnesses to this Knights Trials—as prescribed by the Measure. These now muttered and shook their heads as their leaders conferred.

From a table directly in front of the three Knights Seated in Judgment, Lord Derek rose and bowed to Lord Gunthar. His testimony had reached its end. There remained now only the Knight's Answer and the Judgment itself. Derek returned to his place among the other knights, laughing and talking with them.

Only one person in the hall was silent. Sturm Brightblade sat unmoving throughout all of Lord Derek Crownguard's damning accusations. He had heard charges of insubordination, failure to obey orders, masquerading as a knight—and not a word or murmur had escaped him. His face was carefully expressionless, his hands were clasped on the top of the table.

Lord Gunthar's eyes were on Sturm now, as they had been throughout the Trials. He began to wonder if the man was even still alive, so fixed and white was his face, so rigid his posture. Gunthar had seen Sturm flinch only once. At the charge of cowardice, a shudder convulsed the man's body. The look on his face . . . well, Gunthar recalled seeing that same look once previously—on a man who had just been run through by a spear. But Sturm quickly regained his composure.

Gunthar was so interested in watching Brightblade that he nearly lost track of the conversation of the two knights next to him. He caught only the end of Lord Alfred's sentence.

" . . . not allow Knight's Answer."

"Why not?" Lord Gunthar asked sharply, though keeping his voice low. "It is his right according to the Measure."

"We have never had a case like this," Lord Alfred, Knight of the Sword, stated flatly. "Always before, when a squire has been brought up before the Council of the Order to attain his knighthood, there have been witnesses, many witnesses. He is given an opportunity to explain his reasons for his actions. No one ever questions that he committed the acts. But Brightblade's only defense—"

"Is to tell us that Derek lies," finished Lord Michael Jeoffrey, Knight of the Crown. "And that is unthinkable. To take the word of a squire over a Knight of the Rose."

"Nonetheless, the young man will have his say," Lord Gunthar said, glancing sternly at each of the men. "That is the Law according to the Measure. Do either of you question it?"

"No . . ."

"No, of course not. But—"

"Very well." Gunthar smoothed his moustaches and, leaning forward, tapped gently on the wooden table with the hilt of the sword—Sturm's sword—that lay upon it. The other two knights exchanged looks behind his back, one raising his eyebrows, the other shrugging slightly. Gunthar was aware of this, as he was aware of all the covert scheming and plotting now pervasive in the Knighthood. He chose to ignore it.

Not yet strong enough to claim the vacant position of Grand Master, but still the strongest and most powerful of the knights currently seated on the Council, Gunthar had been forced to ignore a great deal of what he would have—in another day and age—quashed without hesitation. He expected this disloyalty of Alfred MarKenin—the knight had long been in Derek's camp—but he was surprised at Michael, whom he had thought loyal to him. Apparently Derek had gotten to him, too.

Gunthar watched Derek Crownguard as the knights returned to their places. Derek was the only rival with the money and backing capable of claiming the rank of Grand Master. Hoping to earn additional votes, Derek had eagerly volunteered to undertake the perilous quest in search of the legendary dragon orbs. Gunthar was given little choice but to agree. If he had refused, he would appear frightened of Derek's growing power. Derek was undeniably the most qualified—if one strictly followed the Measure. But Gunthar, who had known Derek a long time, would have prevented his going if he could have—not because he feared the knight but because he truly did not trust him. The man was vainglorious and power-hungry, and—when it came down to it—Derek's first loyalties lay to Derek.

And now it appeared that Derek's successful return with a dragon orb had won the day. It had brought many knights into his camp who had been heading that direction anyway and actually enticed away some in Gunthar's own faction. The only ones who opposed him still were the younger knights in the lowest order of the Knighthood—Knights of the Crown.

These young men had little use for the strict and rigid interpretation of the Measure that was life's blood to the older knights. They pushed for change—and had been severely chastened by Lord Derek Crownguard. Some came close to losing their knighthood. These young knights were firmly behind Lord Gunthar. Unfortunately, they were few in number and, for the most part, had more loyalty than money. The young knights had, however, adopted Sturm's cause as their own.

But this was Derek Crownguard's master stroke, Gunthar

thought bitterly. With one slice of his sword, Derek was going to get rid of a man he hated and his chief rival as well.

Lord Gunthar was a well-known friend of the Brightblade family, a friendship that traced back generations. It was Gunthar who had advanced Sturm's claim when the young man appeared out of nowhere five years before to seek his father and his inheritance. Sturm had been able, with letters from his mother, to prove his right to the Brightblade name. A few insinuated this had been accomplished on the wrong side of the sheets, but Gunthar quickly squelched those rumors. The young man was obviously the son of his old friend—that much could be seen in Sturm's face. By backing Sturm, however, the lord was risking a great deal.

Gunthar's gaze went to Derek, walking among the knights, smiling and shaking hands. Yes, this trial was making him—Lord Gunthar Uth Wistan—appear a fool.

Worse still, Gunthar thought sadly, his eyes returning to Sturm, it was probably going to destroy the career of what he believed to be a very fine man, a man worthy of walking his father's path.

"Sturm Brightblade," Lord Gunthar said when silence descended on the hall, "you have heard the accusations made against you?"

"I have, my lord," Sturm answered. His deep voice echoed eerily in the hall. Suddenly a log in the huge fireplace behind Gunthar split, sending a flare of heat and a shower of sparks up the chimney. Gunthar paused while the servants hustled in efficiently to add more wood. When the servants were gone, he continued the ritual questioning.

"Do you, Sturm Brightblade, understand the charges made against you, and do you further understand that these are grievous charges and could cause this Council to find you unfit for the knighthood?"

"I do," Sturm started to reply. His voice broke. Coughing, he repeated more firmly, "I do, my lord."

Gunthar smoothed his moustaches, trying to think how to lead into this, knowing that anything the young man said against Derek was going to reflect badly upon Sturm himself.

"How old are you, Brightblade?" Gunthar asked.

Sturm blinked at this unexpected question.

"Over thirty, I believe?" Gunthar continued, musing.

"Yes, my lord," Sturm answered.

"And, from what Derek tells us about your exploits in Ice Wall Castle, a skilled warrior—"

"I never denied that, my lord," Derek said, rising to his feet once again. His voice was tinged with impatience.

"Yet you accuse him of cowardice," Gunthar snapped. "If my memory serves me correctly, you stated that when the elves attacked, he refused to obey your order to fight."

Derek's face was flushed. "May I remind your lordship that *I* am not on trial—"

"You charge Brightblade with cowardice in the face of the enemy," Gunthar interrupted. "It has been many years since the elves were our enemies."

Derek hesitated. The other knights appeared uncomfortable. The elves were members of the Council of Whitestone, but they were not allowed a vote. Because of the discovery of the dragon orb, the elves would be attending the upcoming Council, and it would never do to have word get back to them that the knights considered them enemies.

"Perhaps 'enemy' *is* too strong a word, my lord." Derek recovered smoothly. "If I am at fault, it is simply that I am being forced to go by what is written in the Measure. At the time I speak of, the elves—though not our enemies in point of fact—were doing everything in their power to prevent us from bringing the dragon orb to Sancrist. Since this was my mission—and the elves opposed it—I therefore am forced to define them as 'enemies'—according to the Measure."

Slick swine, Gunthar thought grudgingly.

With a bow to apologize for speaking out of turn, Derek sat down again. Many of the older knights nodded in approval.

"It also says in the Measure," Sturm said slowly, "that we are not to take life needlessly, that we fight only in defense—either our own or the defense of others. The elves did not threaten our lives. At no time were we in actual physical danger."

"They were shooting arrows at you, man!" Lord Alfred struck the table with his gloved hand.

"True, my lord," Sturm replied, "but all know the elves are expert marksmen. If they had wanted to kill us, they would not have been hitting trees!"

"What do you believe would have happened if you had attacked the elves?" Gunthar questioned.

"The results would have been tragic in my view, my lord," Sturm said, his voice soft and low. "For the first time in generations, elves and humans would be killing each other. I think the Dragon Highlords would have laughed."

Several of the young knights applauded.

Lord Alfred glared at them, angry at this serious breach of the Measure's rules of conduct. "Lord Gunthar, may I remind you that Lord Derek Crownguard is not on trial here. He has proven his valor time and again upon the field of battle. I think we may safely take his word for what is an enemy action and what isn't. Sturm Brightblade, do you say that the charges made against you by Lord Derek Crownguard are false?"

"My lord," Sturm began, licking his lips which were cracked and dry, "I do not say the knight has lied. I say, however, that he has misrepresented me."

"To what purpose?" Lord Michael asked.

Sturm hesitated. "I would prefer not to answer that, my lord," he said so quietly that many knights in the back row could not hear and called for Gunthar to repeat the question. He did so and received the same reply—this time louder.

"On what grounds do you refuse to answer that question, Brightblade?" Lord Gunthar asked sternly.

"Because—according to the Measure—it impinges on the honor of the Knighthood," Sturm replied.

Lord Gunthar's face was grave. "That is a serious charge. Making it, you realize you have no one to stand with you in evidence?"

"I do, my lord," Sturm answered, "and that is why I prefer not to respond."

"If I command you to speak?"

"That, of course, would be different."

"Then speak, Sturm Brightblade. This is an unusual situation, and I do not see how we can make a fair judgment without hearing everything. Why do you believe Lord Derek Crownguard misrepresents you?"

Sturm's face flushed. Clasping and unclasping his hands, he raised his eyes and looked directly at the three knights who sat in judgment on him. His case was lost, he knew that. He would never be a knight, never attain what had been dearer to him than life itself. To have lost it through fault of his own would have been bitter enough, but to lose it like this was a festering wound. And so he spoke the words that he knew would make Derek his bitter enemy for the rest of his days.

"I believe Lord Derek Crownguard misrepresents me in an effort to further his own ambition, my lord."

Tumult broke out. Derek was on his feet. His friends restrained him forcibly, or he would have attacked Sturm in the Council Hall. Gunthar banged the sword hilt for order and eventually the assembly quieted down, but not before Derek had challenged Sturm to test his honor in the field.

Gunthar stared at the knight coldly.

"You know, Lord Derek, that in this—a declared time of war—the contests of honor are forbidden! Come to order or I'll have you expelled from this assembly."

Breathing heavily, his face splotched with red, Derek relapsed back into his seat.

Gunthar gave the Assembly a few more moments to settle down, then resumed. "Have you anything more to say in your defense, Sturm Brightblade?"

"No, my lord," Sturm said.

"Then you may withdraw while this matter is considered."

Sturm rose and bowed to the lords. Turning, he bowed to the Assembly. Then he left the room, escorted by two knights who led him to an antechamber. Here, the two knights, not unkindly, left Sturm to himself. They stood near the closed door, talking softly of matters unrelated to the trial.

Sturm sat on a bench at the far end of the chamber. He appeared composed and calm, but it was all an act. He was determined not to let these knights see the tumult in his soul. It was hopeless, he knew. Gunthar's grieved expression told him that much. But what would the judgment be? Exile, being stripped of lands and wealth? Sturm smiled bitterly. He had nothing they could take from him. He had lived outside of Solamnia so long, exile would be meaningless. Death? He would almost welcome that. Anything was better than this hopeless existence, this dull throbbing pain.

Hours passed. The murmur of three voices rose and fell from within the corridors around the Hall, sometimes angrily. Most of the other knights had gone out, since only

the three as Heads of the Council could pass judgment. The other knights were split into differing factions.

The young knights spoke openly of Sturm's noble bearing, his acts of courage, which even Derek could not suppress. Sturm was right in not fighting the elves. The Knights of Solamnia needed all the friends they could get these days. Why attack needlessly, and so forth. The older knights had only one answer—the Measure. Derek had given Sturm an order. He had refused to obey. The Measure said this was inexcusable. Arguments raged most of the afternoon.

Then, near evening, a small silver bell rang.

"Brightblade," said one of the knights.

Sturm raised his head. "Is it time?"

The knight nodded.

Sturm bowed his head for a moment, asking Paladine for courage. Then he rose to his feet. He and his guards waited for the other knights to reenter and be seated. He knew that they were learning the verdict as soon as they entered.

Finally, the two knights detailed as escort opened the door and motioned for Sturm to enter. He walked into the Hall, the knights following behind. Sturm's gaze went at once to the table before Lord Gunthar.

The sword of his father—a sword that legend said was passed down from Berthel Brightblade himself, a sword that would break only if its master broke—lay on the table. Sturm's eyes went to the sword. His head dropped to hide the burning tears in his eyes.

Wreathed around the blade was the ancient symbol of guilt, black roses.

"Bring the man, Sturm Brightblade, forward," called Lord Gunthar.

The man, Sturm Brightblade, *not the knight!* thought Sturm in despair. Then he remembered Derek. His head came up swiftly, proudly, as he blinked away his tears. Just as he would have hidden his pain from his enemy on the field of battle, so he was determined to hide it now from Derek. Throwing back his head defiantly, his eyes on Lord Gunthar and on no one else, the disgraced squire walked forward to stand before the three officers of the Order to await his fate.

"Sturm Brightblade, we have found you guilty. We are prepared to render judgment. Are you prepared to receive it?"

"Yes, my lord," Sturm said tightly.

Gunthar tugged his moustaches, a sign that the men who had served with him recognized. Lord Gunthar always tugged his moustaches just before riding into battle.

"Sturm Brightblade, it is our judgment that you henceforth cease wearing any of the trappings or accoutrements of a Knight of Solamnia."

"Yes, my lord," Sturm said softly, swallowing.

"And, henceforth, you will not draw pay from the coffers of the Knights, nor obtain any property or gift from them. . . ."

The knights in the hall shifted restlessly. This was ridiculous! No one had drawn pay in the service of the Order since the Cataclysm. Something was up. They smelled thunder before the storm.

"Finally—" Lord Gunthar paused. He leaned forward, his hands toying with the black roses that graced the antique sword. His shrewd eyes swept the Assembly, gathering up his audience, allowing the tension to build. By the time he spoke, even the fire behind him had ceased to crackle.

"Sturm Brightblade. Assembled Knights. Never before has a case such as this come before the Council. And that, perhaps, is not as odd as it may seem, for these are dark and unusual days. We have a young squire—and I remind you that Sturm Bright-blade is young by all standards of the Order—a young squire noted for his skill and valor in battle. Even his accuser admits that. A young squire charged with disobeying orders and cowardice in the face of the enemy. The young squire does not deny this charge, but states that he has been misrepresented.

"Now, by the Measure, we are bound to accept the word of a tried and tested knight such as Derek Crownguard over the word of a man who has not yet won his shield. But the Measure also states that this man shall be able to call witnesses in his own behalf. Due to the unusual circumstances occasioned by these dark times, Sturm Brightblade is not able to call witnesses. Nor, for that matter, was Derek Crownguard able to produce witnesses to support his own cause. Therefore, we have agreed on the following, slightly irregular, procedure."

Sturm stood before Gunthar, confused and troubled. What was happening? He glanced at the other two knights. Lord Alfred was not bothering to conceal his anger. It was obvious, therefore, that this "agreement" of Gunthar's had been hard won.

"It is the judgment of this Council," Lord Gunthar continued, "that the young man, Sturm Brightblade, be accepted into the lowest order of the knights—the Order of the Crown—*on my honor . . .*"

There was a universal gasp of astonishment.

"And that, furthermore, he be placed as third in command of the army that is due to set sail shortly for Palanthas. As prescribed by the Measure, the High Command must have a representative from each of the Orders. Therefore, Derek Crownguard will be High Commander, representing the Order of the Rose. Lord Alfred MarKenin will represent the Order of the Sword, and Sturm Brightblade will act—on my honor—as commander for the Order of the Crown."

Amid the stunned silence, Sturm felt tears course down his cheeks, but now he need hide them no longer. Behind him, he heard the sound of someone rising, of a sword rattling in anger. Derek stalked furiously out of the Hall, the other knights of his faction following him. There were scattered cheers, too. Sturm saw through his tears that about half the knights in the room—particularly the younger knights, the knights he would command—were applauding. Sturm felt swift pain well deep from inside his soul. Though he had won his victory, he was appalled by what the knighthood had become, divided into factions by power-hungry men. It was nothing more than a corrupt shell of a once-honored brotherhood.

"Congratulations, Brightblade," Lord Alfred said stiffly. "I hope you realize what Lord Gunthar has done for you."

"I do, my lord," Sturm said, bowing, "and I swear by my father's sword"—he laid his hand upon it—"that I will be worthy of his trust."

"See to it, young man," Lord Alfred replied and left. The younger lord, Michael, accompanied him without a word to Sturm.

But the other young knights came forward then, offering their enthusiastic congratulations. They pledged his health in wine and would have stayed for an all-out drinking bout if Gunthar had not sent them on their way.

When the two of them were alone in the Hall, Lord Gunthar smiled expansively at Sturm and shook his hand. The young knight returned the handshake warmly, if not the smile. The pain was too fresh.

Then, slowly and carefully, Sturm took the black roses from his sword. Laying them on the table, he slid the blade back in the scabbard at his side. He started to brush the roses aside, but paused, then picked up one and thrust it into his belt.

"I must thank you, my lord," Sturm began, his voice quivering.

"You have nothing to thank me for, son," Lord Gunthar said. Glancing around the room, he shivered. "Let's get out of this place and go somewhere warm. Mulled wine?"

The two knights walked down the stone corridors of Gunthar's ancient castle, the sounds of the young knights leaving drifting up from below—horses's hooves clattering on the cobblestone, voices shouting, some even raising in a military song.

"I must thank you, my lord," Sturm said firmly. "The risk you take is very great. I hope I will prove worthy—"

"Risk! Nonsense, my boy." Rubbing his hands to restore the circulation, Gunthar led Sturm into a small room decorated for the approaching Yule celebration—red winter roses, grown indoors, kingfisher feathers, and tiny, delicate golden crowns. A fire blazed brightly. At Gunthar's command, servants brought in two mugs of steaming liquid that gave off a warm, spicy odor. "Many were the times your father threw his shield in front of me and stood over me, protecting me when I was down."

"And you did the same for him," Sturm said. "You owe him nothing. Pledging your honor for me means that, if I fail, you will suffer. You will be stripped of your rank, your title, your lands. Derek would see to that," he added gloomily.

As Gunthar took a deep drink of his wine, he studied the young man before him. Sturm merely sipped at his wine out of politeness, holding the mug with a hand that trembled visibly. Gunthar laid his hand kindly on Sturm's shoulder, pushing the young man down gently into a chair.

"Have you failed in the past, Sturm?" Gunthar asked.

Sturm looked up, his brown eyes flashing. "No, my lord," he answered. "I have not. I swear it!"

"Then I have no fear for the future," Lord Gunthar said, smiling. He raised his mug. "I pledge your good fortune in battle, Sturm Brightblade."

MARGARET WEIS & TRACY HICKMAN

Sturm shut his eyes. The strain had been too much. Dropping his head on his arm, he wept—his body shaking with painful sobs. Gunthar gripped his shoulder.

"I understand . . ." he said, his eyes looking back to a time in Solamnia when this young man's father had broken down and cried that same way—the night Lord Brightblade had sent his young wife and infant son on a journey into exile—a journey from which he would never see them return.

Exhausted, Sturm finally fell asleep, his head lying on the table. Gunthar sat with him, sipping the hot wine, lost in memories of the past, until he, too, drifted into slumber.

The few days left before the army sailed to Palanthas passed swiftly for Sturm. He had to find armor—used; he couldn't afford new. He packed his father's carefully, intending to carry it since he had been forbidden to wear it. Then there were meetings to attend, battle dispositions to study, information on the enemy to assimilate.

The battle for Palanthas would be a bitter one, determining control of the entire northern part of Solamnia. The leaders were agreed upon their strategy. They would fortify the city walls with the city's army. The knights themselves would occupy the High Clerist's Tower that stood blocking the pass through the Vingaard Mountains. But that was all they agreed upon. Meetings between the three leaders were tense, the air chill.

Finally the day came for the ships to sail. The knights gathered on board. Their families stood quietly on the shore. Though faces were pale, there were few tears, the women standing as tight-lipped and stern as their men. Some wives wore swords buckled around their own waists. All knew that, if the battle in the north was lost, the enemy would come across the sea.

Gunthar stood upon the pier, dressed in his bright armor, talking with the knights, bidding farewell to his sons. He and Derek exchanged a few ritual words as prescribed by the Measure. He and Lord Alfred embraced perfunctorily. At last, Gunthar sought out Sturm. The young knight, clad in plain, shabby armor, stood apart from the crowd.

"Brightblade," Gunthar said in a low voice as he came near him, "I have been meaning to ask this but never found a moment in these last few days. You mentioned that these friends of yours would be coming to Sancrist. Are there any who could serve as witnesses before the Council?"

Sturm paused. For a wild moment the only person he could think of was Tanis. His thoughts had been with his friend during these last trying days. He'd even had a surge of hope that Tanis might arrive in Sancrist. But the hope had died. Wherever Tanis was, he had his own problems, he faced his own dangers. There was another person, too, whom he had hoped against hope he might see. Without conscious thought, Sturm placed his hand over the Starjewel that hung around his neck against his breast. He could almost feel its warmth, and he knew—without knowing how—that though far away, Alhana was with him. Then—

"Laurana!" he said.

"A woman?" Gunthar frowned.

"Yes, but daughter of the Speaker of the Suns, a member of the royal household of the Qualinesti. And there is her brother, Gilthanas. Both would testify for me."

"The royal household . . ." Gunthar mused. His face brightened. "That would be perfect, especially since we have received word that the Speaker himself will attend the High Council to discuss the dragon orb. If that happens, my boy, somehow I'll get word to you, and you can put that armor back on! You'll be vindicated! Free to wear it without shame!"

"And you will be free of your pledge," Sturm said, shaking hands with the knight gratefully.

"Bah! Don't give that a thought." Gunthar laid his hand on Sturm's head, as he had laid his hand on the heads of his own sons. Sturm knelt before him reverently. "Receive my blessing, Sturm Brightblade, a father's blessing I give in the absence of your own father. Do your duty, young man, and remain your father's son. May Lord Huma's spirit be with you."

"Thank you, my lord," Sturm said, rising to his feet. "Farewell."

"Farewell, Sturm," Gunthar said. Embracing the young knight swiftly, he turned and walked away.

The knights boarded the ships. It was dawn, but no sun shone in the winter sky. Gray clouds hung over a lead-gray sea. There were no cheers, the only sounds were the shouted commands of the captain and the responses of his crew, the creaking of the winches, and the flapping of the sails in the wind.

Slowly the white-winged ships weighed anchor and sailed north. Soon the last sail was out of sight, but still no one left the pier, not even when a sudden rain squall struck, pelting them with sleet and icy drops, drawing a fine gray curtain across the chill waters.

THE DRAGON ORB. CARAMON'S PLEDGE.

7

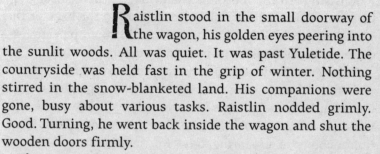

Raistlin stood in the small doorway of the wagon, his golden eyes peering into the sunlit woods. All was quiet. It was past Yuletide. The countryside was held fast in the grip of winter. Nothing stirred in the snow-blanketed land. His companions were gone, busy about various tasks. Raistlin nodded grimly. Good. Turning, he went back inside the wagon and shut the wooden doors firmly.

The companions had been camped here for several days, on the outskirts of Kendermore. Their journey was nearing an end. It had been unbelievably successful. Tonight they would leave, traveling to Flotsam under the cover of darkness. They had money enough to hire a ship, plus some left over for supplies and payment for a week's lodging in Flotsam. This afternoon had been their final performance.

The young mage made his way through the clutter to the back of the wagon. His gaze lingered on the shimmering red robe that hung on a nail. Tika had started to pack it away, but Raistlin had snarled at her viciously. Shrugging, she let it remain, going outside to walk in the woods, knowing Caramon—as usual—would find her.

Raistlin's thin hand reached out to touch the robe, the slender fingers stroking the shining, sequined fabric wistfully, regretting that this period in his life was over.

"I have been happy," he murmured to himself. "Strange. There have not been many times in my life I could make that claim. Certainly not when I was young, nor in these past few years, after they tortured my body and cursed me with these eyes. But then I never expected happiness. How paltry it is, compared to my magic! Still . . . still, these last few weeks have been weeks of peace. Weeks of happiness. I don't suppose any will come again. Not after what I must do—"

Raistlin held the robe a moment longer, then, shrugging, he tossed it in a corner and continued on to the back of the wagon which he had curtained off for his own private use. Once inside, he pulled the curtains securely together.

Excellent. He would have privacy for several hours, until nightfall, in fact. Tanis and Riverwind had gone hunting. Caramon had, too, supposedly, though everyone knew this was just an excuse for him to find time alone with Tika. Goldmoon was preparing food for their journey. No one would bother him. The mage nodded to himself in satisfaction.

Sitting down at the small drop-leaf table Caramon had constructed for him, Raistlin carefully withdrew from the very innermost pocket of his robes an ordinary-looking sack, the sack that contained the dragon orb. His skeletal fingers trembled as he tugged on the drawstring. The bag opened. Reaching in, Raistlin grasped the dragon orb and brought it forth. He held it easily in his palm, inspecting it closely to see if there had been any change.

No. A faint green color still swirled within. It still felt as cold to the touch as if he held a hailstone. Smiling, Raistlin clasped the orb tightly in one hand while he fumbled through the props beneath the table. He finally found what he sought—a crudely carved, three-legged wooden stand. Lifting it up, Raistlin set it on the table. It wasn't much to look at—Flint would have scoffed. Raistlin had neither the love nor the skill needed to work wood. He had carved it laboriously, in secret, shut up inside the jouncing wagon during the long days on the road. No, it was not much to look at, but he didn't care. It would suit his purpose.

Placing the stand upon the table, he set the dragon orb on it. The marble-sized orb looked ludicrous, but Raistlin sat back, waiting patiently. As he had expected, soon the orb began to grow. Or did it? Perhaps *he* was shrinking. Raistlin couldn't tell. He knew only that suddenly the orb was the right size. If anything was different, it was he that was too small, too insignificant to even be in the same room with the orb.

The mage shook his head. He must stay in control, he knew, and he was immediately aware of the subtle tricks the orb was playing to undermine that control. Soon these tricks would not be subtle. Raistlin felt his throat tighten. He coughed, cursing his weak lungs. Drawing a shuddering breath, he forced himself to breathe deeply and easily.

Relax, he thought. I must relax. I do not fear. I am strong. Look what I have done! Silently he called upon the orb: Look at the power I have attained! Witness what I did in Darken Wood. Witness what I did in Silvanesti. I am strong. I do not fear.

The orb's colors swirled softly. It did not answer.

The mage closed his eyes for a moment, blotting the orb from sight. Regaining control, he opened them again, regarding the orb with a sigh. The moment approached.

The dragon orb was now back to its original size. He could almost see Lorac's wizened hands grasping it. The young

mage shuddered involuntarily. No! Stop it! he told himself firmly, and immediately banished the vision from his mind.

Once more he relaxed, breathing regularly, his hourglass eyes focused on the orb. Then—slowly—he stretched forth his slender, metallic-colored fingers. After a moment's final hesitation, Raistlin placed his hands upon the cold crystal of the dragon orb and spoke the ancient words.

"Ast bilak moiparalan/Suh akvlar tantangusar." How did he know what to say? How did he know what ancient words would cause the orb to understand him, to be aware of his presence? Raistlin did not know. He knew only that—somehow, somewhere—inside of him, he *did* know the words! The voice that had spoken to him in Silvanesti? Perhaps. It didn't matter. Again he said the words aloud.

"Ast bilak moiparalan/Suh akvlar tantangusar!" Slowly the drifting green color was submerged in a myriad of swirling, gliding colors that made him dizzy to watch. The crystal was so cold beneath his palms that it was painful to touch. Raistlin had a terrifying vision of pulling away his hands and leaving the flesh behind, frozen to the orb. Gritting his teeth, he ignored the pain and whispered the words again.

The colors ceased to swirl. A light glowed in the center, a light neither white nor black, all colors, yet none. Raistlin swallowed, fighting the choking phlegm that rose in his throat.

Out of the light came two hands! He had a desperate urge to withdraw his own, but before he could move, the two hands grasped his in a grip both strong and firm. The orb vanished! The room vanished! Raistlin saw nothing around him. No light. No darkness. Nothing! Nothing . . . but two hands, holding his. Out of sheer terror, Raistlin concentrated on those hands.

Human? Elven? Old? Young? He could not tell. The fingers

were long and slender, but their grip was the grip of death. Let go and he would fall into the void to drift until merciful darkness consumed him. Even as he clung to those hands with strength lent him by fear, Raistlin realized the hands were slowly drawing him nearer, drawing him into . . . into . . .

Raistlin came to himself suddenly, as if someone had dashed cold water in his face. No! he told the mind that he sensed controlled the hands. I will not go! Though he feared losing that saving grip, he feared even more being dragged where he did not want to go. He would not let loose. I *will* maintain control, he told the mind of the hands savagely. Tightening his own grip, the mage summoned all of his strength, all of his will, and pulled the hands toward him!

The hands stopped. For a moment, the two wills vied together, locked in a life-or-death contest. Raistlin felt the strength ebb from his body, his hands weakened, the palms began to sweat. He felt the hands of the orb begin to pull him again, ever so slightly. In agony, Raistlin summoned every drop of blood, focused every nerve, sacrificed every muscle in his frail body to regain control.

Slowly . . . slowly . . . just when he thought his pounding heart would burst from his chest or his brain explode in fire—Raistlin felt the hands cease their tug. They still maintained their firm grip on him—as he maintained his firm grip on them. But the two were no longer in contest. His hands and the hands of the dragon orb remained locked together, each conceding respect, neither seeking dominance.

The ecstasy of the victory, the ecstasy of the magic flowed through Raistlin and burst forth, wrapping him in a warm, golden light. His body relaxed. Trembling, he felt the hands hold him gently, support him, lend him strength.

What are you? he questioned silently. Are you good? Evil?

I am neither. I am nothing. I am everything. The essence of dragons captured long ago is what I am.

How do you work? Raistlin asked. How do you control the dragons?

At your command, I will call them to me. They cannot resist my call. They will obey.

Will they turn upon their masters? Will they fall under my command?

That depends on the strength of the master and the bond between the two. In some instances, this is so strong that the master can maintain control of the dragon. But most will do what you ask of them. They cannot help themselves.

I must study this, Raistlin murmured, feeling himself growing weaker. I do not understand. . . .

Be easy. I will aid you. Now that we have joined, you may seek my help often. I know of many secrets long forgotten. They can be yours.

What secrets? . . . Raistlin felt himself losing consciousness. The strain had been too much. He struggled to keep his hold on the hands, but he felt his grip slipping.

The hands held onto him gently, as a mother holds a child.

Relax, I will not let you fall. Sleep. You are weary.

Tell me! I must know! Raistlin cried silently.

This only I will tell you, then you must rest. In the library of Astinus of Palanthas are books, hundreds of books, taken there by the mages of old in the days of the Lost Battle. To all who look at these books, they seem nothing more than encyclopedias of magic, dull histories of mages who died in the caverns of time.

Raistlin saw darkness creeping toward him. He clutched at the hands.

What do the books really contain? he whispered.

Then he knew, and with the knowledge, darkness crashed over him like the wave of an ocean.

In a cave near the wagon, hidden by shadows, warmed by the heat of their passion, Tika and Caramon lay in each other's arms. Tika's red hair clung around her face and forehead in tight curls, her eyes were closed, her full lips parted. Her soft body clad in her gaily-colored skirt and puffy-sleeved white blouse pressed against Caramon. Her legs twined around his, her hand caressed his face, her lips brushed his.

"Please, Caramon," she whispered. "This is torture. We want each other. I'm not afraid. Please love me!"

Caramon closed his eyes. His face shone with sweat. The pain of his love seemed impossible to bear. He could end it, end it all in sweet ecstasy. For a moment he hesitated. Tika's fragrant hair was in his nostrils, her soft lips on his neck. It would be so easy . . . so wonderful. . . .

Caramon sighed. Firmly he closed his strong hands around Tika's wrists. Firmly he drew them away from his face and pushed the girl from him.

"No," he said, his passion choking him. Rolling over, he stood up."No," he repeated. "I'm sorry. I didn't mean to . . . to let things get this far."

"Well, I did!" Tika cried. "I'm *not* frightened! Not anymore."

No, he thought, pressing his hands against his pounding head. I feel you trembling in my hands like a snared rabbit. Tika began to tie the string on her white blouse. Unable to see it through her tears, she jerked at the drawstring so viciously it snapped.

"Now! See there!" She hurled the broken silken twine across the cave. "I've ruined my blouse! I'll have to mend it. They'll all know what happened, of course! Or think they know! I—I . . . Oh, what's the use!" Weeping in frustration,

Tika covered her face with her hands, rocking back and forth.

"I don't care what they think!" Caramon said, his voice echoing in the cave. He did not comfort her. He knew if he touched her again, he would yield to his passion. "Besides, they don't think anything at all. They are our friends. They care for us—"

"I know!" Tika cried brokenly. "It's Raistlin, isn't it? He doesn't approve of me. He *hates* me!"

"Don't say that, Tika." Caramon's voice was firm. "If he did and if he were stronger, it wouldn't matter. I wouldn't care what anyone said or thought. The others want us to be happy. They don't understand why we—we don't become—er—lovers. Tanis even told me to my face I was a fool—"

"He's right." Tika's voice was muffled by tear-damp hair.

"Maybe. Maybe not."

Something in Caramon's voice made the girl quit crying. She looked up at him as Caramon turned around to face her.

"You don't know what happened to Raist in the Towers of High Sorcery. None of you know. None of you ever will. But I know. I was there. I saw. They *made* me see!" Caramon shuddered, putting his hands over his face. Tika held very still. Then, looking at her again, he drew a deep breath. "They said, 'His strength will save the world.' What strength? Inner strength? I'm his outer strength! I—I don't understand, but Raist said to me in the dream that we were one whole person, cursed by the gods and put into two bodies. We need each other—right now at least." The big man's face darkened. "Maybe someday that will change. Maybe some day he'll find the outer strength—"

Caramon fell silent. Tika swallowed and wiped her hand across her face. "I—" she began, but Caramon cut her off.

"Wait a minute," he said. "Let me finish. I love you, Tika, as truly as any man loves any woman in this world. I want you. If we weren't involved in this stupid war, I'd make you mine today. This minute. But I can't. Because if I did, it would be a commitment to you that I would dedicate my life to keeping. You must come first in all my thoughts. You deserve no less than that. But I can't make that commitment, Tika. My first commitment is to my brother." Tika's tears flowed again—this time not for herself, but for him. "I must leave you free to find someone who can—"

"Caramon!" A call split the afternoon's sweet silence. "Caramon, come quickly!" It was Tanis.

"Raistlin!" said the big man, and without another word, ran out of the cave.

Tika stood a moment, watching after him. Then, sighing, she tried to comb her damp hair into place.

"What is it?" Caramon burst into the wagon. "Raist?"

Tanis nodded, his face grave.

"I found him like this." The half-elf drew back the curtain to the mage's small apartment. Caramon shoved him aside.

Raistlin lay on the floor, his skin white, his breathing shallow. Blood trickled from his mouth. Kneeling down, Caramon lifted him in his arms.

"Raistlin?" he whispered. "What happened?"

"*That's* what happened," Tanis said grimly, pointing.

Caramon glanced up, his gaze coming to rest on the dragon orb—now grown to the size Caramon had seen in Silvanesti. It stood on the stand Raistlin had made for it, its swirling colors shifting endlessly as he watched. Caramon sucked in his breath in horror. Terrible visions of Lorac flooded his mind. Lorac insane, dying . . .

"Raist!" he moaned, clutching his brother tightly.

Raistlin's head moved feebly. His eyelids fluttered, and he opened his mouth.

"What?" Caramon bent low, his brother's breath cold upon his skin. "What?"

"Mine . . ." Raistlin whispered. "Spells . . . of the ancients . . . mine . . . Mine . . ." The mage's head lolled, his words died. But his face was calm, placid, relaxed. His breathing grew regular.

Raistlin's thin lips parted in a smile.

Yuletide Guests.

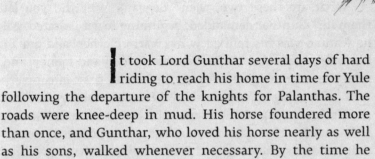

8

It took Lord Gunthar several days of hard riding to reach his home in time for Yule following the departure of the knights for Palanthas. The roads were knee-deep in mud. His horse foundered more than once, and Gunthar, who loved his horse nearly as well as his sons, walked whenever necessary. By the time he returned to his castle, therefore, he was exhausted, drenched, and shivering. The stableman came out to take charge of the horse personally.

"Rub him down well," Gunthar said, dismounting stiffly. "Hot oats and—" He proceeded with his instructions, the stableman nodding patiently, as if he'd never cared for a horse before in his life. Gunthar was, in fact, on the point of walking his horse to the stables himself when his ancient retainer came out in search of him.

"My lord." Wills drew Gunthar to one side in the entryway. "You have visitors. They arrived just a few hours ago."

"Who?" Gunthar asked without much interest, visitors being nothing new, especially during Yule. "Lord Michael? He could not travel with us, but I asked him to stop on his way home—"

"An old man, my lord," Wills interrupted, "and a kender."

"A kender?" Gunthar repeated in some alarm.

"I'm afraid so, my lord. But don't worry," the retainer added hastily. "I've locked the silver in a drawer, and your lady wife has taken her jewelry to the cellar."

"You'd think we were under siege!" Gunthar snorted. He did, however, go through the courtyard faster than usual.

"You can't be too careful around those critters, my lord," Wills mumbled, trotting along behind.

"What are these two, then? Beggars? Why did you let them in?" Gunthar demanded, beginning to get irritated. All he wanted was his mulled wine, warm clothes, and one of his wife's backrubs. "Give them some food and money, and send them on their way. Search the kender first, of course."

"I was going to, my lord," Wills said stubbornly. "But there's something about them—the old man in particular. He's crackers, if you ask me, but he's a smart crackers, for all that. Knows something, and it may be more than's good for him—or us either."

"What do you mean?"

The two had just opened the huge, wooden doors leading into the living quarters of the castle proper. Gunthar stopped and stared at Wills, knowing and respecting his retainer's keen power of observation. Wills glanced around, then leaned close.

"The old man said I was to tell you he had urgent news regarding the dragon orb, my lord!"

"The dragon orb!" Gunthar murmured. The orb was secret, or he presumed it was. The Knights knew of it, of course. Had Derek told anyone else? Was this one of his maneuvers?

"You acted wisely, Wills, as always," Gunthar said finally. "Where are they?"

"I put them in your war room, my lord, figuring they could cause little mischief there."

"I'll change clothes before I catch my death, then see them directly. Have you made them comfortable?"

"Yes, my lord," Wills replied, hurrying after Gunthar, who was on the move again. "Hot wine, a bit of bread and meat. Though I trust the kender's lifted the plates by now—"

Gunthar and Wills stood outside the door of the war room for a moment, eavesdropping on the visitors' conversation.

"Put that back!" ordered a stern voice.

"I won't! It's mine! Look, it was in my pouch."

"Bah! I saw you put it there not five minutes ago!"

"Well, you're wrong," protested the other voice in wounded tones. "It's mine! See, there's my name engraved—"

" 'To Gunthar, my beloved husband on the Day of Life-Gift,' " said the first voice.

There was a moment's silence in the room. Wills turned pale. Then the shrill voice spoke, more subdued this time.

"I guess it must have fallen into my pack, Fizban. That's it! See, my pack was sitting under that table. Wasn't that lucky? It would have broken if it had hit the floor—"

His face grim, Lord Gunthar flung open the door.

"Merry Yuletide to you, sirs," he said. Wills popped in after him, his eyes darting quickly around the room.

The two strangers whirled around, the old man holding a crockery mug in his hand. Wills made a leap for the mug, whisking it away. With an indignant glance at the kender, he placed it upon the mantlepiece, high above the kender's reach.

"Will there be anything else, my lord?" Wills asked, glaring meaningfully at the kender. "Shall I stay and keep an eye on things?"

Gunthar opened his mouth to reply, but the old man waved a negligent hand.

"Yes, thank you, my good man. Bring up some more ale. And don't bring any of that rotgut stuff from the servants' barrels, either!" The old man looked at Wills sternly. "Tap the barrel that's in the dark corner by the cellar stairs. You know—the one that's all cobwebby."

Wills stared at him, open-mouthed.

"Well, go on. Don't stand there gaping like a landed fish! A bit dim-witted, is he?" the old man asked Gunthar.

"N-no," Gunthar stammered. "That's all right, Wills. I—I believe I'll have a mug, too—of—of the ale from the cask by the—uh—stairs. How did *you* know?" He demanded of the old man suspiciously.

"Oh, he's a magic-user," the kender said, shrugging and sitting down without being invited.

"A magic-user?" The old man peered around. "Where?"

Tas whispered something, poking the old man.

"Really? Me?" he said. "You don't say! How remarkable. Now you know, come to think of it, I do seem to remember a spell . . . Fireball. How did it go?"

The old mage began to speak the strange words. Alarmed, the kender leaped out of his seat and grabbed the old man.

"No, Old One!" he said, tugging him back into a chair. "Not now!"

"I suppose not," the old man said wistfully. "Wonderful spell, though . . ."

"I'm certain," murmured Gunthar, absolutely mystified. Then he shook his head, regaining his sternness. "Now, explain yourselves. Who are you? Why are you here? Wills said something about a dragon orb—"

"I'm—" The mage stopped, blinking.

"Fizban," said the kender with a sigh. Standing, he

92

extended his small hand politely to Gunthar. "And I am Tasslehoff Burrfoot." He started to sit down. "Oh," he said, popping up again. "A Merry Yuletide to you, too, sir knight."

"Yes, yes," Gunthar shook hands, nodding absently. "Now about the dragon orb?"

"Ah, yes, the dragon orb!" The befuddled look left Fizban's face. He stared at Gunthar with shrewd, cunning eyes. "Where is it? We've come a long way in search of it."

"I'm afraid I can't tell you," Gunthar said coolly. "If, indeed, such a thing were ever here—"

"Oh, it was here," Fizban replied. "Brought to you by a Knight of the Rose, one Derek Crownguard. And Sturm Brightblade was with him."

"They're friends of mine," explained Tasslehoff, seeing Gunthar's jaw go slack. "I helped get the orb, in fact," the kender added modestly. "We took it away from an evil wizard in a palace made of ice. It's the most wonderful story—" He sat forward eagerly. "Do you want to hear it?"

"No," said Gunthar, staring at them both in amazement. "And if I believed this swimming bird tale—wait—" He sank back in his chair. "Sturm did say something about a kender. Who were the others in your party?"

"Flint the dwarf, Theros the blacksmith, Gilthanas and Laurana—"

"It must be!" Gunthar exclaimed, then he frowned. "But he never mentioned a magic-user. . . ."

"Oh, that's because I'm dead," Fizban stated, propping his feet upon the table.

Gunthar's eyes opened wide, but before he could reply, Wills came in. Glaring at Tasslehoff, the retainer set mugs down on the table in front of his lordship.

"*Three mugs*, here, my lord. And one on the mantle makes four. And there better be *four* when I come back!"

He walked out, shutting the door with a thud.

"I'll keep an eye on them," Tas promised solemnly. "Do you have a problem with people stealing mugs?" he asked Gunthar.

"I—no. . . . Dead?" Gunthar felt he was rapidly losing his grip on the situation.

"It's a long story," said Fizban, downing the liquid in one swallow. He wiped the foam from his lips with the tip of his beard. "Ah, excellent. Now, where was I?"

"Dead," said Tas helpfully.

"Ah, yes. A long story. Too long for now. Must get the orb. Where is it?"

Gunthar stood up angrily, intending to order this strange old man and this kender from his chamber and his castle. He was going to call his guards to extract them. But, instead, he found himself caught by the old man's intense gaze.

The Knights of Solamnia have always feared magic. Though they had not taken part in the destruction of the Towers of High Sorcery—that would have been against the Measure—they had not been sorry to see magic-users driven from Palanthas.

"Why do you want to know?" Gunthar faltered, feeling a cold fear seep into his blood as he felt the old man's strange power engulf him. Slowly, reluctantly, Gunthar sat back down.

Fizban's eyes glittered. "I keep my own counsel," he said softly. "Let it be enough for you to know that I have come seeking the orb. It was made by magic-users, long ago! I know of it. I know a great deal about it."

Gunthar hesitated, wrestling with himself. After all, there were knights guarding the orb, and if this old man really did know something about it, what harm could there be in telling him where it was? Besides, he really didn't feel like he had any choice in the matter.

Fizban absently picked up his empty mug again and started to drink. He peered inside it mournfully as Gunthar answered.

"The dragon orb is with the gnomes."

Fizban dropped his mug with a crash. It broke into a hundred pieces that went skittering across the wooden floor.

"There, what'd I tell you?" Tas said sadly, eyeing the shattered mug.

The gnomes had lived in Mount Nevermind for as long as they could remember—and since they were the only ones who cared, they were the only ones who counted. Certainly they were there when the first knights arrived in Sancrist, traveling from the newly created kingdom of Solamnia to build their keeps and fortress along the westernmost part of their border.

Always suspicious of outsiders, the gnomes were alarmed to see a ship arriving upon their shores, bearing hordes of tall, stern-faced, warlike humans. Determined to keep what they considered a mountain paradise secret from the humans, the gnomes launched into action. Being the most technologically minded of the races on Krynn (they are noted for having invented the steam-powered engine and the coiled spring), the gnomes first thought of hiding within their mountain caverns, but then had a better idea. Hide the mountain itself!

After several months of unending toil by their greatest mechanical geniuses, the gnomes were prepared. Their plan? They were going to make their mountain disappear!

It was at this juncture that one of the members of the gnomish Philosopher's Guild asked if it wasn't likely that the knights would have already noticed the mountain, the tallest on the island. Might not the sudden disappearance of the mountain create a certain amount of curiosity in the humans?

This question threw the gnomes into turmoil. Days were spent in discussion. The question soon divided the Philosopher gnomes into two factions: those who believed that if a tree fell in a forest and no one heard it, it still made a crashing sound; and those who believed it didn't. Just what this had to do with the original question was brought up on the seventh day, but was promptly referred to committee.

Meanwhile, the Mechanical Engineers, in a huff, decided to set off the device anyhow.

And thus occurred the day that is still remembered in the annals of Sancrist (when almost everything else was lost during the Cataclysm) as the Day of Rotten Eggs.

On that day an ancestor of Lord Gunthar woke up wondering sleepily if his son had fallen through the roof of the hen house again. This had happened only a few weeks before. The boy had been chasing a rooster.

"You take him down to the pond," Gunthar's ancestor told his wife sleepily, rolling over in bed and drawing the covers up over his head.

"I can't!" she said drowsily. "The chimney's smoking!"

It was then that both fully woke up, realizing that the smoke filling the house was not coming from the chimney and that the ungodly odor was not coming from the hen house.

Along with every other resident of the new colony, the two rushed outside, choking and gagging with the smell that grew worse by the minute. They could see nothing, however. The land was covered with a thick yellow smoke, redolent of eggs that had been sitting in the sun for three days.

Within hours, everyone in the colony was deathly sick from the smell. Packing up blankets and clothes, they headed for the beaches. Breathing the fresh salt breezes thankfully, they wondered if they could ever go back to their homes.

While discussing this and watching anxiously to see if the yellow cloud on the horizon might lift, the colonists were considerably startled to see what appeared to be an army of short, brown creatures stagger out of the smoke to fall almost lifeless at their feet.

The kindly people of Solamnia immediately went to the aid of the poor gnomes, and thus did the two races of people living on Sancrist meet.

The meeting of the gnomes and the knights turned out to be a friendly one. The Solamnic people had a high regard for four things: individual honor, the Code, the Measure, and technology. They were vastly impressed with the labor-saving devices the gnomes had invented at this time, which included the pulley, the shaft, the screw, and the gear.

It was during this first meeting that Mount Nevermind got its name as well.

The knights soon discovered that, while gnomes appeared to be related to the dwarves—being short and stocky—all similarity ended there. The gnomes were a skinny people with brown skin and pale white hair, highly nervous and hot-tempered. They spoke so rapidly that the knights at first thought they were speaking a foreign language. Instead, it turned out to be Common spoken at an accelerated pace. The reason for this became obvious when an elder made the mistake of asking the gnomes the name of their mountain.

Roughly translated, it went something like this: A Great, Huge, Tall Mound Made of Several Different Strata of Rock of Which We Have Identified Granite, Obsidian, Quartz With Traces of Other Rock We Are Still Working On, That Has Its Own Internal Heating System Which We Are Studying In

Order to Copy Someday That Heats the Rock Up to Temperatures That Convert It Into Both Liquid and Gaseous States Which Occasionally Come to the Surface and Flow Down the Side of the Great, Huge, Tall Mound—

"Nevermind," the elder said hastily.

Nevermind! The gnomes were impressed. To think that these humans could reduce something so gigantic and marvelous into something so simple was wonderful beyond belief. And so, the mountain was called Mount Nevermind from that day forth, to the vast relief of the gnomish Map-Makers Guild.

The knights on Sancrist and the gnomes lived in harmony after that, the knights bringing the gnomes any questions of a technological nature that needed solving, the gnomes providing a steady flood of new inventions.

When the dragon orb arrived, the knights needed to know how the thing worked. They gave it into the keeping of the gnomes, sending along two young knights to guard it. The thought that the orb might be magic did not occur to them.

GNOMEFLINGERS.

9

"Now remember. No gnome living or dead ever in his life completed a sentence. The only way you get anywhere is to interrupt them. Don't worry about being rude. They expect it."

The old mage himself was interrupted by the appearance of a gnome dressed in long brown robes, who came up to them and bowed respectfully.

Tasslehoff studied the gnome with excited curiosity, the kender had never seen a gnome before, although old legends concerning the Graygem of Gargath indicated that the two races were distantly connected. Certainly there was something kenderish in the young gnome, his slender hands, eager expression, and sharp, bright eyes intent on observing everything. But here the resemblance ended. There was nothing of the kender's easy-going manner. The gnome was nervous, serious, and businesslike.

"Tasslehoff Burrfoot," said the kender politely, extending his hand. The gnome took Tas's hand, peered at it intently, then, finding nothing of interest—shook it limply. "And this—"Tas started to introduce Fizban, but stopped when the gnome reached out and calmly took hold of the kender's hoopak.

"Ah . . ." the gnome said, his eyes shining as he grasped the weapon. "SendforamemberoftheWeaponsGuild—"

The guard at the ground-level entrance to the great mountain did not wait for the gnome to finish. Reaching up, he pulled a lever and a shriek sounded. Certain that a dragon had landed behind him, Tas whirled around, ready to defend himself.

"Whistle," said Fizban. "Better get used to it."

"Whistle?" repeated Tas, intrigued. "I never heard one like that before. Smoke comes out of it! How does it wor—Hey! Come back! Bring back my hoopak!" he cried as his staff went speeding down the corridor, carried by three eager gnomes.

"Examinationroom," said the gnome, "uponSkimbosh—"

"What?"

"Examination Room," Fizban translated. "I missed the rest. You really must speak slower," he said, shaking his staff at the gnome.

The gnome nodded, but his bright eyes were fixed on Fizban's staff. Then, seeing it was just plain, slightly battered wood, the gnome returned his attention to the mage and kender.

"Outsiders," he said. "I'lltryand'member . . . I will try and remember, so do not worry because"—he now spoke slowly and distinctly—"your weapon will not be harmed since we are merely going to render a drawing—"

"Really," interrupted Tas, rather flattered. "I could give you a demonstration of how it works, if you like."

The gnome's eyes brightened. "Thatwouldbemuch—"

"And now," interrupted the kender again, feeling pleased that he was learning to communicate, "what is your name?"

Fizban made a quick gesture, but too late.

"Gnoshoshallamarionininillisyylphanitdisdisslishxdie—"

He paused to draw a breath.

"Is that your *name*?" Tas asked, astounded.

The gnome let his breath out. "Yes," he snapped, a bit disconcerted."It's my first name, and now if you'll let me proceed—"

"Wait!" cried Fizban. "What do your friends call you?"

The gnome sucked in a breath again. "Gnoshoshalla-marioninillis—"

"What do the knights call you?"

"Oh"—the gnome seemed downcast—"Gnosh, if you—"

"Thank you," snapped Fizban. "Now, Gnosh, we're in rather a hurry. War going on and all that. As Lord Gunthar stated in his communique, we must see this dragon orb."

Gnosh's small, dark eyes glittered. His hands twisted nervously. "Of course, you may see the dragon orb since Lord Gunthar has requested it, but, if I might ask, what is your interest in the orb besides normalcuri—?"

"I am a magic-user—" Fizban began.

"Magicuser!" the gnome stated, forgetting, in his excitement, to speak slowly. "ComethiswayimmediatelytotheExaminationroomsincethedragonorbwasmadebymagicuser—"

Both Tas and Fizban blinked uncomprehendingly.

"Oh, just come—" the gnome said impatiently.

Before they quite knew what was happening, the gnome, still talking, hustled them through the mountain's entrance, setting off an inordinate number of bells and whistles.

"Examination Room?" Tas said in an undertone to Fizban as they hurried after Gnosh. "What does that mean? They wouldn't have hurt it, would they?"

"I don't think so," Fizban muttered, his bushy white eyebrows coming together in an ominous V-shape over his nose. "Gunthar sent knights to guard it, remember."

"Then what are you worried about?" Tas asked.

"The dragon orbs are strange things. Very powerful. My fear," said Fizban more to himself than to Tas, "is that they may try to *use* it!"

"But the book I read in Tarsis said the orb could control dragons!" Tas whispered. "Isn't that good? I mean, the orbs aren't evil, are they?"

"Evil? Oh, no! Not evil." Fizban shook his head. "That's the danger. They're not good, not evil. They're *not anything*! Or perhaps I should say, they're *everything*."

Tas saw he would probably never get a straight answer out of Fizban, whose mind was far away. In need of diversion, the kender turned his attention to their host.

"What does your name mean?" Tas asked.

Gnosh smiled happily. "In The Beginning, The Gods Created the Gnomes, and One of the First They Created Was Named Gnosh I and these are the Notable Events Which Occurred in His Life: He Married Marioninillis . . ."

Tas had a sinking feeling. "Wait—" he interrupted. "How long is your name?"

"It fills a book this big in the library," Gnosh said proudly, holding his hands out, "because we are a very old family as you will see when I contin—"

"That's all right," Tas said quickly. Not watching where he was going, he stumbled over a rope. Gnosh helped him to his feet. Looking up, Tas saw the rope led up into a nest of ropes connected to each other, snaking out in all directions. He wondered where they led. "Perhaps another time."

"But there are some very good parts," Gnosh said as they walked toward a huge steel door, "and I could skip to those, if you like, such as the part where great-great-great-grand-mother Gnosh invented boiling water—"

"I'd love to hear it." Tas gulped. "But, no time—"

"Yes, I suppose so," Gnosh said, "and anyway, here we are at the entrance to the main chamber, so if you'll excuse me—"

Still talking, he reached up and pulled a cord. A whistle blew. Two bells and a gong rang out. Then, with a tremendous blast of steam that nearly parboiled all of them, two huge steel doors located in the interior of the mountain began to slide open. Almost immediately, the doors stuck, and within minutes the place was swarming with gnomes, yelling and pointing and arguing about whose fault it was.

Tasslehoff Burrfoot had been making plans in the back of his mind as to what he would do after this adventure had ended and all the dragons were slain (the kender tried to maintain a positive outlook).The first thing he had planned to do was to go and spend a few months with his friend, Sestun, the gully dwarf in Pax Tharkas. The gully dwarves led interesting lives, and Tas knew he could settle there quite happily, as long as he didn't have to eat their cooking.

But the moment Tas entered Mount Nevermind, he decided the first thing he would do was come back and live with the gnomes. The kender had never seen anything quite so wonderful in his entire life. He stopped dead in his tracks.

Gnosh glanced at him. "Impressive, isn't it?" he asked.

"Not quite the word *I'd* use," Fizban muttered. They stood in the central portion of the gnome city. Built within an old shaft of a volcano, it was hundreds of yards across and miles high.The city was constructed in levels around the shaft. Tas stared up . . . and up . . . and up. . . .

"How many levels are there?" the kender asked, nearly falling over backward trying to see.

"Thirty-five and—"

"Thirty-five!"Tas repeated in awe. "I'd hate to live on that thirty-fifth level. How many stairs do you have to climb?"

Gnosh sniffed. "Primitive devices we improved upon long

ago and now"—he gestured—"view someofthemarvelsof-technologywehaveinoperat—"

"I can see," said Tas, lowering his eyes to ground level. "You must be preparing for a great battle. I never saw so many catapults in my life . . ."

The kender's voice died. Even as he watched, a whistle sounded, a catapult went off with a twang, and a gnome went sailing through the air. Tas wasn't looking at machines of war, he was looking at the devices that had replaced stairs!

The bottom floor of the chamber was filled with catapults, every type of catapult ever conceived by gnomes. There were sling catapults, cross-bow catapults, willow-sprung cata-pults, steam-driven catapults (still experimental—they were working on adjusting the water temperature).

Surrounding the catapults, over the catapults, under the catapults, and through the catapults were strung miles and miles of rope which operated a crazed assortment of gears and wheels and pulleys, all turning and squeaking and cranking. Out of the floor, out of the machines themselves, and thrusting out from the sides of the walls were huge levers which scores of gnomes were either pushing or pulling or sometimes both at once.

"I don't suppose," Fizban asked in a hopeless tone, "that the Examination Room would be on the ground level?"

Gnosh shook his head. "Examination Room on level fif-teen—"

The old mage heaved a heart-rending sigh.

Suddenly there was a horrible grinding sound that set Tas's teeth on edge.

"Ah, they're ready for us. Come along, " Gnosh said.

Tas leaped after him gleefully as they approached a giant catapult. A gnome gestured at them irritably, pointing to a long line of gnomes waiting their turn. Tas jumped into the seat of the huge sling catapult, staring eagerly up into the shaft. Above him, he could see gnomes peering down at him from various balconies, all of them surrounded by great machines, whistles, ropes, and huge, shapeless things hanging from the sides of the wall like bats. Gnosh stood beside him, scolding.

"Elders first, young man, so get outoftherethisinstant-andlet"—he dragged Tasslehoff out of the seat with remarkable strength—"themagicusergofirst—"

"Uh, that's quite all right," Fizban protested, stumbling backward into a pile of rope. "I—I seem to recall a spell of mine that will take me right to the top. Levitate. How did that g-go? Just give me a moment."

"*You* were the one in a hurry—" Gnosh said severely, glaring at Fizban. The gnomes standing in line began to shout rudely, pushing and shoving and jostling.

"Oh, very well," the old mage snarled, and he climbed into the seat,with Gnosh's help.

The gnome operating the lever that launched the catapult yelled something at Gnosh which sounded like "whalevel?"

Gnosh pointed up, yelling back. "*Skimbosh!*"

The chief walked over to stand in front of the first of a series of five levers. An inordinate number of ropes stretched upward into infinity. Fizban sat miserably in the seat of the catapult, still trying to recall his spell.

"Now," yelled Gnosh, drawing Tas closer so he could have the advantage of an excellent view, "in just a moment, the chief will give the signal—yes, there it is—"

The chief pulled on one of the ropes.

"What does that do?" Tas interrupted.

"The rope rings a bell on *Skimbosh*, er, level fifteen, telling them to expect an arrival—"

"What if the bell doesn't ring?" Fizban demanded loudly.

"Then a second bell rings telling them that the first bell didn't—"

"What happens down here if the bell didn't ring?"

"Nothing. It's Skimbosh'sproblemnotyours—"

"It's my problem if they don't know I'm coming!" Fizban shouted."Or do I just drop in and surprise them!"

"Ah," Gnosh said proudly, "you see—"

"I'm getting out . . ." stated Fizban.

"No, wait," Gnosh said, talking faster and faster in his anguish, "they're ready—"

"Who's ready?" Fizban demanded irritably.

"Skimbosh! With the net tocatchyou,yousee—"

"Net!" Fizban turned pale. "That does it!" He flung a foot over the edge.

But before he could move, the chief reached out and pulled on the first lever. The grinding sound started again as the catapult began pivoting in its mooring. The sudden motion threw Fizban back, knocking his hat over his eyes.

"What's happening?" Tas shouted.

"They're getting him in position," Gnosh yelled. "The longitude and latitude have been precalculated and the catapult set to come into the correct location to send the passenger—"

"What about the net?" Tas yelled.

"The magician flies up to Skimbosh—oh, quite safely, I assure you—we've done studies, in fact, proving that flying is safer than walking—and just when he's at the height of his trajectory, beginning to drop a bit, Skimbosh throws a net out underneath him, catching him just like this"— Gnosh demonstrated with his hand, making a snapping motion like catching a fly—"and hauls him—"

"What incredible timing that must take!"

"The timing is ingenious since it all depends on a certain

hook we've developed, though"—Gnosh pursed his lips, his eyebrows drawing together—"something is throwing the timing off a bit, but there's a committee—"

The gnome pulled down on the lever and Fizban—with a shriek—went sailing through the air.

"Oh dear," said Gnosh, staring, "it appears—"

"What? What?" Tas yelled, trying to see.

"The net's opened too soon again"—Gnosh shook his head—"and that's the second time today that's happened on Skimbosh alone andthisdefinitelywillbebroughtupatthe nextmeetingoftheNet Guild—"

Tas stared, open-mouthed, at the sight of Fizban whizzing through the air, propelled from below by the tremendous force of the catapult, and suddenly the kender saw what Gnosh was talking about. The net on level fifteen—instead of opening *after* the mage had flown past and then catching him as he started to fall—opened *before* the mage reached level fifteen. Fizban hit the net and was flattened like a squashed spider. For a moment he clung there precariously—arms and legs akimbo, then he fell.

Instantly bells and gongs rang out.

"Don't tell me," Tas guessed miserably. "That's the alarm which means the net failed."

"Quite, but don't be alarmed (small joke)," Gnosh chuckled, "because the alarms trip a device to open the net on level thirteen, just in time, oops—a bit late, well, there's still level twelve—"

"Do something!" Tas shrieked.

"Don't get so worked up!" Gnosh said angrily. "And I'll finishwhatIwasabouttosayaboutthefinal emergencybackupsystem andthatis, oh, hereitgoes—"

Tas watched in amazement as the bottoms dropped out of six huge barrels hanging from the walls on level three, sending thousands of sponges tumbling down onto the floor in the center of the chamber. This was done—apparently—in case all the nets on every level failed. Fortunately, the net on level nine actually worked, spreading out beneath the mage just in time. Then it folded up around him and whisked him over to the balcony where the gnomes, hearing the mage cursing and swearing inside, appeared reluctant to let him out.

"Sonoweverything'sfineandit'syourturn," said Gnosh.

"Just one last question!" Tas yelled at Gnosh as he sat down in the seat. "What happens if the emergency backup system with the sponges fails?"

"Ingenious—" said Gnosh happily, "because you see if the sponges come down a little too late, the alarm goes off, releasing a huge barrel of water into the center, and, since the sponges are there already, its easy to clean up the mess—"

The chief pulled the lever.

Tas had been expecting all sorts of fascinating things in the Examination Room, but he found it—to his surprise— nearly empty. It was lighted by a hole drilled through the face of the mountain which admitted the sunlight. (This simple but ingenious device had been suggested to the gnomes by a visiting dwarf who called it a 'window;' the gnomes were quite proud of it.) There were three tables, but little else. On the central table, surrounded by gnomes, rested the dragon orb and his hoopak.

It was back to its original size, Tas noted with interest. It looked the same—still a round piece of crystal, with a kind of milky colored mist swirling around inside. A young Knight of Solamnia with an intensely bored expression on his face stood near the orb, guarding it. His bored expression changed sharply at the approach of strangers.

"Quiteallright," Gnosh told the knight reassuringly, "these are the two Lord Gunthar sent word about—" Still talking, Gnosh hustled them over to the central table. The gnome's eyes were bright as he regarded the orb. "A dragon orb," he murmured happily, "after all these years—"

"What years?" Fizban snapped, stopping at some distance from the table.

"You see," Gnosh explained, "each gnome has a Life Quest assigned to him at birth, and from then on his only ambition in life is to fulfill that Life Quest, and it was my Life Quest to study the dragon orb since—"

"But the dragon orbs have been missing for hundreds of years!" Tas said incredulously. "No one knew about them! How could it be your Life Quest?"

"Oh, we knew about them," Gnosh answered, "because it was my grandfather's Life Quest, and then my father's Life Quest. Both of them died without ever seeing a dragon orb. I feared I might, too, but now finally, one has appeared, and I can establish our family's place in the afterlife—"

"You mean you can't get to the—er—afterlife until you complete the Life Quest?" Tas asked. "But your grandfather and your father—"

"Probably most uncomfortable," Gnosh said, looking sad, "wherever they are—My goodness!"

A remarkable change had come over the dragon orb. It began to swirl and shimmer with many different colors—as if in agitation.

Muttering strange words, Fizban walked to the orb and set his hand upon it. Instantly, it went black. Fizban cast a glance around the room, his expression so severe and frightening that even Tas fell back before him. The knight sprang forward.

"Get out!" the mage thundered. "All of you!"

"I was ordered not to leave and I'm not—" The knight reached for his sword, but Fizban whispered a few words. The knight slumped to the floor.

The gnomes vanished from the room instantly, leaving only Gnosh, wringing his hands, his face twisted in agony.

"Come on, Gnosh!" Tas urged. "I've never seen him like this. We better do as he says. If we don't, he's liable to turn us into gully dwarves or something icky like that!"

Whimpering, Gnosh allowed Tas to lead him out of the room. As he stared back at the dragon orb, the door slammed shut.

"My Life Quest . . ." the gnome moaned.

"I'm sure it will be all right," Tas said, although he wasn't sure, not in the least. He hadn't liked the look on Fizban's face. In fact, it hadn't even seemed to be Fizban's face at all—or anyone Tas wanted to know!

Tas felt chilled and there was a tight knot in the pit of his stomach. The gnomes muttered among themselves and cast baleful glances at him. Tas swallowed, trying to get a bitter taste out of his mouth. Then he drew Gnosh to one side.

"Gnosh, did you discover anything about the orb when you studied it?" Tas asked in a low voice.

"Well," Gnosh appeared thoughtful, "I did find out that there's something inside of it, or seems to be, because I'd stare at it and stare at it without seeing anything for the longest time then, right when I was ready to quit, I'd see words swirling about in the mist—"

"Words?" Tas interrupted eagerly. "What did they say?"

Gnosh shook his head. "I don't know," he said solemnly, "because I couldn't read them; no one could, not even a member of the Foreign Language Guild—"

"Magic, probably," Tas muttered to himself.

"Yes," Gnosh said miserably, "that's what I decided—"

The door blew open, as if something had exploded.

Gnosh whirled around, terrified. Fizban stood in the doorway, holding a small black bag in one hand, his staff and Tasslehoff's hoopak in the other. Gnosh sprang past him.

"The orb!" he screeched, so upset he actually completed a sentence. "You've got it!"

"Yes, Gnosh," said Fizban.

The mage's voice sounded tired, and Tas, looking at him closely, saw that he was on the verge of exhaustion. His skin was gray, his eyelids drooped. He leaned heavily on his staff. "Come with me, my boy," he said to the gnome. "And do not worry. Your Life Quest will be fulfilled. But now the orb must be taken before the Council of Whitestone."

"Come with you," Gnosh repeated in astonishment, "to the Council"—he clasped his hands together in excitement—"where perhaps I'll be asked to make a report, do you think—"

"I wouldn't doubt it in the least," Fizban answered.

"Right away, just give me time to pack, where's my papers—" Gnosh dashed off. Fizban whipped around to face the other gnomes who had been sneaking up behind him, reaching out eagerly for his staff. He scowled so alarmingly that they stumbled backward and vanished into the Examination Room.

"What did you find out?" Tas asked, hesitantly approaching Fizban. The old mage seemed surrounded by darkness. "The gnomes didn't do anything to it, did they?"

"No, no." Fizban sighed. "Fortunately for them. For it is still active and very powerful. Much will depend on the decisions a few make—perhaps the fate of the world."

"What do you mean? Won't the Council make the decisions?"

"You don't understand, my boy," Fizban said gently. "Stop

a moment, I must rest." The mage sat down, leaning against a wall. Shaking his head, he continued. "I concentrated my will on the orb, Tas. Oh, not to control dragons," he added, seeing the kender's eyes widen. "I looked into the future."

"What did you see?" Tas asked hesitantly, not certain from the mage's somber expression that he wanted to know.

"I saw two roads stretching before us. If we take the easiest, it will appear the best at the beginning, but darkness will fall at the end, never to be lifted. If we take the other road, it will be hard and difficult to travel. It could cost the lives of some we love, dear boy. Worse, it might cost others their very souls. But only through these great sacrifices will we find hope." Fizban closed his eyes.

"And this involves the orb?" Tas asked, shivering.

"Yes."

"Do you know what must be done to . . . to take the d-dark road?" Tas dreaded the answer.

"I do," Fizban replied in a low voice. "But the decisions have not been left in my hands. That will be up to others."

"I see," Tas sighed. "Important people, I suppose. People like kings and elflords and knights." Then Fizban's words echoed in his mind. *The lives of some we love . . .*

Suddenly a lump formed in Tas's throat, choking him. His head dropped into his hands. This adventure was turning out all wrong! Where was Tanis? And dear old Caramon? And pretty Tika? He had tried not to think about them, particularly after that dream.

And Flint—I shouldn't have gone without him, Tas thought miserably. He might die, he might be dead right now! *The lives of some you love!* I never thought about any of us dying—not really. I always figured that if we were together we could beat anything! But now, we've gotten scattered somehow. And things are going all wrong!

Tas felt Fizban's hand stroke his topknot, his one great vanity. And for the first time in his life, the kender felt very lost and alone and frightened. The mage's grip tightened around him affectionately. Burying his face in Fizban's sleeve, Tas began to cry.

Fizban patted him gently. "Yes," the mage repeated, "important people."

THE COUNCIL OF WHITESTONE.
AN IMPORTANT PERSON.

10

The Council of Whitestone met upon the twenty-eighth day of December, a day known as Famine Day in Solamnia, for it commemorated the suffering of the people during the first winter following the Cataclysm. Lord Gunthar thought it fitting to hold the Council meeting on this day, which was marked by fasting and meditation.

It had been over a month since the armies sailed for Palanthas. The news Gunthar received from that city was not good. A report had arrived early on the morning of the twenty-eighth, in fact. Reading it twice over, he sighed heavily, frowned, and tucked the paper into his belt.

The Council of Whitestone had met once before within the recent past, a meeting precipitated by the arrival of the refugee elves in Southern Ergoth and the appearance of the dragonarmies in northern Solamnia. This Council meeting was several months in the planning, and so all members—either seated or advisory—were represented. Seated members, those who could vote, included the Knights of Solamnia, the gnomes, the hill dwarves, the dark-skinned, sea-faring people of Northern Ergoth, and a representative of the Solamnic exiles living on Sancrist. Advisory members were the elves, the mountain dwarves, and the kender. These members were invited to express their opinions, but they could not vote.

The first Council meeting, however, had not gone well. Some of the old feuds and animosities between the races represented burst into flame. Arman Kharas, representative of the mountain dwarves, and Duncan Hammerrock, of the hill dwarves, had to be physically restrained at one point, or blood from that ancient feud might have flowed again. Alhana Starbreeze, representative of the Silvanesti in her father's absence, refused to speak a word during the entire session. Alhana had come only because Porthios of the Qualinesti was there. She feared an alliance between the Qualinesti and the humans and was determined to prevent it.

Alhana need not have worried. Such was the distrust between humans and elves, that they spoke to each other only out of politeness. Not even Lord Gunthar's impassioned speech in which he had declared, "Our unity begins peace; our division ends hope!" made an impression.

Porthios's answer to this had been to blame the dragons' reappearance on the humans. The humans, therefore, could extricate themselves from this disaster. Shortly after Porthios made his position clear, Alhana rose haughtily and left, leaving no one with any doubts about the position of the Silvanesti.

The mountain dwarf, Arman Kharas, had declared that his people would be willing to help, but that until the Hammer of Kharas was found, the mountain dwarves could not be united. No one knew at the time that the companions would soon return the Hammer, so Gunthar was forced to discount the aid of the dwarves. The only person, in fact, who offered help was Kronin Thistleknott, chief of the kender. Since the last thing any sane country wanted was the "aid" of an army of kenders, this gesture was received with polite smiles, while the members exchanged horrified looks behind Kronin's back.

The first Council disbanded, therefore, without accomplishing much of anything.

Gunthar had higher hopes for this second Council meeting. The discovery of the dragon orb, of course, put everything in a much brighter light. Representatives from both elven factions had arrived. These included the Speaker of the Suns, who brought with him a human claiming to be a cleric of Paladine. Gunthar had heard a great deal about Elistan from Sturm, and he looked forward to meeting him. Just who would represent the Silvanesti, Gunthar wasn't certain. He assumed it was the lord who had been declared regent following Alhana Starbreeze's mysterious disappearance.

The elves had arrived on Sancrist two days ago. Their tents stood out in the fields, gaily colored silk flags fluttering in brilliant contrast to the gray, stormy sky. They were the only other race to attend. There had not been time to send a message to the mountain dwarves, and the hill dwarves were reported to be fighting for their lives against the dragonarmies; no messenger could reach them.

Gunthar hoped this meeting would unite the humans and the elves in the great fight to drive the dragonarmies from Ansalon. But his hopes were dashed before the meeting began.

After scanning the report from the armies in Palanthas, Gunthar left his tent, preparing to make a final tour of the Glade of the Whitestone to see that everything was in order. Wills, his retainer, came dashing after him.

"My lord," the old man puffed, "return immediately."

"What is it?" Gunthar asked. But the old retainer was too much out of breath to reply.

Sighing, the Solamnic lord went back to his tent where he found Lord Michael, dressed in full armor, pacing nervously.

"What's the matter?" Gunthar said, his heart sinking as he saw the grave expression on the young lord's face.

Michael advanced quickly, seizing Gunthar by the arm. "My lord, we have received word that the elves will demand the return of the dragon orb. If we won't return it, they are prepared to go to war to recover it!"

"What?" Gunthar demanded incredulously. "War! Against us! That's ludicrous! They can't—Are you certain? How reliable is this information?"

"Very reliable, I'm afraid, Lord Gunthar."

"My lord, I present Elistan, cleric of Paladine," Michael said. "I beg pardon for not introducing him earlier, but my mind has been in a turmoil since he first brought me this news."

"I have heard a great deal about you, sir," Lord Gunthar said, extending his hand to the man.

The knight's eyes studied Elistan curiously. Gunthar hardly knew what he had expected to see in a purported cleric of Paladine, perhaps a weak-eyed aesthetic, pale and lean from study. Gunthar was not prepared for this tall, well-built man who might have ridden to battle with the best of the knights. The ancient symbol of Paladine—a platinum medallion engraved with a dragon—hung about his neck.

Gunthar reviewed all he had heard from Sturm concerning Elistan, including the cleric's intention to try and convince the elves to unite with the humans. Elistan smiled wearily, as if aware of every thought passing through Gunthar's mind. They were the thoughts he answered.

"Yes, I have failed," Elistan admitted. "It was all I could do to persuade them to attend the Council meeting, and they have come here only, I fear, to give you an ultimatum: return the orb to the elves or fight to retain it."

Gunthar sank into a chair, gesturing weakly with his hand for the others to be seated. Before him, on a table, were spread maps of the lands of Ansalon, showing in shades of darkness, the insidious advance of the dragonarmies. Gunthar's gaze rested on the maps, then suddenly he swept them to the floor.

"We might as well give up right now!" he snarled. "Send a message to the Dragon Highlords: 'Don't bother to come and wipe us out. We're managing quite nicely on our own.'"

Angrily, he hurled on the table the message he had received."There! That's from Palanthas. The people have insisted the knights leave the city. The Palanthians are negotiating with the Dragon Highlords, and the presence of the knights 'seriously compromises their position.' They refuse to give us any aid. And so an army of a thousand Palanthians sits idle!"

"What is Lord Derek doing, my lord?" Michael asked.

"He and the knights and a thousand footmen, refugees from the occupied lands in Throtyl, are fortifying the High Clerist's tower, south of Palanthas," Gunthar said wearily. "It guards the only pass through the Vingaard Mountains. We'll protect Palanthas for a time, but if the dragonarmies get through . . ." He fell silent. "Damn it," he whispered, beating his fist gently upon the table, "we could hold that pass with two thousand men! The fools! And now this!" He waved his hand in the direction of the elven tents.

Gunthar sighed, letting his head fall into his hands. "Well, what do you counsel, cleric?"

Elistan was quiet for a moment, before he answered. "It is written in the Disks of Mishakal that evil, by its very nature, will always turn in upon itself. Thus it becomes self-defeating." He laid his hand upon Gunthar's shoulder. "I do not know what may come of this meeting. My gods have kept this secret from me. It could be they themselves do not know; that the future of the world stands in balance, and what we decide here will determine it. I do know this: Do not enter with defeat in your heart, for that will be the first victory of evil."

So saying, Elistan rose and left the tent quietly.

Gunthar sat in silence after the cleric had gone. It seemed that the whole world was silent, in fact, he thought. The wind had died during the night. The storm clouds hung low and heavy, muffling sound so that even the clarion trumpet's call marking day's dawning seemed flat. A rustling broke his concentration. Michael was slowly gathering up the spilled maps.

Gunthar raised his head, rubbing his eyes.

"What do you think?"

"Of what? The elves?"

"That cleric," Gunthar said, staring out the tent opening.

"Certainly not what I would have expected," Michael answered, his gaze following Gunthar's. "More like the stories we've heard of the clerics of old, the ones that guided the Knights in the days before the Cataclysm. He's not much like these charlatans we've got now. Elistan is a man who would stand beside you on the field of battle, calling down Paladine's blessing with one hand while wielding his mace with the other. He wears the medallion that none have seen since the gods abandoned us. But is he a true cleric?" Michael shrugged. "It will take a lot more than a medallion to convince me."

"I agree." Gunthar rose to his feet and began to walk toward the tent flap. "Well, it is nearly time. Stay here, Michael, in case any more reports come in." Starting to leave, he paused at the entrance to the tent. "How odd it is, Michael," he murmured, his eyes following Elistan, now no more than a speck of white in the distance. "We have always been a people who looked to the gods for our hope, a people of faith, who distrusted magic. Yet now we look to magic for that hope, and when a chance comes to renew our faith, we question it."

Lord Michael made no answer. Gunthar shook his head and, still pondering, made his way to the Glade of the Whitestone.

As Gunthar said, the Solamnic people had always been faithful followers of the gods. Long ago, in the days before the Cataclysm, the Glade of the Whitestone had been one of the holy centers of worship. The phenomenon of the white rock had attracted the attention of the curious longer than anyone remembered. The Kingpriest of Istar himself had blessed the huge white rock that sat in the middle of a perpetually green glade, declaring it sacred to the gods and forbidding any mortal being to touch it.

Even after the Cataclysm, when belief in the old gods died, the Glade remained a sacred place. Perhaps that was because not even the Cataclysm had affected it. Legend held that when the fiery mountain fell from the sky, the ground around the Whitestone cracked and split apart, but the Whitestone remained intact.

So awesome was the sight of the huge white rock that even now none dared either approach or touch it. What strange powers it possessed, none could say. All they knew was that the air around the Whitestone was always springlike and warm. No matter how bitter the winter, the grass in Whitestone Glade was always green.

Though his heart was heavy, Gunthar relaxed as he stepped inside the glade and breathed the warm, sweet air.

For a moment, he felt once again the touch of Elistan's hand upon his shoulder, imparting a feeling of inner peace.

Glancing around quickly, he saw all in readiness. Massive wooden chairs with ornately carved backs had been placed on the green grass. Five for the voting members of the Council stood to the left side of the Whitestone, three for the advisory members stood on the right. Polished benches for the witnesses to the proceedings as demanded by the Measure, sat facing the Whitestone and the Council members.

Some of the witnesses had already begun arriving, Gunthar noticed. Most of the elven party traveling with the Speaker and the Silvanesti lord were taking their seats. The two estranged elven races sat near each other, apart from the humans who were filing in as well. Everyone sat quietly, some in remembrance of Famine Day; others, like the gnomes, who did not celebrate that holiday, in awe of their surroundings. Seats in the front row were reserved for honored guests or for those with leave to speak before the Council.

Gunthar saw the Speaker's stern-faced son, Porthios, enter with a retinue of elven warriors. They took their seats in the front. Gunthar wondered where Elistan was. He'd intended to ask him to speak. He had been impressed with the man's words (even if he was a charlatan) and hoped he would repeat them.

As he searched in vain for Elistan, he saw three strange figures enter and seat themselves in the front row: it was the old mage in his bent and shapeless hat, his kender friend, and a gnome they had brought back with them from Mount Nevermind. The three had arrived back from their journey only last night.

Gunthar was forced to turn his attention back to the Whitestone. The advisory Council members were entering. There were only two, Lord Quinath of the Silvanesti, and the

Speaker of the Suns. Gunthar looked at the Speaker curiously, knowing he was one of the few beings on Krynn to still remember the horrors of the Cataclysm.

The Speaker was so stooped that he seemed almost crippled. His hair was gray, his face haggard. But as he took his seat and turned his gaze to the witnesses, Gunthar saw the elf's eyes were bright and arresting. Lord Quinath, seated next to him, was known to Gunthar, who considered him as arrogant and proud as Porthios of the Qualinesti, but lacking in the intelligence Porthios possessed.

As for Porthios, Gunthar thought he could probably come to like the Speaker's eldest son quite well. Porthios had every characteristic the knights admired, with one exception, his quick temper.

Gunthar's observations were interrupted, for now it was time for the voting Council members to enter and Gunthar had to take his place. First came Mir Kar-thon of Northern Ergoth, a dark complexioned man with iron-gray hair and the arms of a giant. Next came Serdin MarThasal, representing the Exiles on Sancrist, and finally Lord Gunthar, Knight of Solamnia.

Once seated, Gunthar glanced around a final time. The huge Whitestone glistened behind him, casting its own strange radiance, for the sun would not shine today. On the other side of the Whitestone sat the Speaker, next to him Lord Quinath. Across from them, facing the Council, sat the witnesses upon their benches. The kender was sitting subdued, swinging his short legs on his tall bench. The gnome shuffled through what looked like a ream of paper; Gunthar shuddered, wishing there'd been time to ask for a condensed report. The old magician yawned and scratched his head, peering around vaguely.

All was ready. At Gunthar's signal, two knights entered, bearing a golden stand and a wooden chest. A silence that was almost deathlike descended on the crowd as they watched the entrance of the dragon orb.

The knights came to a halt, standing directly in front of the Whitestone. Here, one of the knights placed the golden stand upon the ground. The other set down the chest, unlocked it, and carefully brought forth the orb that was back to its original size, over two feet in diameter.

A murmur went through the crowd. The Speaker of the Suns shifted uncomfortably, scowling. His son, Porthios, turned to say something to an elflord near him. All of the elves, Gunthar noted, were armed. Not a good sign, from what little he knew of elven protocol.

He had no choice but to proceed. Calling the meeting to order, Lord Gunthar Uth Wistan announced, "Let the Council of Whitestone begin."

After about two minutes, it was obvious to Tasslehoff that things were in a real mess. Before Lord Gunthar had even concluded his speech of welcome, the Speaker of the Suns rose.

"My talk will be brief," the elven leader stated in a voice that matched the steely gray of the storm clouds above him. "The Silvanesti, the Qualinesti, and the Kaganesti met in council shortly after the orb was removed from our camp. It is the first time the members of the three communities have met since the Kinslayer wars." He paused, laying a heavy emphasis on those last words. Then he continued.

"We have decided to set aside our own differences in our perfect agreement that the dragon orb belongs in the hands of the elves, not in the hands of humans or any other race upon Krynn. Therefore, we come before the Council of Whitestone and ask that the dragon orb be given over to us forthwith. In return, we guarantee that we will take it to our lands and keep it safe until such time—if ever—it be needed."

The Speaker sat down, his dark eyes sweeping over the crowd, its silence broken now by a murmur of soft voices. The other Council members, sitting next to Lord Gunthar, shook their heads, their faces grim. The dark-skinned leader of the Northern Ergoth people whispered to Lord Gunthar in a harsh voice, clenching his fist to emphasize his words.

Lord Gunthar, after listening and nodding for several minutes, rose to his feet to respond. His speech was cool, calm, complimentary to the elves. But it said—between the lines—that the Knights would see the elves in the Abyss before they gave them the dragon orb.

The Speaker, understanding perfectly the message of steel couched in the pretty phrases, rose to reply. He spoke only one sentence, but it brought the crowd of witnesses to their feet.

"Then, Lord Gunthar," the Speaker said, "the elves declare that, from this time on—we are at war!"

Humans and elves both headed for the dragon orb that sat upon its golden stand, its milky white insides swirling gently within the crystal. Gunthar shouted for order time and again, banging the hilt of his sword upon the table. The Speaker spoke a few words sharply in elven, staring hard at his son, Porthios, and finally order was restored.

But the atmosphere snapped like the air before a storm. Gunthar talked. The Speaker answered. The Speaker talked. Gunthar answered. The dark-skinned mariner lost his temper and made a few cutting remarks about elves. The lord of the Silvanesti reduced him to quivering anger with his sarcastic rejoinders. Several of the knights left, only to return armed to the teeth. They came to stand near Gunthar, their hands on their weapons. The elves, led by Porthios, rose to surround their own leaders.

Gnosh, his report held fast in his hand, began to realize he wasn't going to be asked to give it.

Tasslehoff looked around despairingly for Elistan. He kept hoping desperately the cleric would come. Elistan could calm these people down. Or maybe Laurana. Where was she? There'd been no word of his friends, the elves had told the kender coldly. She and her brother had apparently vanished in the wilderness. I shouldn't have left them, Tas thought. I shouldn't be here. Why, why did this crazy old mage bring me? I'm useless! Maybe Fizban could do something? Tas looked at the mage hopefully, but Fizban was sound asleep!

"Please, wake up!" Tas begged, shaking him. "Somebody's got to do something!"

At that moment, he heard Lord Gunthar yell, "The dragon orb is *not* yours by right! Lady Laurana and the others were bringing it to *us* when they were shipwrecked! You tried to keep it on Ergoth by force, and your own daughter—"

"Mention not my daughter!" the Speaker said in a deep, harsh voice. "I do not have a daughter."

Something broke within Tasslehoff. Confused memories of Laurana fighting desperately against the evil wizard who guarded the orb, Laurana battling draconians, Laurana firing her bow at the white dragon, Laurana ministering to him so tenderly when he'd been near death. To be cast off by her own people when she was working so desperately to save them, when she had sacrificed so much. . . .

"Stop this!" Tasslehoff heard himself yelling at the top of his voice. "Stop this right now and listen to me!"

Suddenly he saw, to his astonishment, that everyone *had* stopped talking and was staring at him.

Now that he had his audience, Tas realized he didn't have any idea what to say to all of these important people. But he knew he had to say something. After all, he thought, this is my fault—I read about these damn orbs. Gulping, he slid off his bench and walked toward the Whitestone and the two hostile groups clustered around it. He thought he saw—out of the corner of his eye—Fizban grinning from under his hat.

"I—I . . ." The kender stammered, wondering what to say. He was saved by a sudden inspiration.

"I demand the right to represent my people," Tasslehoff said proudly, "and take my place on the advisory council."

Flipping his tassle of brown hair over his shoulder, the kender came to stand right in front of the dragon orb. Looking up, he could see the Whitestone towering over it and over him. Tas stared at the stone, shivering, then quickly turned his gaze from the rock to Gunthar and the Speaker of the Suns.

And then Tasslehoff knew what he had to do. He began to shake with fear. He—Tasslehoff Burrfoot—who'd never been afraid of anything in his life! He'd faced dragons without trembling, but the knowledge of what he was going to do now appalled him. His hands felt as if he'd been making snowballs without gloves on. His tongue seemed to belong in some larger person's mouth. But Tas was resolute. He just had to keep them talking, keep them from guessing what he planned.

"You've never taken us kenders very seriously, you know," Tas began, his voice sounding too loud and shrill in his own ears, "and I can't say I blame you much. We don't have a strong sense of responsibility, I guess, and we are probably too curious for own good—but, I ask you, how are you going to find out anything if you're not curious?"

Tas could see the Speaker's face turn to steel, even Lord Gunthar was scowling. The kender edged nearer the dragon orb.

"We cause lots of trouble, I suppose, without meaning to, and occasionally some of us do happen to acquire certain things which aren't ours. But one thing the kender know is—"

Tasslehoff broke into a run. Quick and lithe as a mouse, he slipped easily through the hands that tried to catch him, reaching the dragon orb within a matter of seconds. Faces blurred around him, mouths opened, shrieking and yelling at him. But they were too late.

In one swift, smooth movement, Tasslehoff hurled the dragon orb at the huge, gleaming Whitestone.

The round, gleaming crystal—its insides swirling in agitation—hung suspended in the air for long, long seconds. Tas wondered if the orb had the power to halt its flight. But it was just a fevered impression in the kender's mind.

The dragon orb struck the rock and shattered, bursting into a thousand sparkling pieces. For an instant, a ball of milky white smoke hung in the air, as if trying desperately to hold itself together. Then the warm, springlike breeze of the glade caught it and swept it apart.

There was intense, awful silence.

The kender stood, looking calmly down at the shattered dragon orb.

"We know," he said in a small voice that dropped into the dreadful silence like a tiny drop of rain, "we should be fighting dragons. Not each other."

No one moved. No one spoke. Then there was a thump. Gnosh had fainted.

The silence broke—almost as shattering as the breaking of the orb. Lord Gunthar and the Speaker both lunged at Tas. One caught hold of the kender's left shoulder, one his right.

"What have you done?" Lord Gunthar's face was livid, his eyes wild as he gripped the kender with trembling hands.

"You have brought death upon us all!" The Speaker's fingers bit into Tas's flesh like the claws of a predatory bird. "You have destroyed our only hope!"

"And for that, he himself will be the first to die!"

Porthios—tall, grim-faced elflord—loomed above the cowering kender, his sword glistening in his hand. The kender stood his ground between the elven king and the knight, his small face pale, his expression defiant. He had known when he committed his crime that death would be the penalty.

Tanis will be unhappy over what I've done, Tas thought sadly. But at least he'll hear that I died bravely.

"Now, now, now . . ." said a sleepy voice. "No one's going to die! At least not at this moment. Quit waving that sword around, Porthios! Someone'll get hurt."

Tas peered out from under a heaving sea of arms and shining armor to see Fizban, yawning, step over the inert body of the gnome and totter toward them. Elves and humans made way for him to pass, as if compelled to do so by an unseen force.

Porthios whirled to face Fizban, so angry that saliva bubbled on his lips and his speech was nearly incoherent.

"Beware, old man, or you will share in the punishment!"

"I said quit waving that sword around," Fizban snapped irritably, wiggling a finger at the sword.

Porthios dropped his weapon with a wild cry. Clutching his stinging, burning hand, he stared down at the sword in astonishment—the hilt had grown thorns! Fizban came to stand next to the elflord and regarded him angrily.

"You're a fine young man, but you should have been taught some respect for your elders. I said to put that sword down and I meant it! Maybe you'll believe me next time!" Fizban's baleful gaze switched to the Speaker. "And you, Solostaran, were a good man about two hundred years ago. Managed to raise three fine children—*three* fine children, I said. Don't give me any of this nonsense about not having a daughter. You have one, and a fine girl she is. More sense than her father. Must take after her mother's side. Where was I? Oh, yes. You brought up Tanis Half-Elven, too. You know, Solostaran, between the four of these young people, we might save this world yet.

"Now I want everyone to take his seat. Yes, you, too, Lord Gunthar. Come along, Solostaran, I'll help. We old men have to stick together. Too bad you're such a damn fool."

Muttering into his beard, Fizban led the astounded Speaker to his chair. Porthios, his face twisted in pain, stumbled back to his seat with the help of his warriors.

Slowly the assembled elves and knights sat down, murmuring among themselves—all casting dark looks at the shattered dragon orb that lay beneath the Whitestone.

Fizban settled the Speaker in his seat, glowered at Lord Quinath, who thought he had something to say but quickly decided he didn't. Satisfied, the old mage came back to the front of the Whitestone where Tas stood, shaken and confused.

"You," Fizban looked at the kender as if he'd never seen him before, "go and attend to that poor chap." He waved a hand at the gnome, who was still out cold.

Feeling his knees tremble, Tasslehoff walked slowly over to Gnosh and knelt down beside him, glad to look at something other than the angry, fear-filled faces.

"Gnosh," he whispered miserably, patting the gnome on the cheek, "I'm sorry. I truly am. I mean about your Life Quest and your father's soul and everything. But there just didn't seem to be anything else to do."

Fizban turned around slowly and faced the assembled group, pushing his hat back on his head. "Yes, I'm going to lecture you. You deserve it, every one of you—so don't sit there looking self-righteous. That kender"—he pointed at Tasslehoff, who cringed—"has more brains beneath that ridiculous topknot of his than the lot of you have put together. Do you know what would have happened to you if the kender hadn't had the guts to do what he did? Do you? Well, I'll tell you. Just let me find a seat here. . . ." Fizban peered around vaguely. "Ah, yes, there . . ." Nodding in satisfaction, the old mage toddled over and sat down on the ground, leaning his back against the sacred Whitestone!

The assembled knights gasped in horror. Gunthar leaped to his feet, appalled at this sacrilege.

"No mortal can touch the Whitestone!" he yelled, striding forward.

Fizban slowly turned his head to regard the furious knight. "One more word," the old mage said solemnly, "and I'll make your moustaches fall off. Now sit down and shut up!"

Sputtering, Gunthar was brought up short by an imperious gesture from the old man. The knight could do nothing but return to his seat.

"Where was I before I was interrupted?" Fizban scowled. Glancing around, his gaze fell on the broken pieces of the orb. "Oh, yes. I was about to tell you a story. One of you would have won the orb, of course. And you would have taken it—either to keep it 'safe' or to 'save the world.' And, yes, it is capable of saving the world, but only if you know how to use it. Who of you has this knowledge? Who has the strength? The orb was created by the greatest, most powerful mages of old. *All* the most powerful—do you understand? It was created by those of the White Robes and those of the Black Robes. It has the essence of both evil and good. The Red Robes brought both essences together and bound them with their force. Few there are now with the power and strength to understand the orb, to fathom its secrets, and to gain mastery over it. Few indeed"—Fizban's eyes gleamed—"and none who sit here!"

Silence had fallen now, a profound silence as they listened to the old mage, whose voice was strong and carried above the rising wind that was blowing the storm clouds from the sky.

"One of you would have taken the orb and used it, and you would have found that you had hurled yourself upon disaster. You would have been broken as surely as the kender broke the orb. As for hope being shattered, I tell you that hope was lost for a time, but now it has been new born—"

A sudden gust of wind caught the old mage's hat, blowing it off his head and tossing it playfully away from him. Snarling in irritation, Fizban crawled forward to pick it up.

Just as the mage leaned over, the sun broke through the clouds. There was a blazing flash of silver, followed by a splintering, deafening crack as though the land itself had split apart.

Half-blinded by the flaring light, people blinked and gazed in fear and awe at the terrifying sight before their eyes.

The Whitestone had been split asunder.

The old magician lay sprawled at its base, his hat clutched in his hand, his other arm flung over his head in terror. Above him, piercing the rock where he had been sitting, was a long weapon made of gleaming silver. It had been thrown by the silver arm of a black man, who walked over to stand beside it. Accompanying him were three people: an elven woman dressed in leather armor, an old, white-bearded dwarf, and Elistan.

Amid the stunned silence of the crowd, the black man reached out and lifted the weapon from the splintered remains of the rock. He held it high above his head, and the silver barbed point glittered brightly in the rays of the midday sun.

"I am Theros Ironfeld," the man called out in a deep voice, "and for the last month I have been forging these!" He shook the weapon in his hand. "I have taken molten silver from the well hidden deep within the heart of the Monument of the Silver Dragon. With the silver arm given me by the gods, I have forged the weapon as legend foretold. And this I bring to you—to all the people of Krynn—that we may join together and defeat the great evil that threatens to engulf us in darkness forever.

"I bring you—the Dragonlance!"

With that, Theros thrust the weapon deep into the ground. It stood, straight and shining, amid the broken pieces of the dragon orb.

An unexpected journey

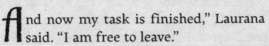

11

"And now my task is finished," Laurana said. "I am free to leave."

"Yes," Elistan said slowly, "and I know why you leave"—Laurana flushed and lowered her eyes—"but where will you go?"

"Silvanesti," she replied. "The last place I saw him."

"Only in a dream—"

"No, that was more than a dream," Laurana replied, shuddering. "It was real. He was there. He is alive and I must find him."

"Surely, my dear, you should stay here, then," Elistan suggested. "You say that in the dream he had found a dragon orb. If he has it, he will come to Sancrist."

Laurana did not answer. Unhappy and irresolute, she stared out the window of Lord Gunthar's castle where she, Elistan, Flint, and Tasslehoff were staying as his guests.

She should have been with the elves. Before they left Whitestone Glade, her father had asked her to come back with them to Southern Ergoth. But Laurana refused. Although she did not say it, she knew she would never live among her people again.

Her father had not pressed her, and—in his eyes—she saw that he heard her unspoken words. Elves aged by years, not by days, as did humans. For her father, it seemed as if time had accelerated and he was changing even as she watched. She felt as though she were seeing him through Raistlin's hourglass eyes, and the thought was terrifying. Yet the news she brought him only increased his bitter unhappiness.

Gilthanas had not returned. Nor could Laurana tell her father where his beloved son had gone, for the journey he and Silvara made was dark and fraught with peril. Laurana told her father only that Gilthanas was not dead.

"You know where he is?" the Speaker asked after a pause.

"I do," Laurana answered, "or rather—I know where he goes."

"And you cannot speak of this, even to me, his father?"

Laurana shook her head steadfastly. "No, Speaker, I cannot. Forgive me, but we agreed when the decision was made to undertake this desperate action that those of us who knew would tell no one. No one," she repeated.

"So you do not trust me—"

Laurana sighed. Her eyes went to the shattered Whitestone. "Father," she said, "you nearly went to war . . . with the only people who can help save us. . . ."

Her father had not replied, but—in his cool farewell and in the way he leaned upon the arm of his elder child—he made it clear to Laurana that he now had only *one* child.

Theros went with the elves. Following his dramatic presentation of the dragonlance, the Council of Whitestone had voted unanimously to make more of these weapons and unite all races in the fight against the dragonarmies.

"At present," Theros announced, "we have only those few lances I was able to forge by myself within a month's time, and I bring several ancient lances the silver dragons hid at the time the dragons were banished from the world. But we'll need more, many more. I need men to help me!"

The elves agreed to provide men to help make the dragon-lances, but whether or not they would help fight—

"That remains a matter we must discuss," the Speaker said.

"Don't discuss it too long," Flint Fireforge snapped, "or you might find yourself discussing it with a Dragon High-lord."

"The elves keep their own counsel and ask for no advice from dwarves," the Speaker replied coldly. "Besides, we do not even know if these lances work! The legend said they were to be forged by one of the Silver Arm, that is certain. But it also says that the Hammer of Kharas was needed in the forging. Where is the Hammer now?" he asked Theros.

"The Hammer could not be brought here in time, even if it could be kept from the dragonarmies. The Hammer of Kharas was required in days of old, because man's skill was not sufficient by itself to produce the lances. Mine is," he added proudly. "You saw what the lance did to that rock."

"We shall see what it does to dragons," the Speaker said, and the Second Council of Whitestone drew to a close. Gunthar proposed at the last that the lances Theros had brought with him be sent to the knights in Palanthas.

These thoughts passed through Laurana's mind as she stared out across the bleak winter landscape. It would be snowing in the valley soon, Lord Gunthar said.

I cannot stay here, Laurana thought, pressing her face against the chill glass. I shall go mad.

"I've studied Gunthar's maps," she murmured, almost speaking to herself, "and I've seen the location of the dragon-armies. Tanis will never reach Sancrist. And if he does have the orb, he may not know the danger it poses. I must warn him."

"My dear, you're not talking sensibly," Elistan said mildly. "If Tanis cannot reach Sancrist safely, how will you reach him? Think logically, Laurana—"

"I don't want to think logically!" Laurana cried, stomping her foot and glaring angrily at the cleric. "I'm sick of being sensible! I'm tired of this whole war. I've done my part—more than my part. I just want to find Tanis!"

Seeing Elistan's sympathetic face, Laurana sighed. "I'm sorry, my dear friend. I know what you say is true," she said, ashamed. "But I can't stay here and do nothing!"

Though Laurana didn't mention it, she had another concern. That human woman, that Kitiara. Where was she? Were they together as she had seen in the dream? Laurana realized now, suddenly, that the remembered image of Kitiara standing with Tanis's arm around her was more disturbing than the image she had seen of her own death.

At that moment, Lord Gunthar suddenly entered the room.

"Oh!" he said, startled, seeing Elistan and Laurana. "I'm sorry, I hope I am not disturbing—"

"Please, no, come in," Laurana said quickly.

"Thank you," Gunthar said, stepping inside and carefully shutting the door, first glancing down the hallway to make certain no one was near. He joined them at the window. "Actually I needed to talk to you both, anyway. I sent Wills looking for you. This is best, however. No one knows we're speaking."

More intrigue, Laurana thought wearily. Throughout their journey to Gunthar's castle, she had heard about nothing but the political infighting that was destroying the Knighthood.

Shocked and outraged at Gunthar's story of Sturm's trial, Laurana had gone before a Council of Knights to speak in Sturm's defense. Although the appearance of a woman at a

Council was unheard of, the knights were impressed by this vibrant, beautiful young woman's eloquent speech on Sturm's behalf. The fact that Laurana was a member of the royal elven household, and that she had brought the dragonlances, also spoke highly in her favor.

Even Derek's faction—those that remained—were hard-pressed to fault her. But the knights had been unable to reach a decision. The man appointed to stand in Lord Alfred's place was strongly in Derek's tent—as the phrase went—and Lord Michael had vacillated to such a degree that Gunthar had been forced to throw the matter to an open vote. The knights demanded a period of reflection and the meeting was adjourned. They had reconvened this afternoon. Apparently, Gunthar had just come from this meeting.

Laurana knew, from the look on Gunthar's face, that things had gone favorably. But if so, why the maneuvering?

"Sturm's been pardoned?" she asked.

Gunthar grinned and rubbed his hands together. "Not pardoned, my dear. That would have implied his guilt. No. He has been completely vindicated! I pushed for that. Pardon would not have suited us at all. His knighthood is granted. He has his command officially bestowed upon him. And Derek is in serious trouble!"

"I am happy, for Sturm's sake," Laurana said coolly, exchanging worried looks with Elistan. Although she liked what she had seen of Lord Gunthar, she had been brought up in a royal household and knew Sturm was being made a game piece.

Gunthar caught the edge of ice in her voice, and his face became grave. "Lady Laurana," he said, speaking more somberly, "I know what you are thinking—that I am dangling Sturm from puppet strings. Let us be brutally frank, lady. The Knights are divided, split into two factions—

139

Derek's and my own. And we both know what happens to a tree split in two: both sides wither and die. This battle between us must end, or it will have tragic consequences. Now, lady and Elistan, for I have come to trust and rely on your judgment, I leave this in your hands. You have met me and you have met Lord Derek Crownguard. Who would you choose to head the Knights?"

"You, of course, Lord Gunthar," Elistan said sincerely.

Laurana nodded her head. "I agree. This feud is ruinous to the Knighthood. I saw that myself, in the Council meeting. And—from what I've heard of the reports coming from Palanthas—it is hurting our cause there as well. My first concern must be for my friend, however."

"I quite understand, and I am glad to hear you say so," Gunthar said approvingly, "because it makes the very great favor I am about to ask of you easier." Gunthar took Laurana's arm. "I want you to go to Palanthas."

"What? Why? I don't understand!"

"Of course not. Let me explain. Please sit down. You, too, Elistan. I'll pour some wine—"

"I think not," Laurana said, sitting near the window.

"Very well." Gunthar's face became grave. He laid his hand over Laurana's. "We know politics, you and I, lady. So I am going to arrange all my game pieces before you. Ostensibly you will be traveling to Palanthas to teach the knights to use the dragonlances. It is a legitimate reason. Without Theros, you and the dwarf are the only ones who understand their usage. And—let's face it—the dwarf is too short to handle one."

Gunthar cleared his throat. "You will take the lances to Palanthas. But more importantly, you will carry with you a Writ of Vindication from the Council fully restoring Sturm's honor. That will strike the death's blow to Derek's ambition.

The moment Sturm puts on his armor, all will know I have the Council's full support. I shouldn't wonder if *Derek* won't go on trial when he returns."

"But why me?" Laurana asked bluntly. "I can teach anyone—Lord Michael, for example—to use a dragonlance. He can take them to Palanthas. He can carry the Writ to Sturm—"

"Lady"—Lord Gunthar gripped her hand hard, drawing near and speaking barely above a whisper—"you still do not understand! I cannot trust Lord Michael! I cannot—I dare not trust any one of the knights with this! Derek has been knocked from his horse—so to speak—but he hasn't lost the tourney yet. I need someone I can trust implicitly! Someone who knows Derek for what he is, who has Sturm's best interests at heart!"

"I *do* have Sturm's interests at heart," Laurana said coldly. "I put them above the interests of the Knighthood."

"Ah, but remember, Lady Laurana," Gunthar said, rising to his feet and bowing as he kissed her hand, "Sturm's *only* interest is the Knighthood. What would happen to him, do you think, if the Knighthood should fall? What will happen to him if Derek seizes control?"

In the end, of course, Laurana agreed to go to Palanthas, as Gunthar had known she must. As the time of her departure drew nearer, she began to dream almost nightly of Tanis arriving on the island just hours after she left. More than once she was on the verge of refusing to go, but then she thought of facing Tanis, of having to tell him she had refused to go to Sturm to warn him of this peril. This kept her from changing her mind. This—and her regard for Sturm.

It was during the lonely nights, when her heart and her arms ached for Tanis and she had visions of him holding that human woman with the dark, curly hair, flashing brown eyes, and the charming, crooked smile, that her soul was in turmoil.

Her friends could give her little comfort. One of them, Elistan, left when a messenger arrived from the elves, requesting the cleric's presence, and asking that an emissary from the knights accompany him. There was little time for farewells. Within a day of the arrival of the elven messenger, Elistan and Lord Alfred's son, a solemn, serious young man named Douglas, began their journey back to Southern Ergoth. Laurana had never felt so alone as she bid her mentor good-bye.

Tasslehoff faced a sad parting as well.

In the midst of the excitement over the dragonlance, everyone forgot poor Gnosh and his Life Quest, which lay in a thousand sparkling pieces on the grass. Everyone but Fizban. The old magician rose from where he lay cowering on the ground before the shattered Whitestone and went to the stricken gnome, who was staring woefully at the shattered dragon orb.

"There, there, my boy," said Fizban, "this isn't the end of everything!"

"It isn't?" asked Gnosh, so miserable he finished a sentence.

"No, of course not! You've got to look at this from the proper perspective. Why, now you've got a chance to study a dragon orb from the inside out!"

Gnosh's eyes brightened. "You're right," he said after a short pause, "and, in fact, I bet I could glue—"

"Yes, yes," Fizban said hurriedly, but Gnosh lunged forward, his speech growing faster and faster.

"We could tag the pieces, don'tyousee,andthendrawadiagramofwhereeachpiece waslyingontheground,which—"

"Quite, quite," Fizban muttered.

"Step aside, step aside," Gnosh said importantly, shooing people away from the orb. "Mind where you walk, Lord Gunthar, and, yes, we're going to study it from the inside out now, and I should have a report in a matter of weeks—"

Gnosh and Fizban cordoned off the area and set to work. For the next two days, Fizban stood on the broken Whitestone making diagrams, supposedly marking the exact location of each piece before it was picked up. (One of Fizban's diagrams accidentally ended up in the kender's pouch. Tas discovered later that it was actually a game known as "x's and zeroes" which the mage had been playing against himself and apparently—lost.)

Gnosh, meanwhile, crawled happily around on the grass, sticking bits of parchment adorned with numbers on pieces of glass smaller than the bits of parchment. He and Fizban finally collected the 2,687 pieces of dragon orb in a basket and transported them back to Mount Nevermind.

Tasslehoff had been offered the choice of staying with Fizban or going to Palanthas with Laurana and Flint. The choice was simple. The kender knew two such innocents as the elfmaid and the dwarf could not survive without him. But it was hard leaving his old friend. Two days before the ship sailed, he paid a final visit to the gnomes and to Fizban.

After an exhilarating ride in the catapult, he found Gnosh in the Examination Room. The pieces of the broken dragon orb—tagged and numbered—were spread out across two tables.

"Absolutelyfascinating," Gnosh spoke so fast he stuttered, "because wehaveanalyzedtheglass, curiousmaterial, unlikenothingwe'veeverseen, greatestdiscovery, thiscentury—"

"So your Life Quest is over?" Tas interrupted. "Your father's soul—"

"Restingcomfortably!" Gnosh beamed, then returned to his work." Andsogladyoucouldstopbyandifyou'reeverintheneighborhoodcomebyandseeusagain—"

"I will," Tas said, smiling.

Tas found Fizban two levels down. (A fascinating journey—he simply yelled out the name of his level, then leaped into the void. Nets flapped and fluttered, bells went off, gongs sounded and whistles blew. Tas was finally caught one level above the ground, just as the area was being inundated with sponges.)

Fizban was in Weapons Development, surrounded by gnomes, all gazing at him with unabashed admiration.

"Ah, my boy!" he said, peering vaguely at Tasslehoff. "You're just in time to see the testing of our new weapon. Revolutionize warfare. Make the dragonlance obsolete."

"Really?" Tas asked in excitement.

"A fact!" Fizban confirmed. "Now, you stand over here—" He motioned to a gnome who leaped to do his bidding, running to stand in the middle of the cluttered room.

Fizban picked up what looked, to the kender's confused mind, like a crossbow that had been attacked by an enraged fisherman. It was a crossbow all right. But instead of an arrow, a huge net dangled from a hook on the end. Fizban, grumbling and muttering, ordered the gnomes to stand behind him and give him room.

"Now, you are the enemy," Fizban told the gnome in the center of the room. The gnome immediately assumed a fierce, warlike expression. The other gnomes nodded appreciatively.

Fizban aimed, then let fly. The net sailed out into the air, got snagged on the hook at the end of crossbow, and snapped back like a collapsing sail to engulf the magician.

"Confounded hook!" Fizban muttered.

Between the gnomes and Tas, they got him disentangled.

"I guess this is good-bye," Tas said, slowly extending his small hand.

"It is?" Fizban looked amazed. "Am I going somewhere? No one told me! I'm not packed—"

"*I'm* going somewhere," Tas said patiently, "with Laurana. We're taking the lances and—oh, I don't think I'm supposed to be telling anyone," he added, embarrassed.

"Don't worry. Mum's the word," Fizban said in a hoarse whisper that carried clearly through the crowded room. "You'll love Palanthas. Beautiful city. Give Sturm my regards. Oh, and Tasslehoff"—the old magician looked at him shrewdly—"you did the right thing, my boy!"

"I did?" Tas said hopefully. "I'm glad." He hesitated. "I wondered . . . about what you said—the dark path. Did I—?"

Fizban's face grew grave as he gripped Tas firmly on the shoulder "I'm afraid so. But you have the courage to walk it."

"I hope so," Tas said with a small sigh. "Well, good-bye. I'll be back. Just as soon as the war's over."

"Oh, I probably won't be here," Fizban said, shaking his head so violently his hat slid off. "Soon as the new weapon's perfected, I'll be leaving for—" he paused. "Where was that I was supposed to go? I can't seem to recall. But don't worry. We'll meet again. At least you're not leaving me buried under a pile of chicken feathers!" he muttered, searching for his hat.

Tas picked it up and handed it to him.

"Good-bye," the kender said, a choke in his voice.

"Good-bye, good-bye!" Fizban waved cheerfully. Then— giving the gnomes a hunted glance—he pulled Tas over to him. "Uh, I seem to have forgotten something. What was my name again?"

Someone else said good-bye to the old magician, too, although not under quite the same circumstances.

Elistan was pacing the shore of Sancrist, waiting for the boat that would take him back to Southern Ergoth. The young man, Douglas, walked along beside him. The two were deep in conversation, Elistan explaining the ways of the ancient gods to a rapt and attentive listener.

Suddenly Elistan looked up to see the old, befuddled magician he had seen at the Council meeting. Elistan had tried for days to meet the old mage, but Fizban always avoided him. Thus it was with astonishment Elistan saw the old man come walking toward them now along the shoreline. His head was bowed, he was muttering to himself. For a moment, Elistan thought he would pass by without noticing them, when suddenly the old mage raised his head.

"Oh, I say! Haven't we met?" he asked, blinking.

For a moment Elistan could not speak. The cleric's face turned deathly white beneath its weathered tan. He was finally able to answer the old mage, his voice was husky. "Indeed we have, sir. I did not realize it before now. And though we were but lately introduced, I feel that I have known you a long, long time."

"Indeed?" The old man scowled suspiciously. "You're not making some sort of comment on my age, are you?"

"No, certainly not!" Elistan smiled.

The old man's face cleared.

"Well, have a pleasant journey. And a safe one. Farewell."

Leaning on a bent and battered staff, the old man toddled on past them. Suddenly he stopped and turned around. "Oh, by the way, the name's Fizban."

"I'll remember," Elistan said gravely, bowing. "Fizban."

Pleased, the old magician nodded and continued on his way along the shoreline while Elistan, suddenly thoughtful and quiet, resumed his walk with a sigh.

The Perechon
Memories of Long Ago.

12

"This is crazy, I hope you realize that!" Caramon hissed.

"We wouldn't be here if we were sane, would we?" Tanis responded, gritting his teeth.

"No," Caramon muttered. "I suppose you're right."

The two men stood in the shadows of a dark alleyway, in a town where generally the only things ever found in alleyways were rats, drunks, and dead bodies.

The name of the wretched town was Flotsam, and it was well named, for it lay upon the shores of the Blood Sea of Istar like the wreckage of a broken vessel tossed upon the rocks. Peopled by the dregs of most of the races of Krynn, Flotsam was, in addition, an occupied town now, overrun with draconians, goblins, and mercenaries of all races, attracted to the Highlords by high wages and the spoils of war.

And so, "like the other scum," as Raistlin observed, the companions floated along upon the tides of war and were deposited in Flotsam. Here they hoped to find a ship that would take them on the long, treacherous journey around the northern part of Ansalon to Sancrist—or wherever—

Where they were going was a point that had been much in contention lately—ever since Raistlin's recovery from his illness. The companions had anxiously watched him following his use of the dragon orb, their concern not completely centered on his health. What had happened when he used the orb? What harm might he have brought upon them?

"You need not fear," Raistlin told them in his whispering voice. "I am not weak and foolish like the elven king. I gained control of the orb. It did not gain control of me."

"Then what does it do? How can we use it?" Tanis asked, alarmed by the frozen expression on the mage's metallic face.

"It took all my strength to gain control of the orb," Raistlin replied, his eyes on the ceiling above his bed. "It will require much more study before I learn how to use it."

"Study . . ." Tanis repeated. "Study of the orb?"

Raistlin flicked him a glance, then resumed staring at the ceiling. "No," he replied. "The study of books, written by the ancient ones who created the orb. We must go to Palanthas, to the library of one Astinus, who resides there."

Tanis was silent for a moment. He could hear the mage's breath rattle in his lungs as he struggled to draw breath.

What keeps him clinging to this life? Tanis wondered silently.

It had snowed that morning, but now the snow had changed to rain. Tanis could hear it drumming on the wooden roof of the wagon. Heavy clouds drifted across the sky. Perhaps it was the gloom of the day, but as he looked at Raistlin, Tanis felt a chill creep through his body until the cold seemed to freeze his heart.

"Was this what you meant, when you spoke of ancient spells?" Tanis asked.

"Of course. What else?" Raistlin paused, coughing, then asked, "When did I speak of . . . ancient spells?"

"When we first found you," Tanis answered, watching the mage closely. He noticed a crease in Raistlin's forehead and heard tension in his shattered voice.

"What did I say?"

"Nothing much," Tanis replied warily. "Just something about ancient spells, spells that would soon be yours."

"That was all?"

Tanis did not reply immediately. Raistlin's strange, hourglass eyes focused on him coldly. The half-elf shivered and nodded. Raistlin turned his head away. His eyes closed. "I will sleep now," he said softly. "Remember, Tanis. Palanthas."

Tanis was forced to admit he wanted to go to Sancrist for purely selfish reasons. He hoped against hope that Laurana and Sturm and the others would be there. And it was where he had promised he would take the dragon orb. But against this, he had to weigh Raistlin's steady insistence that they must go to the library of this Astinus to discover how to use the orb.

His mind was still in a quandary when they reached Flotsam. Finally, he decided they would set about getting passage on a ship going north first and decide where to land later.

But when they reached Flotsam, they had a nasty shock. There were more draconians in that city than they had seen on their entire journey from Port Balifor north. The streets were crawling with heavily armed patrols, taking an intense interest in strangers. Fortunately, the companions had sold their wagon before entering the town, so they were able to mingle with the crowds on the streets. But they hadn't been inside the city gates five minutes before they saw a draconian patrol arrest a human for "questioning."

This alarmed them, so they took rooms in the first inn they came to—a run-down place at the edge of town.

151

"How are we going to even get to the harbor, much less buy passage on a ship?" Caramon asked as they settled into their shabby rooms. "What's going on?"

"The innkeeper says a Dragon Highlord is in town. The draconians are searching for spies or something," Tanis muttered uncomfortably. The companions exchanged glances.

"Maybe they're searching for *us*," Caramon said.

"That's ridiculous!" Tanis answered quickly—too quickly. "We're getting spooked. How could anyone know we're here? Or know what we carry?"

"I wonder . . ." Riverwind said grimly, glancing at Raistlin.

The mage returned his glance coolly, not deigning to answer. "Hot water for my drink," he instructed Caramon.

"There's only one way I can think of," Tanis said, as Caramon brought his brother the water as ordered. "Caramon and I will go out tonight and waylay two of the dragonarmy soldiers. We'll steal their uniforms. Not the draconians—" he said hastily, as Caramon's brow wrinkled in disgust. "The human mercenaries. Then we can move around Flotsam freely."

After some discussion, everyone agreed it was the only plan that seemed likely to work. The companions ate dinner without much appetite—dining in their rooms rather than risk going into the common room.

"You'll be all right?" Caramon asked Raistlin uneasily when the two were alone in the room they shared.

"I am quite capable of taking care of myself," Raistlin replied. Rising to his feet, he had picked up a spellbook to study, when a fit of coughing doubled him over.

Caramon reached out his hand, but Raistlin flinched away.

"Be gone!" the mage gasped. "Leave me be!"

Caramon hesitated, then he sighed. "Sure, Raist," he said,

and left the room, shutting the door gently behind him.

Raistlin stood for a moment, trying to catch his breath. Then he moved slowly across the room, setting down the spellbook. With a trembling hand, he picked up one of the many sacks that Caramon had placed on the table beside his bed. Opening it, Raistlin carefully withdrew the dragon orb.

Tanis and Caramon—the half-elf keeping his hood pulled low over his face and ears—walked the streets of Flotsam, watching for two guards whose uniforms might fit them. This would have been relatively easy for Tanis, but finding a guard whose armor fit the giant Caramon was more difficult.

They both knew they had better find something quickly. More than once, draconians looked them over suspiciously. Two draconians even stopped them, insisting roughly on knowing their business. Caramon replied in the crude mercenary dialect that they were seeking employment in the Dragon Highlord's army, and the draconians let them go. But both men knew it was only a matter of time before a patrol caught them.

"I wonder what's going on?" Tanis muttered worriedly.

"Maybe the war's heating up for the Highlords," Caramon began."There, look, Tanis. Going into that bar—"

"I see. Yeah, he's about your size. Duck into that alley. We'll wait until they come out, then—" The half-elf made a motion of wringing a neck. Caramon nodded. The two slipped through the filthy streets and vanished into the alley, hiding where they could keep on eye on the front door of the bar.

It was nearly midnight. The moons would not rise tonight. The rain had ceased, but clouds still obscured the sky. The two men crouched in the alley were soon shivering, despite their heavy cloaks. Rats skittered across their feet, making them cringe in the darkness. A drunken hobgoblin took a wrong turn and lurched past them, falling headfirst into a pile of garbage. The hobgoblin did not get back up again and the stench nearly made Tanis and Caramon sick, but they dared not leave their vantage point.

Then they heard welcome sounds—drunken laughter and human voices speaking Common. The two guards they had been waiting for lurched out of the bar and staggered toward them.

A tall iron brazier stood on the sidewalk, lighting the night. The mercenaries lurched into its light, giving Tanis a close look at them. Both were officers in the dragonarmy, he saw. Newly promoted, he guessed, which may have been what they were celebrating. Their armor was shining new, relatively clean, and undented. It was good armor, too, he saw with satisfaction. Made of blue steel, it was fashioned after the style of the Highlords' own dragon-scale armor.

"Ready?" Caramon whispered. Tanis nodded.

Caramon drew his sword. "Elven scum!" he roared in his deep, barrel-chested bass. "I've found you out, and now you'll come with me to the Dragon Highlord, spy!"

"You'll never take me alive!" Tanis drew his own sword.

At the sound of their voices, the two officers staggered to a stop, peering bleary-eyed into the dark alley.

The officers watched with growing interest as Caramon and Tanis made a few passes at each other, maneuvering themselves into position. When Caramon's back was to the officers and Tanis was facing them, the half-elf made a sudden move. Disarming Caramon, he sent the warrior's sword flying.

"Quick! Help me take him!" Caramon bellowed. "There's a reward out for him—dead or alive!"

The officers never hesitated. Fumbling drunkenly for their weapons, they headed for Tanis, their faces twisted into expressions of cruel pleasure.

"That's it! Nail 'im!" Caramon urged, waiting until they were past him. Then—just as they raised their swords—Caramon's huge hands encircled their necks. He slammed their heads together, and the bodies slumped to the ground.

"Hurry!" Tanis grunted. He dragged one body by the feet away from the light. Caramon followed with the other. Quickly they began to strip off the armor.

"Phew! This one must have been half-troll," Caramon said, waving his hand to clear the air of the foul smell.

"Quit complaining!" Tanis snapped, trying to figure out how the complex system of buckles and straps worked. "At least you're used to wearing this stuff. Give me a hand with this, will you?"

"Sure." Caramon, grinning, helped to buckle Tanis into the armor. "An elf in plate armor. What's the world coming to?"

"Sad times," Tanis muttered. "When are we supposed to meet that ship captain William told you about?"

"He said we could find her on board around daybreak."

"The name's Maquesta Kar-thon," said the woman, her expression cool and businesslike. "And—let me guess—you're *not* officers in the dragonarmy. Not unless they're hiring elves these days."

Tanis flushed, slowly drawing off the helm of the officer. "Is it that obvious?"

The woman shrugged. "Probably not to anyone else. The beard is very good—perhaps I should say half-elf, of course.

And the helm hides your ears. But unless you get a mask, those pretty, almond shaped eyes of yours are a dead give-away. But then, not many draconians are apt to look into your pretty eyes, are they?" Leaning back in her chair, she put a booted foot on a table, and regarded him coolly.

Tanis heard Caramon chuckle, and felt his skin burn.

They were on board the *Perechon*, sitting in the captain's cabin, across from the captain herself. Maquesta Kar-thon was one of the dark-skinned race living in Northern Ergoth. Her people had been sailors for centuries and, it was popularly believed, could speak the languages of seabirds and dolphins. Tanis found himself thinking of Theros Ironfeld as he looked at Maquesta. The woman's skin was shining black, her hair tightly curled and bound with a gold band around her forehead. Her eyes were brown and shining as her skin. But there was the glint of steel from the dagger at her belt, and the glint of steel in her eyes.

"We're here to discuss business, Captain Maque—" Tanis stumbled over the strange name.

"Sure you are," the woman said. "And call me Maq. Easier for both of us. It's well you have this letter from Pig-faced William, or I wouldn't have even talked to you. But he says you're square and your money's good, so I'll listen. Now, where're you bound?"

Tanis exchanged glances with Caramon. That was the question. Besides, he wasn't certain he wanted either of their destinations known. Palanthas was the capital city of Solamnia, while Sancrist was a well-known haven of the Knights.

"Oh, for the love of—" Maq snapped, seeing them hesitate. Her eyes flared. Removing her foot from the table, she stared at them grimly. "You either trust me or you don't!"

"Should we?" Tanis asked bluntly.

Maq raised an eyebrow. "How much money do you have?"

"Enough," Tanis said. "Let's just say that we want to go north, around the Cape of Nordmaar. If, at that point, we still find each other's company agreeable, we'll go on. If not, we'll pay you off, and you put us in a safe harbor."

"Kalaman," said Maq, settling back. She seemed amused. "That's a safe harbor. As safe as any these days. Half your money now. Half at Kalaman. Any farther is negotiable."

"*Safe* delivery to Kalaman," Tanis amended.

"Who can promise?" Maq shrugged. "It's a rough time of year to travel by sea." She rose languidly, stretching like a cat. Caramon, standing up quickly, stared at her admiringly.

"It's a deal," she said. "Come on. I'll show you the ship."

Maq led them onto the deck. The ship seemed fit and trim as far as Tanis, who knew nothing about ships, could tell. Her voice and manner had been cold when they first talked to her, but when she showed them around her ship, she seemed to warm up. Tanis had seen the same expression, heard the same warm tones Maq used in talking about her ship that Tika used when talking about Caramon. The *Perechon* was obviously Maq's only love.

The ship was quiet, empty. Her crew was ashore, along with her first mate, Maq explained. The only other person Tanis saw on board was a man sitting by himself, mending a sail. The man looked up as they passed, and Tanis saw his eyes widen in alarm at the sight of the dragon armor.

"*Nocesta*, Berem," Maq said to him soothingly as they passed. She made a slashing motion with her hand, gesturing to Tanis and Caramon. "*Nocesta*. Customers. Money."

The man nodded and went back to his work.

"Who is he?" Tanis asked Maq in a low voice as they walked toward her cabin once more to conclude their business.

"Who? Berem?" she asked, glancing around. "He's the helmsman. Don't know much about him. He came around a few months back, looking for work. Took him on as a deck-swab. Then my helmsman was killed in a small altercation with—well, never mind. But this fellow turned out to be a damn good hand at the wheel, better than the first, in fact. He's an odd one, though. A mute. Never speaks. Never goes ashore, if he can help it. Wrote his name down for me in the ship's book, or I wouldn't have known that much about him. Why?" she asked, noticing Tanis studying the man intently.

Berem was tall, well-built. At first sight, one might guess him to be middle-aged, by human terms. His hair was gray; his face was clean shaven, deeply tanned, and weathered from months spent on board ship. But his eyes were youthful, clear, and bright. The hands that held the needle were smooth and strong, the hands of a young man. Elven blood, perhaps, Tanis thought, but if so it wasn't apparent in any of his features.

"I've seen him somewhere," Tanis murmured. "How about you, Caramon? Do you remember him?"

"Ah, come on," said the big warrior. "We've seen hundreds of people this past month, Tanis. He was probably in the audience at one of our shows.

"No." Tanis shook his head. "When I first saw him, I thought of Pax Tharkas and Sturm. . . ."

"Hey, I got a lot of work to do, half-elf," Maquesta said. "You coming, or you gonna gawk at a guy stitching a sail?"

She climbed down the hatch. Caramon followed clumsily, his sword and armor clanking. Reluctantly, Tanis went after them. But he turned for one final look at the man, and caught the man regarding him with a strange, penetrating gaze.

"All right, you go back to the inn with the others. I'll buy the supplies. We sail when the ship's ready. Maquesta says about four days."

"I wish it was sooner," muttered Caramon.

"So do I," said Tanis grimly. "There's too damn many draconians around here. But we've got to wait for the tide or some such thing. Go back to the inn and keep everyone inside. Tell your brother to lay in a store of that herb stuff he drinks—we'll be at sea a long time. I'll be back in a few hours, after I get the supplies."

Tanis walked down the crowded streets of Flotsam, no one giving him a second glance in his dragon armor. He would be glad to take it off. It was hot, heavy and itchy. And he had trouble remembering to return the salutes of draconians and goblins. It was beginning to occur to him—as he saw the respect his uniform commanded—that the humans they stole the uniforms from must have held a high rank. The thought was not comforting. Any moment now, someone might recognize his armor.

But he couldn't do without it, he knew. There were more draconians in the streets than ever today. The air of tension in Flotsam was high. Most of the town's citizens were staying home, and most of the shops were closed—with the exception of the taverns. In fact, as he passed one closed shop after another, Tanis began to worry about where he was going to buy supplies for the long ocean voyage.

Tanis was musing on this problem as he stared into a closed shop window, when a hand suddenly wrapped around his boot and yanked him to the ground.

The fall knocked the breath from the half-elf's body. He struck his head heavily on the cobblestones and—for a moment—was groggy with pain. Instinctively he kicked out at whatever had him by the feet, but the hands that grasped him were strong. He felt himself being dragged into a dark alley.

Shaking his head to clear it, he strained to look at his captor. It was an elf! His clothes filthy and torn, his elven features distorted by grief and hatred, the elf stood above him, a spear in his hand.

"Dragon man!" the elf snarled in Common. "Your foul kind slaughtered my family—my wife and my children! Murdered them in their beds, ignoring their pleas for mercy. This is for them!" The elf raised his spear.

"*Shak! It mo dracosali!*" Tanis cried desperately in elven, struggling to pull off his helmet. But the elf, driven insane by grief, was beyond hearing or understanding. His spear plunged downward. Suddenly the elf's eyes grew wide, riveted in shock. The spear fell from his nerveless fingers as a sword punctured him from behind. The dying elf fell with a shriek, landing heavily upon the pavement.

Tanis looked up in astonishment to see who had saved his life. A Dragon Highlord stood over the elf's body.

"I heard you shouting and saw one of my officers in trouble. I guessed you needed some help," said the Highlord, reaching out a gloved hand to help Tanis up.

Confused, dizzy with pain and knowing only that he mustn't give himself away, Tanis accepted the Highlord's hand and struggled to his feet. Ducking his face, thankful for the dark shadows in the alley, Tanis mumbled words of thanks in a harsh voice. Then he saw the Highlord's eyes behind the mask widen.

"Tanis?"

The half-elf felt a shudder run through his body, a pain as swift and sharp as the elven spear. He could not speak, he could only stare as the Highlord swiftly removed the blue and gold dragonmask.

"Tanis! It *is* you!" the Highlord cried, grasping him by the arms. Tanis saw bright brown eyes, a crooked, charming smile.

"Kitiara . . ."

TANIS CAPTURED.

13

So, Tanis! An officer, and in my own command. I should review my troops more often!" Kitiara laughed, sliding her arm through his. "You're shaking. You took a nasty fall. Come on. My rooms aren't far from here. We'll have a drink, patch up that wound, then . . . talk."

Dazed—but not from the head wound—Tanis let Kitiara lead him out of the alley onto the sidewalk. Too much had happened too fast. One minute he had been buying supplies and now he was walking arm in arm with a Dragon Highlord who had just saved his life and who was also the woman he had loved for so many years. He could not help but stare at her, and Kitiara—knowing his eyes were on her—returned his gaze from beneath her long, sooty-black eyelashes.

The gleaming, night-blue dragon-scale armor of the Highlords suited her well, Tanis caught himself thinking. It was tight-fitting, emphasizing the curves of her long legs.

Draconians swarmed around them, hoping for even a brief nod from the Highlord. But Kitiara ignored them, chatting breezily with Tanis as if it were only an afternoon since they had parted, instead of five years. He could not absorb her words, his brain was still fumbling to make sense of this, while his body was reacting—once again—to her nearness.

The mask had left her hair somewhat damp, the curls clung to her face and forehead. Casually she ran her gloved hand through her hair, shaking it out. It was an old habit of hers and that small gesture brought back memories—

Tanis shook his head, struggling desperately to pull his shattered world together and attend to her words. The lives of his friends depended on what he did now.

"It's hot beneath that dragon helm!" she was saying. "I don't need the frightful thing to keep my men in line. Do I?" she asked, winking.

"N-no," Tanis stammered, feeling himself flush.

"Same old Tanis," she murmured, pressing her body against his. "You still blush like a schoolboy. But you were never like the others, never . . ." she added softly. Pulling him close, she put her arms around him. Closing her eyes, her moist lips brushed his. . . .

"Kit—" Tanis said in a strangled voice, wrenching backward. "Not here! Not in the street," he added lamely.

For a moment Kitiara regarded him angrily, then—shrugging, she dropped her hand down to clasp his arm again. Together they continued along the street, the draconians leering and joking.

"Same Tanis," she said again, this time with a little, breathless sigh. "I don't know why I let you get away with it. Any other man who refused me like that would have died on my sword. Ah, here we are."

She entered the best inn in Flotsam, the Saltbreeze. Built high on a cliff, it overlooked the Blood Sea of Istar, whose waves broke on the rocks below. The innkeeper hurried forward.

"Is my room made up?" Kit asked coolly.

"Yes, Highlord," the innkeeper said, bowing again and again. As they ascended the stairs, the innkeeper hustled ahead of them to make certain that all was in order.

Kit glanced around. Finding everything satisfactory, she casually tossed the dragonhelm on a table and began pulling off her gloves. Sitting down in a chair, she raised her leg with sensual and deliberate abandon.

"My boots," she said to Tanis, smiling.

Swallowing, giving her a weak smile in return, Tanis gripped her leg in his hands. This had been an old game of theirs, him taking off her boots. It had always led to—Tanis tried to keep himself from thinking about that!

"Bring us a bottle of your finest wine," Kitiara told the hovering innkeeper, "and two glasses." She raised her other leg, her brown eyes on Tanis. "Then leave us alone."

"But—my lord—" the innkeeper said hesitantly, "there have been messages from Dragon Highlord Ariakas. . . ."

"If you show your face in this room—*after* you bring the wine—I'll cut off your ears," Kitiara said pleasantly. But, as she spoke, she drew a gleaming dagger from her belt.

The innkeeper turned pale, nodded, and left hurriedly.

Kit laughed. "There!" she said, wiggling her toes in their blue silken hose. "Now, I'll take off your boots—"

"I—I really must go," Tanis said, sweating beneath his armor. "My c-company commander will be missing me . . ."

"But *I'm* commander of your company!" Kit said gaily. "And tomorrow *you'll* be commander of your company. Or higher, if you like. Now, sit down."

Tanis could do nothing but obey, knowing, however, that in his heart he *wanted* to do nothing but obey.

"It's so good to see you," Kit said, kneeling before him and tugging at his boot. "I'm sorry I missed the reunion in Solace. How is everyone? How is Sturm? Probably fighting with the

Knights, I suppose. I'm not surprised you two separated. That was one friendship I never could understand—"

Kitiara talked on, but Tanis ceased to listen. He could only look at her. He had forgotten how lovely she was, how sensual, inviting. Desperately he concentrated on his own danger. But all he could think of were nights of bliss spent with Kitiara.

At that moment, Kit looked up into his eyes. Caught and held by the passion she saw in them, she let his boot slip from her hands. Involuntarily, Tanis reached out and drew her near. Kitiara slid her hand around his neck and pressed her lips against his.

At her touch, the desires and longings that had tormented Tanis for five years surged through his body. Her fragrance, warm and womanly—mingled with the smell of leather and steel. Her kiss was like flame. The pain was unbearable. Tanis knew only one way to end it.

When the innkeeper knocked on the door, he received no answer. Shaking his head in admiration—this was the third man in as many days—he set the wine upon the floor and left.

"And now," Kitiara murmured sleepily, lying in Tanis's arms. "Tell me about my little brothers. Are they with you? The last I saw them, you were escaping from Tarsis with that elf woman."

"That was you!" Tanis said, remembering the blue dragons.

"Of course!" Kit cuddled nearer. "I like the beard," she said, stroking his face. "It hides those weak elvish features. How did you get into the army?"

How indeed? thought Tanis frantically.

"We . . . were captured in Silvanesti. One of the officers convinced me I was a fool to fight the D-Dark Queen."

"And my little brothers?"

"We—we were separated," Tanis said weakly.

"A pity," Kit said with a sigh. "I'd like to see them again. Caramon must be a giant by now. And Raistlin—I hear he is quite a skilled mage. Still wearing the Red Robes?"

"I—I guess," Tanis muttered. "I haven't seen him—"

"That won't last long," Kit said complacently. "He's like me. Raist always craved power . . ."

"What about you?" Tanis interrupted quickly. "What are you doing here, so far from the action? The fighting's north—"

"Why, I'm here for the same reason you are," Kit answered, opening her eyes wide. "Searching for the Green Gemstone Man, of course."

"That's where I've seen him before!" Tanis said, memories flooding his mind. The man on the *Perechon!* The man in Pax Tharkas, escaping with poor Eben. The man with the green gemstone embedded in the center of his chest.

"You've found him!" Kitiara said, sitting up eagerly. "Where, Tanis? Where?" Her brown eyes glittered.

"I'm not sure," Tanis said, faltering. "I'm not sure it was him. I—we were just given a rough description. . . ."

"He looks about fifty in human years," Kit said in excitement, "but he has strange, young eyes, and his hands are young. And in the flesh of his chest is a green gemstone. We had reports he was sighted in Flotsam. That's why the Dark Queen sent me here. He's the key, Tanis! Find him—and no force on Krynn can stop us!"

"Why?" Tanis made himself ask calmly. "What's he got that's so essential to—uh—our side winning this war?"

"Who knows?" Shrugging her slender shoulders, Kit lay back in Tanis's arms. "You're shivering. Here, this will warm you." She kissed his neck, running her hands over his body. "We were just told the most important thing we could do to end this war in one swift stroke is to find this man."

Tanis swallowed, feeling himself warming to her touch.

"Just think," Kitiara whispered in his ear, her breath hot and moist against his skin, "if we found him—you and I—we would have all of Krynn at our feet! The Dark Queen would reward us beyond anything we ever dreamed! You and I, together always, Tanis. Let's go now!"

Her words echoed in his mind. The two of them, together, forever. Ending the war. Ruling Krynn. No, he thought, feeling his throat constrict. This is madness! Insanity! My people, my friends. . . . Yet, haven't I done enough? What do I owe any of them, humans or elves? Nothing! They are the ones who have hurt me, derided me! All these years, a cast-out. Why think about them? *Me!* It's time I thought about *me* for a change! This is the woman I've dreamed of for so long. And she can be mine! Kitiara . . . so beautiful, so desirable . . .

"No!" Tanis said harshly, then, "No," he said more gently. Reaching out his hand, he pulled her back near him. "Tomorrow will do. If it was him, he isn't going anywhere. I know. . . ."

Kitiara smiled and, with a sigh, lay back down. Tanis, bending over her, kissed her passionately. Far away, he could hear the waves of the Blood Sea of Istar crashing on the shore.

THE HIGH CLERIST'S TOWER.
THE KNIGHTING.

14

By morning, the storm over Solamnia had blown itself out. The sun rose, a disk of pale gold that warmed nothing. The knights who stood watch upon the battlements of the Tower of the High Clerist went thankfully to their beds, talking of the wonders they had seen during the awful night, for such a storm as this had not been known in the lands of Solamnia since the days after the Cataclysm. Those who took over the watch from their fellow knights were nearly as weary; no one had slept.

Now they looked out upon a plain covered with snow and ice. Here and there the landscape was dotted with flickering flames where trees, blasted by the jagged lightning that had streaked out of the sky during the blizzard, burned eerily. But it was not to those strange flames the eyes of the knights turned as they ascended the battlements. It was to the flames that burned upon the horizon—hundreds and hundreds of flames, filling the clear, cold air with their foul smoke.

The campfires of war. The campfires of the dragonarmies.

One thing stood between the Dragon Highlord and victory in Solamnia. That "thing" (as the Highlord often referred to it) was the Tower of the High Clerist. Built long ago by Vinas Solamnus, founder of the Knights, in the only pass through the snow-capped, cloud-shrouded Vingaard Mountains, the Tower protected Palanthas, capital city of Solamnia, and the harbor known as the Gates of Paladine. Let the Tower fall, and Palanthas would belong to the dragonarmies. It was a soft city—a city of wealth and beauty, a city that had turned its back upon the world to gaze with admiring eyes into its own mirror.

With Palanthas in her hands and the harbor under her control, the Highlord could easily starve the rest of Solamnia into submission and then wipe out the troublesome Knights.

The Dragon Highlord, called the Dark Lady by her troops, was not in camp this day. She was gone on secret business to the east. But she had left loyal and able commanders behind her, commanders who would do anything to win her favor.

Of all the Dragon Highlords, the Dark Lady was known to sit highest in the regard of her Dark Queen. And so the troops of draconians, goblins, hobgoblins, ogres, and humans sat around their campfires, staring at the Tower with hungry eyes, longing to attack and earn her commendation.

The Tower was defended by a large garrison of Knights of Solamnia who had marched out from Palanthas only a few weeks ago. Legend recalled that the Tower had never fallen while men of faith held it, dedicated as it was to the High Clerist—that position which, second only to the Grand Master, was most revered in the Knighthood.

The clerics of Paladine had lived in the High Clerist's Tower during the Age of Dreams. Here young knights had come for their religious training and indoctrination. There were still many traces of the clerics' presence left behind.

It wasn't only fear of the legend that forced the dragon-armies to sit idle. It didn't take a legend to tell their commanders that taking this tower was going to be costly.

"Time is in our favor," stated the Dark Lady before she left. "Our spies tell us the knights have received little help from Palanthas. We've cut off their supplies from Vingaard Keep to the east. Let them sit in their tower and starve. Sooner or later their impatience and their stomachs will cause them to make a mistake. When they do, we will be ready."

"We could take it with a flight of dragons," muttered a young commander. His name was Bakaris, and his bravery in battle and his handsome face had done much to advance him in the Dark Lady's favor. She eyed him speculatively, however, as she prepared to mount her blue dragon, Skie.

"Perhaps not," she said coolly. "You've heard the reports of the discovery of the ancient weapon—the dragonlance?"

"Bah! Children's stories!" The young commander laughed as he assisted her onto Skie's back. The blue dragon stood glaring at the handsome commander with fierce, fiery eyes.

"Never discount children's stories," the Dark Lady said, "for these were the same tales that were told of dragons." She shrugged. "Do not worry, my pet. If my mission to capture the Green Gemstone Man is successful, we will not need to attack the Tower, for its destruction will be assured. If not, perhaps I will bring you that flight of dragons you ask for."

With that, the giant blue lifted his wings and sailed off toward the east, heading for a small and wretched town called Flotsam on the Blood Sea of Istar.

And so the dragonarmies waited, warm and comfortable around their fires, while—as the Dark Lady had predicted—the knights in their Tower starved. But far worse than the lack of food was the bitter dissension within their own ranks.

The young knights under Sturm Brightblade's command had grown to revere their disgraced leader during the hard months that followed their departure from Sancrist. Although melancholy and often aloof, Sturm's honesty and integrity won him his men's respect and admiration. It was a costly victory, causing Sturm a great deal of suffering at Derek's hands. A less noble man might have turned a blind eye to Derek's political maneuvers, or at least kept his mouth shut (as did Lord Alfred), but Sturm spoke out against Derek constantly—even though he knew it worsened his own cause with the powerful knight.

It was Derek who had completely alienated the people of Palanthas. Already distrustful, filled with old hatreds and bitterness, the people of the beautiful, quiet city were alarmed and angered by Derek's threats when they refused to allow the Knights to garrison the city. It was only through Sturm's patient negotiations that the knights received any supplies at all.

The situation did not improve when the knights reached the High Clerist's Tower. The disruption among the knights lowered the morale of the footmen, already suffering from a lack of food. Soon the Tower itself became an armed camp— the majority of knights who favored Derek were now openly opposed by those siding with Lord Gunthar, led by Sturm. It was only because of the knights' strict obedience to the Measure that fights within the Tower itself had not yet broken out. But the demoralizing sight of the dragonarmies camped nearby, as well as the lack of food, led to frayed tempers and taut nerves.

Too late, Lord Alfred realized their danger. He bitterly regretted his own folly in supporting Derek, for he could see clearly now that Derek Crownguard was going insane.

The madness grew on him daily; Derek's lust for power

ate away at him and deprived him of his reason. But Lord Alfred was powerless to act. So locked into their rigid structure were the knights that it would take—according to the Measure—months of Knights Councils to strip Derek of his rank.

News of Sturm's vindication struck this dry and crackling forest like a bolt of lightning. As Gunthar had foreseen, this completely shattered Derek's hopes. What Gunthar had not foreseen was that this would sever Derek's tenuous hold on sanity.

On the morning following the storm, the eyes of the guards turned for a moment from their vigilance over the dragon-armies to look down into the courtyard of the Tower of the High Clerist. The sun filled the gray sky with a chill, pale light that was reflected in the coldly gleaming armor of the Knights of Solamnia as they assembled in the solemn ceremony awarding knighthood.

Above them, the flags with the Knight's Crest seemed frozen upon the battlements, hanging lifeless in the still, cold air. Then a trumpet's pure notes split the air, stirring the blood. At that clarion call, the knights lifted their heads proudly and marched into the courtyard.

Lord Alfred stood in the center of a circle of knights. Dressed in his battle armor, his red cape fluttering from his shoulders, he held an antique sword in an old, battered scabbard. The kingfisher, the rose, and the crown—ancient symbols of the Knighthood—were entwined upon the scabbard. The lord cast a swift, hopeful gaze around the assembly, but then lowered his eyes, shaking his head.

Lord Alfred's worst fears were realized. He had hoped bleakly that this ceremony might reunite the knights. But it was having the opposite effect. There were great gaps in the Sacred Circle, gaps that the knights in attendance stared at uncomfortably. Derek and his entire command were absent.

The trumpet call sounded twice more, then silence fell upon the assembled knights. Sturm Brightblade, dressed in long, white robes, stepped out of the Chapel of the High Clerist where he had spent the night in solemn prayer and meditation as prescribed by the Measure. Accompanying him was an unusual Guard of Honor.

Beside Sturm walked an elven woman, her beauty shining in the bleakness of the day like the sun dawning in the spring. Behind her walked an old dwarf, the sunlight bright on his white hair and beard. Next to the dwarf came a kender dressed in bright blue leggings.

The circle of knights opened to admit Sturm and his escorts. They came to a halt before Lord Alfred. Laurana, holding his helm in her hands, stood on his right. Flint, carrying his shield, stood on his left, and after a poke in the ribs from the dwarf—Tasslehoff hurried forward with the knight's spurs.

Sturm bowed his head. His long hair, already streaked with gray though he was only in his early thirties, fell about his shoulders. He stood a moment in silent prayer, then, at a sign from Lord Alfred, fell reverently to his knees.

"Sturm Brightblade," Lord Alfred declared solemnly, opening a sheet of paper, "the Knights Council, on hearing testimony given by Lauralanthalasa of the royal family of Qualinesti and further testimony by Flint Fireforge, hill dwarf of Solace township, has granted you Vindication from the charges brought against you. In recognition of your deeds of bravery and courage as related by these witnesses, you are hereby declared a Knight of Solamnia." Lord Alfred's voices softened as he looked down upon the knight. Tears streamed unchecked down Sturm's gaunt cheeks. "You have spent the night in prayer, Sturm Brightblade," Alfred said quietly. "Do you consider yourself worthy of this great honor?"

"No, my lord," Sturm answered, according to ancient ritual, "but I most humbly accept it and vow that I shall devote my life to making myself worthy." The knight lifted his eyes to the sky. "With Paladine's help," he said softly, "I shall do so."

Lord Alfred had been through many such ceremonies, but he could not recall such fervent dedication in a man's face.

"I wish Tanis were here," Flint muttered gruffly to Laurana, who only nodded briefly.

She stood tall and straight, wearing armor specially made for her in Palanthas at Lord Gunthar's command. Her honey-colored hair streamed from beneath a silver helm. Intricate gold designs glinted on her breastplate, her soft black leather skirt—slit up the side to allow freedom of movement—brushed the tips of her boots. Her face was pale and grim, for the situation in Palanthas and in the Tower itself was dark and seemingly without hope.

She could have returned to Sancrist. She had been ordered to, in fact. Lord Gunthar had received a secret communique from Lord Alfred relating the desperate straits the knights were in, and he had sent Laurana orders to cut short her stay.

But she had chosen to remain, at least for a while. The people of Palanthas had received her politely—she was, after all, of royal blood and they were charmed with her beauty. They were also quite interested in the dragonlance and asked for one to exhibit in their museum. But when Laurana mentioned the dragonarmies, they only shrugged and smiled.

Then Laurana found out from a messenger what was happening in the High Clerist's Tower. The knights were under siege. A dragonarmy numbering in the thousands waited upon the field. The knights needed the dragonlances, Laurana decided, and there was no one but her to take the lances to the knights and teach them their use. She ignored Lord Gunthar's command to return to Sancrist.

The journey from Palanthas to the Tower was nightmarish. Laurana started out accompanying two wagons filled with meager supplies and the precious dragonlances. The first wagon bogged down in snow only a few miles outside of the city. Its contents were redistributed between the few knights riding escort, Laurana and her party, and the second wagon. It, too, foundered. Time and again they dug it out of the snow drifts until, finally, it was mired fast. Loading the food and the lances onto their horses, the knights and Laurana, Flint, and Tas walked the rest of the way. Theirs was the last group to make it through. After the storm of last night, Laurana knew, as did everyone in the Tower, no more supplies would be coming. The road to Palanthas was now impassable.

Even by strictest rationing, the knights and their footmen had food enough for only a few days. The dragonarmies seemed prepared to wait for the rest of the winter.

The dragonlances were taken from the weary horses who had borne them and, by Derek's orders, were stacked in the courtyard. A few of the knights looked at them curiously, then ignored them. The lances seemed clumsy, unwieldy weapons.

When Laurana timidly offered to instruct the knights in the use of the lances, Derek snorted in derision. Lord Alfred stared out the window at the campfires burning on the horizon. Laurana turned to Sturm to see her fears confirmed.

"Laurana," he said gently, taking her cold hand in his, "I don't think the Highlord will even bother to send dragons. If we cannot reopen the supply lines, the Tower will fall because there will be only the dead left to defend it."

So the dragonlances lay in the courtyard, unused, forgotten, their bright silver buried beneath the snow.

A KENDER'S CURIOSITY.
THE KNIGHTS RIDE FORTH.

15

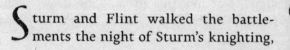

Sturm and Flint walked the battlements the night of Sturm's knighting, reminiscing.

"A well of pure silver—shining like a jewel—within the heart of the Dragon Mountain," Flint said, awe his voice. "And it was from that silver Theros forged the dragonlances."

"I should have liked—above all things—to have seen Huma's Tomb," Sturm said quietly. Staring out at the campfires on the horizon, he stopped, resting his hand on the ancient stone wall. Torchlight from a nearby window shone on his thin face.

"You will," said the dwarf. "When this is finished, we'll go back. Tas drew a map, not that it's likely to be any good—"

As he grumbled on about Tas, Flint studied his other old friend with concern. The knight's face was grave and melancholy—not unusual for Sturm. But there was something new, a calmness about him that came not from serenity, but from despair.

"We'll go there together," he continued, trying to forget about his hunger. "You and Tanis and I. And the kender, too, I suppose, plus Caramon and Raistlin. I never thought I'd miss that skinny mage, but a magic-user might be handy now. It's just as well Caramon's not here. Can you imagine the belly-aching we'd hear about missing a couple of meals?"

Sturm smiled absently, his thoughts far away. When he spoke, it was obvious he hadn't heard a word the dwarf said.

"Flint," he began, his voice soft and subdued, "we need only one day of warm weather to open the road. When that day comes, take Laurana and Tas and leave. Promise me."

"We should all leave if you ask me!" the dwarf snapped. "Pull the knights back to Palanthas. We could hold that town against even dragons, I'll wager. Its buildings are good solid stone. Not like this place!" The dwarf glanced around the human-built Tower with scorn. "Palanthas could be defended."

Sturm shook his head. "The people won't allow it. They care only for their beautiful city. As long as they think it can be saved, they won't fight. No, we must make our stand here."

"You don't have a chance," Flint argued.

"Yes, we do," Sturm replied, "if we can just hold out until the supply lines can be firmly established. We've got enough manpower. That's why the dragonarmies haven't attacked—"

"There's another way," came a voice.

Sturm and Flint turned. The torchlight fell on a gaunt face, and Sturm's expression hardened.

"What way is that, Lord Derek?" Sturm asked with deliberate politeness.

"You and Gunthar believe you have defeated me," Derek said, ignoring the question. His voice was soft and shaking with hatred as he stared at Sturm. "But you haven't! By one heroic act, I will have the Knights in my palm"—Derek held out his mailed hand, the armor flashing in the firelight—

"and you and Gunthar will be finished!" Slowly, he clenched his fist.

"I was under the impression our war was out there, with the dragonarmies," Sturm said.

"Don't give me that self-righteous twaddle!" Derek snarled. "Enjoy your knighthood, Brightblade. You paid enough for it. What did you promise the elfwoman in return for her lies? Marriage? Make a respectable woman of her?"

"I cannot fight you—according to the Measure—but I do not have to listen to you insult a woman who is as good as she is courageous," Sturm said, turning upon his heel to leave.

"Don't you ever walk away from me!" Derek cried. Leaping forward, he grabbed Sturm's shoulder. Sturm whirled in anger, his hand on his sword. Derek reached for his weapon as well, and it seemed for a moment that the Measure might be forgotten. But Flint laid a restraining hand on his friend. Sturm drew a deep breath and lifted his hand away from the hilt.

"Say what you have to say, Derek!" Sturm's voice quivered.

"You're finished, Brightblade. Tomorrow I'm leading the knights onto the field. No more skulking in this miserable rock prison. By tomorrow night, my name will be legend!"

Flint looked up at Sturm in alarm. The knight's face had drained of blood. "Derek," Sturm said softly, "you're mad! There are thousands of them! They'll cut you to ribbons!"

"Yes, that's what you'd like to see, isn't it?" Derek sneered. "Be ready at dawn, Brightblade."

That night, Tasslehoff—cold, hungry, and bored—decided that the best way to take his mind off his stomach was to explore his surroundings. There are plenty of places to hide things here, thought Tas. This is one of the strangest buildings I've ever seen.

The Tower of the High Clerist sat solidly against the west side of the Westgate Pass, the only canyon pass that crossed the Habbakuk Range of mountains separating eastern Solamnia from Palanthas. As the Dragon Highlord knew, anyone trying to reach Palanthas other than by this route would have to travel hundreds of miles around the mountains, or through the desert, or by sea. And ships entering the Gates of Paladine were easy targets for the gnomes' fire-throwing catapults.

The High Clerist's Tower had been built during the Age of Might. Flint knew a lot about the architecture of this period—the dwarves having been instrumental in designing and building most of it. But they had not built or designed this Tower. In fact, Flint wondered who had—figuring the person must have been either drunk or insane.

An outer curtain wall of stone formed an octagon as the Tower's base. Each point of the octagonal wall was surmounted by a turret. Battlements ran along the top of the curtain wall between turrets. An inner octagonal wall formed the base of a series of towers and buttresses that swept gracefully upward to the central Tower itself.

This was fairly standard design, but what puzzled the dwarf was the lack of internal defense points. Three great steel doors breached the outer wall, instead of one door—as would seem most reasonable, since three doors took an incredible number of men to defend. Each door opened into a narrow courtyard at the far end of which stood a portcullis leading directly into a huge hallway. Each of these three hallways met in the heart of the Tower itself!

"Might as well invite the enemy inside for tea!" the dwarf had grumbled. "Stupidest way to build a fortress I ever saw."

No one entered the Tower. To the knights, it was inviolate. The only one who could enter the Tower was the High Clerist himself, and since there was no High Clerist, the knights would defend the Tower walls with their lives, but not one of them could set foot in its sacred halls.

Originally the Tower had merely guarded the pass, not blocked it. But the Palanthians had later built an addition to the main structure that sealed off the pass. It was in this addition that the knights and the footmen were living. No one even thought of entering the Tower itself.

No one except Tasslehoff.

Driven by his insatiable curiosity and his gnawing hunger, the kender made his way along the top of the outer wall. The knights on guard duty eyed him warily, gripping their swords in one hand, their purses in the other. But they relaxed as soon as he passed, and Tas was able to slip down the steps and into the central courtyard.

Only shadows walked down here. No torches burned, no guard was posted. Broad steps led up to the steel portcullis. Tas padded up the stairs toward the great, yawning archway and peered eagerly through the bars. Nothing. He sighed. The darkness beyond was so intense he might have been staring into the Abyss itself.

Frustrated, he pushed up on the portcullis, more out of habit than hope, for only Caramon or ten knights would have the strength necessary to raise it.

To the kender's astonishment, the portcullis began to rise, making the most god-awful screeching! Grabbing for it, Tas dragged it slowly to a halt. The kender looked fearfully up at the battlements, expecting to see the entire garrison thundering down to capture him. But apparently the knights were listening only to the growlings of their empty stomachs.

Tas turned back to the portcullis. There was a small space open between the sharp iron spikes and the stone work, a space just big enough for a kender. Tas didn't waste any time or stop to consider the consequences. Flattening himself, he wriggled beneath the spikes.

He found himself in a large, wide hall, nearly fifty feet across. He could see just a short distance. There were old torches on the wall, however. After a few jumps, Tas reached one and lit it from Flint's tinder box he found in his pouch.

Now Tas could see the gigantic hall clearly. It ran straight ahead, right into the heart of the Tower. Strange columns ranged along either side, like jagged teeth. Peering behind one, he saw nothing but an alcove.

The hall itself was empty. Disappointed, Tas continued walking down it, hoping to find something interesting. He came to a second portcullis, already raised, much to his chagrin. "Anything easy is more trouble than it's worth," was an old kender saying. Tas walked beneath that portcullis into a second hallway, narrower than the first—only about ten feet wide—but with the same strange, toothlike columns on either side.

Why build a tower so easy to enter? Tas wondered. The outer wall was formidable, but once past that, five drunken dwarves could take this place. Tas peered up. And why so huge? The main hall was thirty feet high!

Perhaps the knights back in those days had been giants, the kender speculated with interest as he crept down the hall, peering into open doors and poking into corners.

At the end of the second hallway, he found a third portcullis. This one was different from the other two, and as strange as the rest of the Tower. This portcullis had two halves, which slid together to join in the center. Oddest of all, there was a large hole cut right through the middle of the doors!

Crawling through this hole, Tas found himself in a smaller room. Across from him stood two huge steel doors. Pushing on them casually, he was startled to find them locked. None of the portcullises had been locked. There was nothing to protect.

Well, at least here was something to keep him occupied and make him forget about his empty stomach. Climbing onto a stone bench, Tas stuck his torch into a wall sconce, then began to fumble through his pouches. He finally discovered the set of lock-picking devices that are a kender's birthright—"Why insult the door's purpose by locking it?" is a favorite kender expression.

Quickly Tas selected the proper tool and set to work. The lock was simple. There was a slight click, and Tas pocketed his tools with satisfaction as the door swung inward. The kender stood a moment, listening carefully. He could hear nothing. Peering inside, he could see nothing. Climbing up on the bench again, he retrieved his torch and crept carefully through the steel doors.

Holding his torch aloft, he found himself in a great, wide, circular room. Tas sighed. The great room was empty except for a dust-covered object that resembled an ancient fountain standing squarely in the center. This was the end of the corridor, too, for though there were two more sets of double doors leading out of the room, it was obvious to the kender that they only led back up the other two giant hallways. This was the heart of the Tower. This was the sacred place. This was what all the fuss was about.

Nothing.

Tas walked around a bit, shining his torchlight here and there. Finally the disgruntled kender went to examine the fountain in the center of the room before leaving.

As Tas drew closer, he saw it wasn't a fountain at all, but

185

the dust was so thick, he couldn't figure it out. It was about as tall as the kender, standing four feet off the ground. The round top was supported on a slender three-legged stand.

Tas inspected the object closely, then he took a deep breath and blew as hard as he could. Dust flew up his nose and he sneezed violently, nearly dropping the torch. For a moment he couldn't see a thing. Then the dust settled and he could see the object. His heart leaped into his throat.

"Oh, no!" Tas groaned. Diving into another pouch, he pulled out a handkerchief and rubbed the object. The dust came off easily, and he knew now what it was. "Drat!" he said in despair. "I was right. Now what do I do?"

The sun rose red the next morning, glimmering through a haze of smoke hovering above the dragonarmies. In the courtyard of the Tower of the High Clerist, the shadows of night had not yet lifted before activity began. One hundred knights mounted their horses, adjusted the girths, called for shields, or buckled on armor, while a thousand footmen milled around, searching for their proper places in line.

Sturm, Laurana, and Lord Alfred stood in a dark doorway, watching in silence as Lord Derek, laughing and calling out jokes to his men, rode into the courtyard. The knight was resplendent in his armor, the rose glistening on his breastplate in the first rays of the sun. His men were in good spirits, the thought of battle making them forget their hunger.

"You've got to stop this, my lord," Sturm said quietly.

"I can't!" Lord Alfred said, pulling on his gloves. His face was haggard in the morning light. He had not slept since Sturm awakened him in the waning hours of the night. "The Measure gives him the right to make this decision."

In vain had Alfred argued with Derek, trying to convince him to wait just a few more days! Already the wind was starting to shift, bringing warm breezes from the north.

But Derek had been adamant. He would ride out and challenge the dragonarmies on the field. As for being outnumbered, he laughed in scorn. Since when do goblins fight like Knights of Solamnia? The Knights had been outnumbered fifty to one in the Goblin and Ogre wars of the Vingaard Keep one hundred years ago, and they'd routed the creatures with ease!

"But you'll be fighting draconians," Sturm warned. "They are not like goblins. They are intelligent and skilled. They have magic-users among their ranks, and their weapons are the finest in Krynn. Even in death they have the power to kill—"

"I believe we can deal with them, Brightblade," Derek interrupted harshly. "And now I suggest you wake your men and tell them to make ready."

"I'm not going," Sturm said steadily. "And I'm not ordering my men to go, either."

Derek paled with fury. For a moment he could not speak, he was so angry. Even Lord Alfred appeared shocked.

"Sturm," Alfred began slowly, "do you know what you are doing?"

"Yes, my lord," Sturm answered. "We are the only thing standing between the dragonarmies and Palanthas. We dare not leave this garrison unmanned. I'm keeping my command here."

"Disobeying a direct order," Derek said, breathing heavily. "You are a witness, Lord Alfred. I'll have his *head* this time!" He stalked out. Lord Alfred, his face grim, followed, leaving Sturm alone.

In the end, Sturm had given his men a choice. They could stay with him at no risk to themselves—since they were simply obeying the orders of their commanding officer—or they could accompany Derek. It was, he mentioned, the same choice Vinas Solamnus had given his men long ago, when the Knights rebelled against the corrupt Emperor of Ergoth. The men did not need to be reminded of this legend. They saw it as a sign and, as with Solamnus, most of them chose to stay with the commander they had come to respect and admire.

Now they stood watching, their faces grim, as their friends prepared to ride out. It was the first open break in the long history of the Knighthood, and the moment was grievous.

"Reconsider, Sturm," Lord Alfred said as the knight helped him mount his horse. "Lord Derek is right. The dragonarmies have not been trained, not like the Knights. There's every probability we'll route them with barely a blow being struck."

"I pray that is true, my lord," Sturm said steadily.

Alfred regarded him sadly. "If it *is* true, Brightblade, Derek will see you tried and executed for this. There'll be nothing Gunthar can do to stop him."

"I would willingly die that death, my lord, if it would stop what I fear will happen," Sturm replied.

"Damn it, man!" Lord Alfred exploded. "If we are defeated, what will you gain by staying here? You couldn't hold off an army of gully dwarves with your small contingent of men! Suppose the roads do open up? You won't be able to hold the Tower long enough for Palanthas to send reinforcements."

"At the least we can buy Palanthas time to evacuate her citizens, if—"

Lord Derek Crownguard edged his horse between those of his men. Glaring down at Sturm, his eyes glittering from behind the slits in his helm, Lord Derek raised his hand for silence.

"According to the Measure, Sturm Brightblade," Derek began formally, "I hereby charge you with conspiracy and—"

"To the Abyss with the Measure!" Sturm snarled, his patience snapping. "Where has the Measure gotten us? Divided, jealous, crazed! Even our own people prefer to treat with the armies of our enemies! The Measure has failed!"

A deathly hush settled over the knights in the courtyard, broken only by the restless pawing of a horse or the jingle of armor as here and there a man shifted in his saddle.

"Pray for my death, Sturm Brightblade," Derek said softly, "or by the gods I'll slit your throat at your execution myself!" Without another word, he wheeled his horse around and cantered to the head of the column.

"Open the gates!" he called.

The morning sun climbed above the smoke, rising into the blue sky. The winds blew from the north, fluttering the flag flying bravely from the top of the Tower. Armor flashed. There was a clatter of swords against shields and the sound of a trumpet call as men rushed to open the thick wooden gates.

Derek raised his sword high in the air. Lifting his voice in the Knight's salute to the enemy, he galloped forward. The knights behind him picked up his ringing challenge and rode forth out onto the fields where—long ago—Huma had ridden to glorious victory. The footmen marched, their footsteps beating a tattoo upon the stone pavement. For a moment, Lord Alfred seemed about to speak to Sturm and the young knights who stood watching. But he only shook his head and rode away.

The gates swung shut behind him. The heavy iron bar was dropped down to lock them securely. The men in Sturm's command ran to the battlements to watch.

Sturm stood silently in the center of the courtyard, his gaunt face expressionless.

The young and handsome commander of the dragon-armies in the Dark Lady's absence was just waking to breakfast and the start of another boring day when a scout galloped into camp.

Commander Bakaris glared at the scout in disgust. The man was riding through camp wildly, his horse scattering cooking pots and goblins. Draconian guards leaped to their feet, shaking their fists and cursing. But the scout ignored them.

"The Highlord!" he called, sliding off his horse in front of the tent. "I must see the Highlord."

"The Highlord's gone," said the commander's aide.

"I'm in charge," snapped Bakaris. "What's your business?"

The ranger looked around quickly, not wanting to make a mistake. But there was no sign of the dread Dark Lady or the big blue dragon she rode.

"The Knights have taken the field!"

"What?" The commander's jaw sagged. "Are you certain?"

"Yes!" The scout was practically incoherent. "Saw them! Hundreds on horseback! Javelins, swords. A thousand foot."

"She was right!" Bakaris swore softly to himself in admiration. "The fools have made their mistake!"

Calling for his servants, he hurried back to his tent. "Sound the alarm," he ordered, rattling off instructions. "Have the captains here in five minutes for final orders." His hands shook in eagerness as he strapped on his armor. "And

MARGARET WEIS & TRACY HICKMAN

send the wyvern to Flotsam with word for the Highlord."

Goblin servants ran off in all directions, and soon blaring horn calls were echoing throughout the camp. The commander cast one last, quick glance at the map on his table, then left to meet with his officers.

"Too bad," he reflected coolly as he walked away. "The fight will probably be over by the time she gets the news. A pity. She would have wanted to be present at the fall of the High Clerist's Tower. Still," he reflected, "perhaps tomorrow night we'll sleep in Palanthas, she and I."

DEATH ON THE PLAINS.
TASSLEHOFF'S DISCOVERY.

16

The sun climbed high in the sky. The knights stood upon the battlements of the Tower, staring out across the plains until their eyes ached. All they could see was a great tide of black, crawling figures swarming over the fields, ready to engulf the slender spear of gleaming silver that advanced steadily to meet it.

The armies met. The knights strained to see, but a misty gray veil crept across the land. The air became tainted with a foul smell, like hot iron. The mist grew thicker, almost totally obscuring the sun.

Now they could see nothing. The Tower seemed afloat on a sea of fog. The heavy mist even deadened sound, for at first they heard the clash of weapons and the cries of the dying. But even that faded, and all was silent.

The day wore on. Laurana, pacing restlessly in her darkening chamber, lit candles that sputtered and flickered in the foul air. The kender sat with her. Looking down from her tower window, Laurana could see Sturm and Flint, standing on the battlements below her, reflected in ghostly torchlight.

A servant brought her the bit of maggoty bread and dried meat that was her ration for the day. It must be only midafternoon, she realized. Then movement down on the battlements caught her attention. She saw a man dressed in mud-splattered leather approach Sturm. A messenger, she thought. Hurriedly, she began to strap on her armor.

"Coming?" she asked Tas, thinking suddenly that the kender had been awfully quiet. "A messenger's arrived from Palanthas!"

"I guess," Tas said without interest.

Laurana frowned, hoping he wasn't growing weak from lack of food. But Tas shook his head at her concern.

"I'm all right," he mumbled. "Just this stupid gray air."

Laurana forgot about him as she hurried down the stairs.

"News?" she asked Sturm, who peered over the walls in a vain effort to see out onto the field of battle. "I saw the messenger—"

"Oh, yes." He smiled wearily. "Good news, I suppose. The road to Palanthas is open. The snow melted enough to get through. I have a rider standing by to take a message to Palanthas in case we are def—" He stopped abruptly, then drew a deep breath. "I want you to be ready to go back to Palanthas with him."

Laurana had been expecting this and her answer was prepared. But now that the time had come for her speech, she could not give it. The bitter air dried her mouth, her tongue seemed swollen. No, that wasn't it, she chided herself. She was frightened. Admit it. She *wanted* to go back to Palanthas! She wanted to get out of this grim place where death lurked in the shadows. Clenching her fist, she beat her gloved hand nervously on the stone, gathering her courage.

"I'm staying here, Sturm," she said. After pausing to get her voice under control, she continued, "I know what you're going to say, so listen to me first. You're going to need all the skilled fighters you can get. You know my worth."

Sturm nodded. What she said was true. There were few in his command more accurate with a bow. She was a trained swordsman, as well. She was battle-tested—something he couldn't say about many of the young knights under his command. So he nodded in agreement. He meant to send her away anyhow.

"I am the only one trained to use the dragonlance—"

"Flint's been trained," Sturm interrupted quietly.

Laurana fixed the dwarf with a penetrating stare.

Caught between two people he loved and admired, Flint flushed and cleared his throat. "That's true," he said huskily, "but—uh—I—must admit—er, Sturm, that I *am* a bit short."

"We've seen no sign of dragons, anyhow," Sturm said as Laurana flashed him a triumphant glance. "The reports say they're south of us, fighting for control of Thelgaard."

"But you believe the dragons are on the way, don't you?" Laurana returned.

Sturm appeared uncomfortable. "Perhaps," he muttered.

"You can't lie, Sturm, so don't start now. I'm staying. It's what Tanis would do—"

"Damn it, Laurana!" Sturm said, his face flushed. "Live your own life! You *can't* be Tanis! *I* can't be Tanis! He isn't here! We've got to face that!" The knight turned away suddenly. "He isn't here," he repeated harshly.

Flint sighed, glancing sorrowfully at Laurana. No one noticed Tasslehoff, who sat huddled miserably in a corner.

Laurana put her arm around Sturm. "I know I'm not the friend Tanis is to you, Sturm. I can never take his place. But I'll do my best to help you. That's what I meant. You don't have to treat me any differently from your knights—"

"I know, Laurana," Sturm said. Putting his arm around

195

her, he held her close. "I'm sorry I snapped at you." Sturm sighed. "And you know why I must send you away. Tanis would never forgive me if anything happened to you."

"Yes, he would," Laurana answered softly. "He would understand. He told me once that there comes a time when you've got to risk your life for something that means more than life itself. Don't you see, Sturm? If I fled to safety, leaving my friends behind, he would say he understood. But, deep inside, he wouldn't. Because it is so far from what he would do himself. Besides"—she smiled—"even if there were no Tanis in this world, I still could not leave my friends."

Sturm looked into her eyes and saw that no words of his would make any difference. Silently, he held her close. His other arm went around Flint's shoulder and drew the dwarf near.

Tasslehoff, bursting into tears, stood up and flung himself on them, sobbing wildly. They stared at him in astonishment.

"Tas, what is it?" Laurana asked, alarmed.

"It's all my fault! I broke one! Am I doomed to go around the world breaking these things?" Tas wailed incoherently.

"Calm down," Sturm said, his voice stern. He gave the kender a shake. "What are you talking about?"

"I found another one," Tas blubbered. "Down below, in a big empty chamber."

"Another what, you doorknob?" Flint said in exasperation.

"Another dragon orb!" Tas wailed.

Night settled over the Tower like a thicker, heavier fog. The knights lighted torches, but the flame only peopled the darkness with ghosts. The knights kept silent watch from the battlements, straining to hear or see something, anything. . . .

Then, when it was nearly midnight, they were startled to hear, not the victorious shouts of their comrades or the flat, blaring horns of the enemy, but the jingle of harness, the soft whinny of horses approaching the fortress.

Rushing to the edge of the battlements, the knights shone torches down into the fog. They heard the hoofbeats slowly come to a halt. Sturm stood above the gate.

"Who rides to the Tower of the High Clerist?" he called.

A single torch flared below. Laurana, staring down into the misty darkness, felt her knees grow weak and grabbed the stone wall to support herself. The knights cried out in horror.

The rider who held the flaming torch was dressed in the shining armor of an officer in the dragonarmy. He was blonde, his features handsome, cold, and cruel. He led a second horse across which were thrown two bodies—one of them headless, both bloody, mutilated.

"I have brought back your officers," the man said, his voice harsh and blaring. "One is quite dead, as you can see. The other, I believe, still lives. Or he did when I started on my journey. I hope he is still living, so that he can recount for you what took place upon the field of battle today. If you could even call it a battle."

Bathed in the glare of his own torch, the officer dismounted. He began to untie the bodies, using one hand to strip away the ropes binding them to the saddle. Then he glanced up.

"Yes, you could kill me now. I am a fine target, even in this fog. But you won't. You're Knights of Solamnia"—his sarcasm was sharp—"and your honor is your life. You wouldn't shoot an unarmed man returning the bodies of your leaders." He gave the ropes a yank. The headless body slid to the ground. The officer dragged the other body off the saddle. He tossed the torch down into the snow next to the bodies. It sizzled, then went out, and the darkness swallowed him.

"You have a surfeit of honor out there on the field," he called. The knights could hear the leather creak, his armor clang as he remounted his horse. "I'll give you until morning to surrender. When the sun rises, lower your flag. The Dragon Highlord will deal with you mercifully—"

Suddenly there was the twang of a bow, the thunk of an arrow striking into flesh, and the sound of startled swearing from below them. The knights turned around to stare in astonishment at a lone figure standing on the wall, a bow in its hand.

"I am not a knight," Laurana called out, lowering her bow. "I am Lauralanthalasa, daughter of the Qualinesti. We elves have our own code of honor and, as I'm sure you know, I can see you quite well in this darkness. I could have killed you. As it is, I believe you will have some difficulty using that arm for a long time. In fact, you may never hold a sword again."

"Take that as our answer to your Highlord," Sturm said harshly. "We will lie cold in death before we lower our flag!"

"Indeed you will!" the officer said through teeth clenched in pain. The sound of galloping hooves was lost in the darkness.

"Bring in the bodies," Sturm ordered.

Cautiously, the knights opened the gates. Several rushed out to cover the others who gently lifted the bodies and bore them inside. Then the guard retreated back into the fortress and bolted the gates behind them.

Sturm knelt in the snow beside the body of the headless knight. Lifting the man's hand, he removed a ring from the stiff, cold fingers. The knight's armor was battered and black with blood. Dropping the lifeless hand back into the snow,

Sturm bowed his head. "Lord Alfred," he said tonelessly.

"Sir," said one of the young knights, "the other is Lord Derek. The foul dragon officer was right—he is still alive."

Sturm rose and walked over to where Derek lay on the cold stone. The lord's face was white, his eyes wide and glittering feverishly. Blood caked his lips, his skin was clammy. One of the young knights supporting him, held a cup of water to his lips, but Derek could not drink.

Sick with horror, Sturm saw Derek's hand was pressed over his stomach, where his life's blood was welling out, but not fast enough to end the agonizing pain. Giving a ghastly smile, Derek clutched Sturm's arm with a bloody hand.

"Victory!" he croaked. "They ran before us and we pursued! It was glorious, glorious! And I—I will be Grand Master!" He choked and blood spewed from his mouth as he fell back into the arms of the young knight, who looked up at Sturm, his youthful face hopeful.

"Do you suppose he's right, sir? Maybe that was a ruse—" His voice died at the sight of Sturm's grim face, and he looked back at Derek with pity. "He's mad, isn't he, sir?"

"He's dying—bravely—like a true knight," Sturm said.

"Victory!" Derek whispered, then his eyes fixed in his head and he gazed sightlessly into the fog.

"No, you mustn't break it," said Laurana.

"But Fizban said—"

"I know what he said," Laurana replied impatiently. "It isn't evil, it isn't good, it's not anything, it's everything. That"—she muttered—"is so like Fizban!"

She and Tas stood in front of the dragon orb. The orb rested on its stand in the center of the round room, still covered with dust except for the spot Tas had rubbed clean. The room was dark and eerily silent, so quiet, in fact, that Tas and Laurana felt compelled to whisper.

Laurana stared at the orb, her brow creased in thought. Tas stared at Laurana unhappily, afraid he knew what she was thinking.

"These orbs have to work, Tas!" Laurana said finally. "They were created by powerful magic-users! People like Raistlin who do not tolerate failure. If only we knew how—"

"I know how," Tas said in a broken whisper.

"What?" Laurana asked. "You know! Why didn't you—"

"I didn't know I knew—so to speak," Tas stammered. "It just came to me. Gnosh—the gnome—told me that he discovered writing inside the orb, letters that swirled around in the mist. He couldn't read them, he said, because they were written in some sort of strange language—"

"The language of magic."

"Yes, that's what I said and—"

"But that won't help us! We can't either of us speak it. If only Raistlin—"

"We don't need Raistlin," Tas interrupted. "I can't speak it, but I can read it. You see, I have these glasses—glasses of true seeing, Raistlin called them. They let me read languages—even the language of magic. I know because he said if he caught me reading any of his scrolls he'd turn me into a cricket and swallow me whole."

"And you think you can read the orb?"

"I can try," Tas hedged, "but, Laurana, Sturm said there probably wouldn't be any dragons. Why should we risk even bothering with the orb? Fizban said only the most powerful magic-users dared use it."

"Listen to me, Tasslehoff Burrfoot," Laurana said softly, kneeling down beside the kender and staring him straight in the eye. "If they bring even one dragon here, we're finished. That's why they gave us time to surrender instead of just storming the place. They're using the extra time to bring in dragons. We must take this chance!"

A dark path and a light path. Tasslehoff remembered Fizban's words and hung his head. *Death of those you love, but you have the courage.*

Slowly Tas reached into the pocket of his fleecy vest, pulled out the glasses, and fit the wire frames over his pointed ears.

THE SUN RISES.
DARKNESS DESCENDS.

17

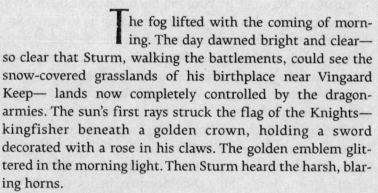

The fog lifted with the coming of morning. The day dawned bright and clear— so clear that Sturm, walking the battlements, could see the snow-covered grasslands of his birthplace near Vingaard Keep— lands now completely controlled by the dragonarmies. The sun's first rays struck the flag of the Knights— kingfisher beneath a golden crown, holding a sword decorated with a rose in his claws. The golden emblem glittered in the morning light. Then Sturm heard the harsh, blaring horns.

The dragonarmies marched upon the Tower at dawn.

The young knights—the hundred or so that were left— stood silently on the battlements watching as the vast army crawled across the land with the inexorability of devouring insects.

At first Sturm had wondered about the knight's dying words. "They ran before us!" Why had the dragonarmy run? Then it became clear to him—the dragonmen had used the knights' own vainglory against them in an ancient, yet simple, maneuver. Fall back before your enemy . . . not too fast, just let the front lines show enough fear and terror to be believable. Let them seem to break in panic. Then let your enemy charge after you, overextending his lines. And let your armies close in, surround him, and cut him to shreds.

It didn't need the sight of the bodies—barely visible in the distant trampled, bloody snow—to tell Sturm he had judged correctly. They lay where they had tried desperately to regroup for a final stand. Not that it mattered how they died. He wondered who would look on his body when it was all over.

Flint peered out from a crack in the wall. "At least I'll die on dry land," the dwarf muttered.

Sturm smiled slightly, stroking his moustaches. His eyes went to the east. As he thought about dying, he looked upon the land where he'd been born—a home he had barely known, a father he barely remembered, a country that had driven his family into exile. He was about to give his life to defend that country. Why? Why didn't he just leave and go back to Palanthas?

All of his life he had followed the Code and the Measure. The Code: *Est Sularus oth Mithas*—My Honor Is My Life. The Code was all he had left. The Measure was gone. It had failed. Rigid, inflexible, the Measure had encased the Knights in steel heavier than their armor. The Knights, isolated, fighting to survive, had clung to the Measure in despair—not realizing that it was an anchor, weighing them down.

Why was I different? Sturm wondered. But he knew the answer, even as he listened to the dwarf grumble. It was because of the dwarf, the kender, the mage, the half-elf. . . . They had taught him to see the world through other eyes: slanted eyes, smaller eyes, even hourglass eyes. Knights like Derek saw the world in stark black and white. Sturm had seen the world in all its radiant colors, in all its bleak grayness.

"It's time," he said to Flint. The two descended from the high lookout point just as the first of the enemy's poison-tipped arrows arched over the walls.

With shrieks and yells, the blaring of horns, and clashing of shield and sword, the dragonarmies struck the Tower of the High Clerist as the sun's brittle light filled the sky.

By nightfall, the flag still flew. The Tower stood.

But half its defenders were dead.

The living had no time during the day to shut the staring eyes or compose the contorted, agonized limbs. The living had all they could do to stay alive. Peace came at last with the night, as the dragonarmies withdrew to rest and wait for the morrow.

Sturm paced the battlements, his body aching with weariness. Yet every time he tried to rest, taut muscles twitched and danced, his brain seemed on fire. And so he was driven to pace again—back and forth, back and forth with slow, measured tread. He could not know that his steady pace drove the day's horrors from the thoughts of the young knights who listened. Knights in the courtyard, laying out the bodies of friends and comrades, thinking that tomorrow someone might be doing this for them, heard Sturm's steady pacing and felt their fears for tomorrow eased.

The ringing sound of the knight's footfalls brought comfort to everyone, in fact, except to the knight himself. Sturm's thoughts were dark and tormented: thoughts of defeat; thoughts of dying ignobly, without honor; tortured memories of the dream, seeing his body hacked and mutilated by the foul creatures camped beyond. Would the dream come true? he wondered, shivering. Would he falter at the end, unable to conquer fear? Would the Code fail him, as had the Measure?

Step . . . step . . . step . . . step . . .

Stop this! Sturm told himself angrily. You'll soon be mad as poor Derek. Spinning abruptly on his heel to break his stride, the knight turned to find Laurana behind him. His eyes met hers, and the black thoughts were brightened by her light. As long as such peace and beauty as hers existed in this world there was hope. He smiled at her and she smiled back—a strained smile—but it erased lines of fatigue and worry in her face.

"Rest," he told her. "You look exhausted."

"I tried to sleep," she murmured, "but I had terrible dreams—hands encased in crystal, huge dragons flying through stone hallways." She shook her head, then sat down, exhausted, in a corner sheltered from the chill wind.

Sturm's gaze moved to Tasslehoff, who lay beside her. The kender was fast asleep, curled into a ball. Sturm looked at him with a smile. Nothing bothered Tas. The kender'd had a truly glorious day, one that would live in his memory forever.

"I've never been at a siege before," Sturm had heard Tas confide to Flint just seconds before the dwarf's battle-axe swept off a goblin's head.

"You know we're all going to die," Flint growled, wiping black blood from his axe blade.

"That's what you said when we faced that black dragon in Xak Tsaroth," Tas replied. "Then you said the same thing in Thorbardin, and then there was the boat—"

"This time we're going to die!" Flint roared in a rage. "If I have to kill you myself!"

But they hadn't died—at least not today. There's always tomorrow, Sturm thought, his gaze resting on the dwarf who leaned against a stone wall, carving at a block of wood.

Flint looked up. "When will it start?" he asked.

Sturm sighed, his gaze shifting out to the eastern sky. "Dawn," he replied. "A few hours yet."

The dwarf nodded. "Can we hold?" His voice was matter-of-fact, the hand that held the wood firm and steady.

"We must," Sturm replied. "The messenger will reach Palanthas tonight. If they act at once, it's still a two-day march to reach us. We must give them two days—"

"If they act at once!" Flint grunted.

"I know . . ." Sturm said softly, sighing. "You should leave," he turned to Laurana, who came out of her reverie with a start. "Go to Palanthas. Convince them of the danger."

"Your messenger must do that," Laurana said tiredly. "If not, no words of mine will sway them."

"Laurana," he began.

"Do you need me?" she asked abruptly. "Am I of use here?"

"You know you are," Sturm answered. He had marveled at the elfmaid's unflagging strength, her courage, and her skill with the bow.

"Then I'm staying," Laurana said simply. Drawing the blanket up more closely around her, she closed her eyes. "I can't sleep," she whispered. But within a few moments, her breathing became soft and regular as the slumbering kender's.

Sturm shook his head, swallowing a choking thickness in his throat. His glance met Flint's. The dwarf sighed and went back to his carving. Neither spoke, both men thinking the same thing. Their deaths would be bad if the draconians overran the Tower. Laurana's death could be a thing of nightmares.

The eastern sky was brightening, foretelling the sun's approach, when the knights were roused from their fitful

207

slumber by the blaring of horns. Hastily they rose, grabbed their weapons, and stood to the walls, peering out across the dark land.

The campfires of the dragonarmies burned low, allowed to go out as daylight neared. They could hear the sounds of life returning to the horrible body. The knights gripped their weapons, waiting. Then they turned to each other, bewildered.

The dragonarmies were retreating! Although only dimly seen in the faint half-light, it was obvious that the black tide was slowly withdrawing. Sturm watched, puzzled. The armies moved back, just over the horizon. But they were still out there, Sturm knew. He sensed them.

Some of the younger knights began to cheer.

"Keep quiet!" Sturm commanded harshly. Their shouts grated on his raw nerves. Laurana came to stand beside him and glanced at him in astonishment. His face was gray and haggard in the flickering torchlight. His gloved fists, resting atop the battlements, clenched and unclenched nervously His eyes narrowed as he leaned forward, staring eastward.

Laurana, sensing the rising fear within him, felt her own body grow chill. She remembered what she had told Tas.

"Is it what we feared?" she asked, her hand on his arm.

"Pray we are wrong!" he spoke softly, in a broken voice.

Minutes passed. Nothing happened. Flint came to join them, clambering up on a huge slab of broken stone to see over the edge of the wall. Tas woke, yawning.

"When's breakfast?" the kender inquired cheerfully, but no one paid any attention to him.

Still they watched and waited. Now all the knights, each of them feeling the same rising fear, lined the walls, staring eastward without any clear idea why.

"What is it?" Tas whispered. Climbing up to stand beside

Flint, he saw the small red sliver of sun burning on the horizon, its orange fire turning the night sky purple, dimming the stars.

"What are we looking at?" Tas whispered, nudging Flint.

"Nothing," Flint grumbled.

"Then why are we looking—" The kender caught his breath with a sharp gulp. "Sturm—" he quavered.

"What is it?" the knight demanded, turning in alarm.

Tas kept staring. The rest followed his gaze, but their eyes were no match for the kender's.

"Dragons . . ." Tasslehoff replied. "Blue dragons."

"I thought as much," Sturm said softly. "The dragonfear. That's why they pulled the armies back. The humans fighting among them could not withstand it. How many dragons?"

"Three," answered Laurana. "I can see them now."

"Three," Sturm repeated, his voice empty, expressionless.

"Listen, Sturm—" Laurana dragged him back away from the wall. "I—we—weren't going to say anything. It might not have mattered, but it does now. Tasslehoff and I know how to use the dragon orb!"

"Dragon orb?" Sturm muttered, not really listening.

"The orb here, Sturm!" Laurana persisted, her hands clutching him eagerly. "The one below the Tower, in the very center. Tas showed it to me. Three long, wide hallways lead to it and—and—" Her voice died. Suddenly she saw vividly, as her subconscious had seen during the night, dragons flying down stone halls. . . .

"Sturm!" she shouted, shaking him in her excitement. "I know how the orb works! I know how to kill the dragons! Now, if we just have the time—"

Sturm caught hold of her, his strong hands grasping her by the shoulders. In all the months he had known her, he

209

could not recall seeing her more beautiful. Her face, pale with weariness, was alight with excitement.

"Tell me, quickly," he ordered. Laurana explained, her words falling over themselves as she painted the picture for him that became clearer to her as she talked. Flint and Tas watched from behind Sturm, the dwarf's face aghast, the kender's face filled with consternation.

"Who'll use the orb?" Sturm asked slowly.

"I will," Laurana replied.

"But, Laurana," Tasslehoff cried, "Fizban said—"

"Tas, shut up!" Laurana said through clenched teeth. "Please, Sturm!" she urged. "It's our only hope. We have the dragon-lances—and the dragon orb!"

The knight looked at her, then toward the dragons speeding out of the ever-brightening east.

"Very well," he said finally. "Flint, you and Tas go down and gather the men together in the center courtyard. Hurry!"

Tasslehoff, giving Laurana a last, troubled glance, jumped down from the rock where he and the dwarf had been standing. Flint came after him more slowly, his face somber and thoughtful. Reaching the ground, he walked up to Sturm.

Must you? Flint asked Sturm silently, as their eyes met.

Sturm nodded once. Glancing at Laurana, he smiled sadly. "I'll tell her," he said softly. "Take care of the kender. Good-bye, my friend."

Flint swallowed, shaking his old head. Then, his face a mask of sorrow, the dwarf brushed his gnarled hand across his eyes and gave Tas a shove in the back.

"Get moving!" the dwarf snapped.

Tas turned to look at him in astonishment, then shrugged and ran skipping along the top of the battlements, his shrill voice shouting out to the startled knights.

Laurana's face glowed. "You come, too, Sturm!" she said, tugging at him like a child eager to show a parent a new toy. "I'll explain this to the men if you want. Then you can give the orders and arrange the battle disposition—"

"You're in command, Laurana," Sturm said.

"What?" Laurana stopped, fear replacing the hope in her heart so suddenly the pain made her gasp.

"You said you needed time," Sturm said, adjusting his swordbelt, avoiding her eyes. "You're right. You must get the men in position. You must have time to use the orb. I will gain you that time." He picked up a bow and a quiver of arrows.

"No! Sturm!" Laurana shivered with terror. "You can't mean this! I can't command! I need you! Sturm, don't do this to yourself!" Her voice died to a whisper. "Don't do this to me!"

"You can command, Laurana," Sturm said, taking her head in his hands. Leaning forward, he kissed her gently. "Farewell, elfmaid," he said softly. "Your light will shine in this world. It is time for mine to darken. Don't grieve, dear one. Don't cry." He held her close. "The Forestmaster said to us, in Darken Wood, that we should not mourn those who have fulfilled their destiny. Mine is fulfilled. Now, hurry, Laurana. You'll need every second."

"At least take the dragonlance with you," she begged.

Sturm shook his head, his hand on the antique sword of his father. "I don't know how to use it. Good-bye, Laurana. Tell Tanis—" He stopped, then he sighed. "No," he said with a slight smile. "He will know what was in my heart."

"Sturm . . ." Laurana's tears choked her into silence. She could only stare at him in mute appeal.

"Go," he said.

Stumbling blindly, Laurana turned around and somehow

made her way down the stairs to the courtyard below. Here she felt a strong hand grasp hers.

"Flint," she began, sobbing painfully, "he, Sturm . . ."

"I know, Laurana," the dwarf replied. "I saw it in his face. I think I've seen it there for as long as I can remember. It's up to you now. You can't fail him."

Laurana drew a deep breath, then wiped her eyes with her hands, cleaning her tear-streaked face as best she could. Taking another breath, she lifted her head.

"There," she said, keeping her voice firm and steady. "I'm ready. Where's Tas?"

"Here," said a small voice.

"Go on down. You read the words in the orb once before. Read them again. Make absolutely certain you've got it right."

"Yes, Laurana." Tas gulped and ran off.

"The knights are assembled," Flint said. "Waiting your command."

"Waiting my command," Laurana repeated absently.

Hesitating, she looked up. The red rays of the sun flashed on Sturm's bright armor as the knight climbed the narrow stairs that led to a high wall near the central Tower. Sighing, she lowered her gaze to the courtyard where the knights waited.

Laurana drew another deep breath, then walked toward them, the red crest fluttering from her helmet, her golden hair flaming in the morning light.

The cold and brittle sun stained the sky blood red, deepening into the velvet blue-blackness of receding night. The Tower stood in shadow still, though the sun's rays sparkled off the golden threads in the fluttering flag.

Sturm reached the top of the wall. The Tower soared above him. The parapet Sturm stood upon extended a hundred feet or more to his left. Its stone surface was smooth, providing no shelter, no cover.

Looking east, Sturm saw the dragons.

They were blue dragons, and on the back of the lead dragon in the formation sat a Dragon Highlord, the blue-black dragon-scale armor gleaming in the sunlight. He could see the hideous horned mask, the black cape fluttering behind. Two other blue dragons with riders followed the Dragon Highlord. Sturm gave them a brief, perfunctory glance. They did not concern him. His battle was with the leader, the Highlord.

The knight looked into the courtyard far below him. Sunlight was just climbing the walls. Sturm saw it flicker red off the tips of the silver dragonlances that each man held now in his hand. He saw it burn on Laurana's golden hair. He saw the men look up at him. Grasping his sword, he raised it into the air. Sunlight flashed from the ornately carved blade.

Smiling up at him, though she could barely see him through her tears, Laurana raised her dragonlance into the air in answer—in good-bye.

Comforted by her smile, Sturm turned back to face his enemy.

Walking to the center of the wall, he seemed a small figure poised halfway between land and sky. The dragons could fly past him, or circle around him, but that wasn't what he wanted. They must see him as a threat. They must take time to fight him.

Sheathing his sword, Sturm fit an arrow to his bow and took careful aim at the lead dragon. Patiently he waited, holding his breath. I cannot waste this, he thought. Wait . . . wait . . .

The dragon was in range. Sturm's arrow sped through the morning brilliance. His aim was true. The arrow struck the blue dragon in the neck. It did little damage, bouncing off the dragon's blue scales, but the dragon reared its head in pain and irritation, slowing its flight. Quickly Sturm fired again, this time at the dragon flying directly behind the leader.

The arrow tore into a wing, and the dragon shrieked in rage. Sturm fired once more. This time the lead dragon's rider steered it clear. But the knight had accomplished what he set out to do: capture their attention, prove he was a threat, force them to fight him. He could hear the sound of running footsteps in the courtyard and the shrill squeak of the winches raising the portcullises.

Now Sturm could see the Dragon Highlord rise to his feet in the saddle. Built like a chariot, the saddle could accommodate its rider in a standing position for battle. The Highlord carried a spear in his gloved hand. Sturm dropped his bow. Picking up his shield and drawing his sword, he stood upon the wall, watching as the dragon flew closer and closer, its red eyes flaring, its white teeth gleaming.

Then—far away—Sturm heard the clear, clarion call of a trumpet, its music cold as the air from the snow-covered mountains of his homeland in the distance. Pure and crisp, the trumpet call pierced his heart, rising bravely above the darkness and death and despair that surrounded him.

Sturm answered the call with a wild battle-cry, raising his sword to meet his enemy. The sunlight flashed red on his blade. The dragon swooped in low.

Again the trumpet sounded, and again Sturm answered, his voice rising in a shout. But this time his voice faltered, for suddenly Sturm realized he had heard this trumpet before.

The dream!

Sturm stopped, gripping his sword in a hand that was sweating inside its glove. The dragon loomed above him. Astride the dragon was the Highlord, the horns of his mask flickering blood-red, his spear poised and ready.

Fear knotted Sturm's stomach, his skin grew cold. The horn call sounded a third time. It had sounded three times in the dream, and after the third call he had fallen. The dragon fear was overwhelming him. Escape! his brain screamed.

Escape! The dragons would swoop into the courtyard. The knights could not be ready yet, they would die, Laurana, Flint, and Tas. . . . The Tower would fall.

No! Sturm got hold of himself. Everything else was gone: his ideals, his hopes, his dreams. The Knighthood was collapsing. The Measure had been found wanting. Everything in his life was meaningless. His death must not be so. He would buy Laurana time, buy it with his life, since that was all he had to give. And he would die according to the Code, since that was all he had to cling to.

Raising his sword in the air, he gave the knight's salute to an enemy. To his surprise, it was returned with grave dignity by the Dragon Highlord. Then the dragon dove, its jaws open, prepared to slash the knight apart with its razor-sharp teeth. Sturm swung his sword in a vicious arc, forcing the dragon to rear its head back or risk decapitation. Sturm hoped to disrupt its flight. But the creature's wings held it steady, its rider guiding it with a sure hand while holding the gleaming-tipped spear in the other.

Sturm faced east. Half-blinded by the sun's brilliance, Sturm saw the dragon as a thing of blackness. He saw the creature dip in its flight, diving below the level of the wall, and he realized the blue was going to come up from beneath,

giving its rider the room needed to attack. The other two dragon riders held back, watching, waiting to see if their lord required help finishing this insolent knight.

For a moment the sun-drenched sky was empty, then the dragon burst up over the edge of the wall, its horrifying scream splitting Sturm's eardrums, filling his head with pain. The breath from its gaping mouth gagged him. He staggered dizzily but managed to keep his feet as he slashed out with his sword. The ancient blade struck the dragon's left nostril. Black blood spurted into the air. The dragon roared in fury.

But the blow was costly. Sturm had no time to recover.

The Dragon Highlord raised his spear, its tip flaming in the sun. Leaning down, he thrust it deep, piercing through armor, flesh, and bone.

Sturm's sun shattered.

18

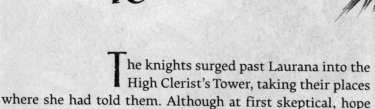

The knights surged past Laurana into the High Clerist's Tower, taking their places where she had told them. Although at first skeptical, hope dawned as Laurana explained her plan.

The courtyard was empty after the knights' departure. Laurana knew she should hurry. Already she should be with Tas, preparing herself to use the dragon orb. But Laurana could not leave that gleaming, solitary figure standing alone—waiting—upon the wall.

Then, silhouetted in the rising sun, she saw the dragons. Sword and spear flashed in the brilliant sunlight.

Laurana's world stopped turning. Time slowed to a dream. The sword drew blood. The dragon screamed. The spear held poised for an eternity. The sun stood still.

The spear struck.

A glittering object fell slowly from the top of the wall into the courtyard. The object was Sturm's sword, dropped from his lifeless hand, and it was—to Laurana—the only movement in a static world. The knight's body stood still, impaled upon the spear of the Dragon Highlord. The dragon hovered above, its wings poised. Nothing moved, everything held perfectly still.

MARGARET WEIS & TRACY HICKMAN

Then the Highlord jerked the spear free and Sturm's body crumpled where he stood, a dark mass against the sun. The dragon roared in outrage and a bolt of lightning streaked from the blue's blood-frothed mouth and struck the High Clerist's Tower. With a booming explosion, the stone burst apart. Flames flared, brighter than the sun. The other two dragons dove for the courtyard as Sturm's sword clattered to the pavement with a ringing sound.

Time began.

Laurana saw the dragons diving at her. The ground around her shook as stone and rock rained down upon her and smoke and dust filled the air. Still Laurana could not move. To move would make the tragedy real. Some inane voice kept whispering in her brain—if you stand perfectly still, this will not have happened.

But there lay the sword, only a few feet from her. And as she watched, she saw the Dragon Highlord wave the spear, signaling to the dragonarmies that waited out upon the plains, telling them to attack. Laurana heard the blaring of the horns. In her mind's eye, she could see the dragonarmies surging across the snow-covered land.

Again the ground shook beneath her feet. Laurana hesitated one instant more, bidding a silent farewell to the spirit of the knight. Then she ran forward, stumbling as the ground heaved and the air crackled with terrifying lightning blasts. Reaching down, she grabbed Sturm's sword and raised it defiantly in the air.

"*Soliasi Arath!!*" she cried in elven, her voice ringing above the sounds of destruction in challenge to the attacking dragons.

The dragon riders laughed, shouting their scornful challenges in return. The dragons shrieked in cruel enjoyment of the kill. Two dragons who had accompanied the Highlord plummeted after Laurana into the courtyard.

Laurana ran toward the huge, gaping portcullis, the entryway into the Tower that made so little sense. The stone walls were a blur as she fled past them. Behind her she could hear a dragon swooping after her. She could hear its stertorous breathing, the rush of air past its wings. She heard the dragon rider's command that stopped the dragon from following her right into the Tower. Good! Laurana smiled grimly to herself.

Running through the wide hallway, she sped swiftly past the second portcullis. Knights stood there, poised and ready to drop it.

"Keep it open!" she gasped breathlessly. "Remember!"

They nodded. She sped on. Now she was in the dark, narrower chamber where the oddly shaped, toothlike pillars slanted toward her with razor sharpness. Behind the pillars, she saw white faces beneath gleaming helms. Here and there, light sparkled on a dragonlance. The knights peered at her as she ran past.

"Get back!" she shouted. "Stay behind the pillars."

"Sturm?" one asked.

Laurana shook her head, too exhausted to talk. She ran through the third portcullis—the strange one, the one with a hole in the center. Here stood four knights, along with Flint. This was the key position. Laurana wanted someone here she could depend on. She had no time for more than an exchange of glances with the dwarf, but that was enough. Flint read the story of his friend in her face. The dwarf's head bowed for a moment, his hand covering his eyes.

Laurana ran on. Through this small room, beneath double doors made of solid steel and then into the chamber of the dragon orb.

Tasslehoff had dusted the orb with his handkerchief. Laurana could see inside it now, a faint red mist swirling with a myriad colors. The kender stood before it, staring into it, his magical glasses perched upon his small nose.

"What do I do?" Laurana gasped, out of breath.

"Laurana," Tas begged, "don't do this! I've read—if you fail to control the essence of the dragons within the orb, the dragons will come, Laurana, and take control of you!"

"Tell me what I need to do!" Laurana said firmly.

"Put your hands on the orb," Tas faltered, "and—no—wait, Laurana!"

It was too late. Laurana had already placed both slender hands upon the chill crystal globe. There was a flash of color from inside the orb, so bright Tas had to avert his eyes.

"Laurana!" he cried in his shrill voice. "Listen! You must concentrate, clear your mind of everything except bending the orb to your will! Laurana . . ."

If she heard him, she made no response, and Tas realized she was already caught up in the battle for control of the orb. Fearfully he remembered Fizban's warning, death for those you love, worse—the loss of the soul. Only dimly did he understand the dire words written in the flaming colors of the orb, but he knew enough to realize that Laurana's soul was at balance here.

In agony he watched her, longing to help—yet knowing that he did not dare do anything. Laurana stood for long moments without moving, her hands upon the orb, her face slowly draining of all life. Her eyes stared deep into the spinning, swirling colors. The kender grew dizzy looking at it and turned away, feeling sick. There was another explosion outside. Dust drifted down from the ceiling. Tas stirred uneasily. But Laurana never moved.

Her eyes closed, her head bent forward. She clutched the orb, her hands whitening from the pressure she exerted. Then she began to whimper and shake her head. "No," she moaned, and it seemed as if she were trying desperately to pull her hands away. But the orb held them fast.

Tas wondered bleakly what he should do. He longed to run up and pull her away. He wished he had broken this orb, but there was nothing he could do now. He could only stand and watch helplessly.

Laurana's body gave a convulsive shudder. Tas saw her drop to her knees, her hands still holding fast to the orb. Then Laurana shook her head angrily. Muttering unfamiliar words in elven, she fought to stand, using the orb to drag herself up. Her hands turned white with the strain and sweat trickled down her face. She was exerting every ounce of strength she possessed. With agonizing slowness, Laurana stood.

The orb flared a final time, the colors swirled together, becoming many colors and none. Then a bright, beaming, pure white light poured from the orb. Laurana stood tall and straight before it. Her face relaxed. She smiled.

And then she collapsed, unconscious, to the floor.

In the courtyard of the High Clerist's Tower, the dragons were systematically reducing the stone walls to rubble. The army was nearing the Tower, draconians in the forefront, preparing to enter through the breached walls and kill anything left alive inside. The Dragon Highlord circled above the chaos, his blue dragon's nostril black with dried blood. The Highlord supervised the destruction of the Tower. All was proceeding well when the bright daylight was pierced by a pure white light beaming out from the three huge, gaping entryways into the Tower.

The dragon riders glanced at these light beams, wondering casually what they portended. Their dragons, however, reacted differently. Lifting their heads, their eyes lost all focus. The dragons heard the call.

Captured by ancient magic-users, brought under control by an elfmaiden, the essence of the dragons held within the orb did as it was bound to do when commanded. It sent forth its irresistible call. And the dragons had no choice but to answer that call and try desperately to reach its source.

In vain the startled dragon riders tried to turn their mounts. But the dragons no longer heard the riders' commanding voices, they heard only a single voice, that of the orb. Both dragons swooped toward the inviting portcullises while their riders shouted and kicked wildly.

The white light spread beyond the Tower, touching the front ranks of the dragonarmies, and the human commanders stared as their army went mad.

The orb's call sounded clearly to dragons. But draconians, who were only part dragon, heard the call as a deafening voice shouting garbled commands. Each one heard the voice differently, each one received a different call.

Some draconians fell to their knees, clutching their heads in agony. Others turned and fled an unseen horror lurking in the Tower. Still others dropped their weapons and ran wildly, straight *toward* the Tower. Within moments an organized, well-planned attack had turned into mass confusion as a thousand draconians dashed off shrieking in a thousand directions. Seeing the major part of their force break and run, the goblins promptly fled the battlefield, while the humans stood bewildered amidst the chaos, waiting for orders that were not forthcoming.

The Dragon Highlord's own mount was barely kept in control by the Highlord's powerful force of will. But there was no stopping the other two dragons or the madness of the army. The Highlord could only fume in impotent fury, trying to determine what this white light was and where it was coming from. And—if possible—try to eradicate it.

The first blue dragon reached the first portcullis and sped inside the huge entryway, its rider ducking just in time to avoid having his head taken off by the wall. Obeying the call of the orb, the blue dragon flew easily through the wide stone halls, the tips of her wings just barely brushing the sides.

Through the second portcullis she darted, entering the chamber with the strange, toothlike pillars. Here in this second chamber she smelled human flesh and steel, but she was so in thrall to the orb she paid no attention to them. This chamber was smaller, so she was forced to pull her wings close to her body, letting momentum carry her forward.

Flint watched her coming. In all his one hundred forty-some years, he had never seen a sight like this . . . and he hoped he never would again. The dragonfear broke over the men confined in the room like a stupifying wave. The young knights, lances clutched in their shaking hands, fell back against the walls, hiding their eyes as the monstrous, blue-scaled body thundered past them.

The dwarf staggered back against the wall, his nerveless hand resting feebly on the mechanism that would slide shut the portcullis. He had never been so terrified in his life. Death would be welcome if it would end this horror. But the dragon sped on, seeking only one thing—to reach the orb. Her head glided under the strange portcullis.

Acting instinctively, knowing only that the dragon must not reach the orb, Flint released the mechanism. The portcullis closed around the dragon's neck, holding it fast. The dragon's head was now trapped within the small chamber.

Her struggling body lay helpless, wings pressed against her sides, in the chamber where the knights stood, dragonlances ready.

Too late, the dragon realized she was trapped. She howled in such fury the rocks shuddered and cracked as she opened her mouth to blast the dragon orb with her lightning breath. Tasslehoff, trying frantically to revive Laurana, found himself staring into two flaming eyes. He saw the dragon's jaws part, he heard the dragon suck in her breath.

Lightning crackled from the dragon's throat, the concussion knocking the kender flat. Rock exploded into the room and the dragon orb shuddered on its stand. Tas lay on the floor, stunned by the blast. He could not move, did not even want to move, in fact. He just lay there, waiting for the next bolt which he knew would kill Laurana—if she wasn't already dead—and him, too. At this point, he really didn't much care.

But the blast never came.

The mechanism finally activated. The double steel door slammed shut in front of the dragon's snout, sealing the creature's head inside the small room.

At first it was deathly silent. Then the most horrible scream imaginable reverberated through the chamber. It was high-pitched, shrill, wailing, bubbling in agony, as the knights lunged out of their hiding places behind the toothlike pillars and drove the silver dragonlances into the blue, writhing body of the trapped dragon.

Tas covered his ears with his hands, trying to block out the awful sound. Over and over he pictured the terrible destruction he had seen the dragons wreak on towns, the innocent people they had slaughtered. The dragon would have killed him, too, he knew—killed him without mercy. It had probably already killed Sturm. He kept reminding himself of that, trying to harden his heart.

But the kender buried his head in his hands and wept.

Then he felt a gentle hand touch him.

"Tas," whispered a voice.

"Laurana!" He raised his head. "Laurana! I'm sorry. I shouldn't care what they do to the dragon, but I can't stand it, Laurana! Why must there be killing? I can't stand it!" Tears streaked his face.

"I know," Laurana murmured, vivid memories of Sturm's death mingling with the shrieks of the dying dragon. "Don't be ashamed, Tas. Be thankful you can feel pity and horror at the death of an enemy. The day we cease to care, even for our enemies, is the day we have lost this battle."

The fearful wailing grew even louder. Tas held out his arms and Laurana gathered him close. The two clung to each other, trying to blot out the screams of the dying dragon. Then they heard another sound—the knights calling out a warning. A second dragon had entered the other chamber, slamming its rider into the wall as it struggled to enter the smaller entryway in response to the beaming call of the dragon orb. The knights were sounding the alarm.

At that moment, the Tower itself shuddered from top to foundation, shaken by the violent flailings of the tortured dragon.

"Come on!" Laurana cried. "We've got to get out of here!" Dragging Tas to his feet, she ran stumbling toward a small door in the wall that would lead them out into the courtyard. Laurana yanked open the door, just as the dragon's head burst into the room with the orb. Tas could not help stopping, just a moment, to watch. The sight was so fascinating. He could see the dragon's flaring eyes—mad with rage at the sounds of his dying mate, knowing—too late—that he had flown into the same trap. The dragon's mouth twisted into a vicious snarl, he sucked in his breath. The double steel doors dropped in front of the dragon—but only halfway.

"Laurana, the door's stuck!" Tas shouted. "The dragon orb—"

"Come on!" Laurana yanked at the kender's hand. Lightning flashed, and Tas turned and fled, hearing the room behind him explode into flame. Rock and stone filled the chamber. The white light of the dragon orb was buried in the debris as the Tower of the High Clerist collapsed on top of it.

The shock threw Laurana and Tas off balance, sending them slamming against the wall. Tas helped Laurana to her feet, and the two of them kept going, heading for the bright daylight.

Then the ground was still. The thunder of falling rock ceased. There was only a sharp crack now and again or a low rumble. Pausing a moment to catch their breath, Tas and Laurana looked behind them. The end of the passage was completely blocked, choked by the huge boulders of the Tower.

"What about the dragon orb?" Tas gasped.

"It is better destroyed."

Now that Tas could see Laurana more clearly in the daylight, he was stunned at the sight. Her face was deathly white, even her lips drained of blood. The only color was in her green eyes, and they seemed disturbingly large, shadowed by purple smudges.

"I could not use it again," she whispered, more to herself than to him. "I nearly gave up. Hands . . . I can't talk about it!" Shivering, she covered her eyes.

"Then I remembered Sturm, standing upon the wall, facing his death alone. If I gave in, his death would be meaningless. I couldn't let that happen. I couldn't let him down." She shook her head, trembling. "I forced the orb to obey my command, but I knew I could do it only once. And I can never, never go through that again!"

"Sturm's dead?" Tas's voice quavered.

Laurana looked at him, her eyes softened. "I'm sorry, Tas," she said "I didn't realize you didn't know. He—he died fighting a Dragon Highlord."

"Was it—was it . . ." Tas choked.

"Yes, it was quick," Laurana said gently. "He did not suffer long."

Tas bowed his head, then raised it again quickly as another explosion shook what was left of the fortress.

"The dragonarmies . . ." Laurana murmured. "Our fight is not ended." Her hand went to the hilt of Sturm's sword, which she had buckled around her slender waist. "Go find Flint."

Laurana emerged from the tunnel into the courtyard, blinking in the bright light, almost surprised to see it was still day. So much had happened, it seemed to her years might have passed. But the sun was just lifting over the courtyard wall.

The tall Tower of the High Clerist was gone, fallen in upon itself, a heap of stone rubble in the center of the courtyard. The entryways and halls leading to the dragon orb were not damaged, except where the dragons had smashed into them. The walls of the outer fortress still stood, although breached in places, their stone blackened by the dragons' lightning bolts.

But no armies poured through the breaches. It was quiet, Laurana realized. In the tunnels behind her, she could hear the dying screams of the second dragon, the hoarse shouts of the knights finishing the kill.

What had happened to the army? Laurana wondered, looking around in confusion. They must be coming over the walls. Fearfully she looked up at the battlements, expecting to see the fierce creatures pouring over them.

And then she saw the flash of sunlight shining on armor. She saw the shapeless mass lying on the top of the wall.

Sturm. She remembered the dream, remembered the bloody hands of the draconians hacking at Sturm's body.

It must not happen! she thought grimly. Drawing Sturm's sword, she ran across the courtyard and immediately realized the ancient weapon would be too heavy for her to wield. But what else was there? She glanced around hurriedly. The dragonlances! Dropping the sword, she grabbed one. Then, carrying the lightweight footman's lance easily, she climbed the stairs.

Laurana reached the top of the battlements and stared out across the plain, expecting to see the black tide of the army surging forward. But the plain was empty. There were only a few groups of humans standing, staring vaguely around.

What could it mean? Laurana had no idea, and she was too exhausted to think. Her wild elation died. Weariness descended on her now, as did her grief. Dragging the lance behind her, she stumbled over to Sturm's body lying in the blood-stained snow.

Laurana knelt beside the knight. Putting her hand out, she brushed back the wind-blown hair to look once more upon the face of her friend. For the first time since she had met him, Laurana saw peace in Sturm's lifeless eyes.

Lifting his cold hand, she pressed it to her cheek. "Sleep, dear friend," she murmured, "and let not your sleep be troubled by dragons." Then, as she lay the cold white hand upon the shattered armor, she saw a bright sparkle in the blood-stained snow. She picked up an object so covered with blood she could not see what it was. Carefully Laurana brushed the snow and blood away. It was a piece of jewelry. Laurana stared at it in astonishment.

But before she could wonder how it came to be here, a dark shadow fell over her. Laurana heard the creak of huge wings, the intake of breath into a gigantic body. Fearfully she leaped to her feet and whirled around.

A blue dragon landed upon the wall behind her. Stone gave way as the great claws scrabbled for a hold. The creature's great wings beat the air. From the saddle upon the dragon's back, a Dragon Highlord gazed at Laurana with cold, stern eyes from behind the hideous mask.

Laurana took a step backward as the dragonfear overcame her. The dragonlance slipped from her nerveless hand, and she dropped the jewel into the snow. Turning, she tried to flee, but she could not see where she was going. She slipped and fell into the snow to lie trembling beside Sturm's body.

In her paralyzing fear, all she could think of was the dream! Here she had died—as Sturm had died. Laurana's vision was filled with blue scales as the creature's great neck reared above her.

The dragonlance! Scrambling for it in the blood-wet snow, Laurana's fingers closed over its wooden shaft. She started to rise, intending to plunge it into the dragon's neck.

But a black boot slammed down upon the lance, narrowly missing her hand. Laurana stared at the shining black boot, decorated with gold work that gleamed in the sun. She stared at the black boot standing in Sturm's blood, and she drew a deep breath.

"Touch his body, and you will die," Laurana said softly. "Your dragon will not be able to save you. This knight was my friend, and I will not let his killer defile his body."

"I have no intention of defiling the body," the Dragon Highlord said. Moving with elaborate slowness, the Highlord reached down and gently shut the knight's eyes, which were fixed upon the sun he would see no more.

The Dragon Highlord stood up, facing the elfmaid who knelt in the snow, and removed the booted foot from the

230

dragonlance. "You see, he was my friend, too. I knew—the moment I killed him."

Laurana stared up at the Highlord. "I don't believe you," she said tiredly. "How could that be?"

Calmly, the Dragon Highlord removed the hideous horned dragon mask. "I think you might have heard of me, Lauralanthalasa. That is your name, isn't it?"

Laurana nodded dumbly, rising to her feet.

The Dragon Highlord smiled, a charming, crooked smile. "And my name is—"

"Kitiara."

"How did you know?"

"A dream . . ." Laurana murmured.

"Oh, yes—the dream." Kitiara ran her gloved hand through her dark, curly hair. "Tanis told me about the dream. I guess you all must have shared it. He thought his friends might have." The human woman glanced down at the body of Sturm, lying at her feet. "Odd, isn't it—the way Sturm's death came true? And Tanis said the dream came true for him as well: the part where I saved his life."

Laurana began to tremble. Her face, which had already been white with exhaustion, was so drained of blood it seemed transparent. "Tanis? . . . You've seen Tanis?"

"Just two days ago," Kitiara said. "I left him in Flotsam, to look after matters while I was gone."

Kitiara's cold, calm words drove through Laurana's soul like the Highlord's spear had driven through Sturm's flesh. Laurana felt the stones start to shift from under her. The sky and ground mixed, the pain cleaved her in two. She's lying, Laurana thought desperately. But she knew with despairing certainty that, though Kitiara might lie when she chose—she was not lying now.

Laurana staggered and nearly fell. Only the grim determination not to reveal any weakness before this human woman kept the elfmaiden on her feet.

Kitiara had not noticed. Stooping down, she picked up the weapon Laurana had dropped and studied it with interest.

"So this is the famed dragonlance?" Kitiara remarked.

Laurana swallowed her grief, forcing herself to speak in a steady voice. "Yes," she replied. "If you want to see what it's capable of, go look within the walls of the fortress at what's left of your dragons."

Kitiara glanced down into the courtyard briefly, without a great deal of interest. "It was not these that lured my dragons into your trap," she said, her brown eyes appraising Laurana coolly, "nor scattered my army to the four winds."

Once more Laurana glanced across the empty plains.

"Yes," Kitiara said, seeing the dawning comprehension on Laurana's face. "You have won—today. Savor your victory now, Elf, for it will be short-lived." The Dragon Highlord dexterously flipped the lance in her hand and held it aimed at Laurana's heart. The elfmaid stood unmoving before her, the delicate face empty of expression.

Kitiara smiled. With a quick motion, she reversed the killing stroke "Thank you for this weapon,"she said, standing the lance in the snow. "We've received reports of these. Now we can find out if it as formidable a weapon as you claim."

Kitiara made Laurana a slight bow from the waist. Then, replacing the dragonmask over her head, she grasped the dragonlance and turned to go. As she did, her gaze went once more to the body of the knight.

"See that he is given a knight's funeral," Kitiara said. "It will take at least three days to rebuild the army. I give you that time to prepare a ceremony befitting him."

"We will bury our own dead," Laurana said proudly. "We ask you for nothing!"

The memory of Sturm's death, the sight of the knight's body, brought Laurana back to reality like cold water poured on the face of a dreamer. Moving to stand protectively between Sturm's body and the Dragon Highlord, Laurana looked into the brown eyes, glittering behind the dragonmask.

"What will you tell Tanis?" she asked abruptly.

"Nothing," Kit said simply. "Nothing at all." Turning, she walked away.

Laurana watched the Dragon Highlord's slow, graceful walk, the black cape fluttering in the warm breeze blowing from the north. The sun glinted off the prize Kitiara held in her hand. Laurana knew she should get the lance away. There was an army of knights below. She had only to call.

But Laurana's weary brain and her body refused to act. It was an effort just to remain standing. Pride alone kept her from falling to the cold stones.

Take the dragonlance, Laurana told Kitiara silently. Much good it will do you.

Kitiara walked to the giant blue dragon. Down below, the knights had come into the courtyard, dragging with them the head of one of her blue dragons. Skie tossed his own head angrily at the sight, a savage growl rumbling deep within his chest. The knights turned their amazed faces toward the wall where they saw the dragon, the Dragon Highlord, and Laurana. More than one drew his weapon, but Laurana raised her hand to stop them. It was the last gesture she had strength to make.

Kitiara gave the knights a disdainful look and laid her hand upon Skie's neck, stroking him, reassuring him. She took her time, letting them see she was not afraid of them.

Reluctantly, the knights lowered their weapons.

Laughing scornfully, Kitiara swung herself onto the dragon. "Farewell, Lauralanthalasa," she called.

Lifting the dragonlance in the air, Kitiara commanded Skie to fly. The huge blue dragon spread his wings, rising effortlessly into the air. Guiding him skillfully, Kitiara flew just above Laurana.

The elfmaid looked up into the dragon's fiery red eyes. She saw the wounded, bloodied nostril, the gaping mouth twisted in a vicious snarl. On his back, sitting between the giant wings, was Kitiara, the dragon-scale armor glistening, the sun glinting off the horned mask. Sunlight flashed from the point of the dragonlance.

Then, glittering as it turned over and over, the dragonlance fell from the Dragon Highlord's gloved hand. Clattering on the stones, it landed at Laurana's feet.

"Keep it," Kitiara called to her in a ringing voice. "You're going to need it!"

The blue dragon lifted his wings, caught the air currents, and soared into the sky to vanish into the sun.

The Funeral

inter's night was dark and starless. The wind had become a gale, bringing driving sleet and snow that pierced armor with the sharpness of arrows, freezing blood and spirit. No watch was set. A man standing upon the battlements of the High Clerist's Tower would have frozen to death at his post.

There was no need for the watch. All day, as long as the sun shone, the knights had stared across the plains, but there was no sign of the dragonarmies' return. Even after darkness fell, the knights could see few campfires on the horizon.

On this winter's night, as the wind howled among the ruins of the crumbled Tower like the shrieks of the slaughtered dragons, the Knights of Solamnia buried their dead.

The bodies were carried into a cavelike sepulcher beneath the Tower. Long ago, it had been used for the dead of the Knighthood. But that had been in ages past, when Huma rode to glorious death upon the fields beyond. The sepulcher might have remained forgotten but for the curiosity of a kender. Once it must have been guarded and well kept, but time had touched even the dead, who are thought to be beyond time. The stone coffins were covered with a fine sifting of thick dust. When it was brushed away, nothing could be read of the writings carved into the stone.

Called the Chamber of Paladine, the sepulcher was a large rectangular room, built far below the ground where the destruction of the Tower did not affect it. A long, narrow staircase led down to it from two huge iron doors marked with the symbol of Paladine—the platinum dragon, ancient symbol of death and rebirth. The knights brought torches to light the chamber, fitting them into rusted iron sconces upon the crumbling stone walls.

The stone coffins of the ancient dead lined the walls of the room. Above each one was an iron plaque giving the name of the dead knight, his family, and the date of his death. A center aisle led between the rows of coffins toward a marble altar at the head of the room. In this central aisle of the Chamber of Paladine, the knights lay their dead.

There was no time to build coffins. All knew the dragon-armies would return. The knights must spend their time fortifying the ruined walls of the fortress, not building homes for those who no longer cared. They carried the bodies of their comrades down to the Chamber of Paladine and laid them in long rows upon the cold stone floor. The bodies were draped with ancient winding sheets which had been meant for the ceremonial wrapping. There was no time for that either. Each dead knight's sword was laid upon his breast, while some token of the enemy—an arrow perhaps, a battered shield, or the claws of a dragon—were laid at his feet.

When the bodies had been carried to the torch-lit chamber, the knights assembled. They stood among their dead, each man standing beside the body of a friend, a comrade, a brother. Then, amid a silence so profound each man could hear his own heart beating, the last three bodies were brought inside. Carried upon stretchers, they were attended by a solemn Guard of Honor.

This should have been a state funeral, resplendent with the trappings detailed by the Measure. At the altar should have stood the Grand Master, arrayed in ceremonial armor. Beside him should have been the High Clerist, clad in armor covered with the white robes of a cleric of Paladine. Here should have stood the High Justice, his armor covered by the judicial robes of black. The altar itself should have been banked with roses. Golden emblems of the kingfisher, the crown, and the sword should have been placed upon it.

But here at the altar stood only an elfmaiden, clad in armor that was dented and stained with blood. Beside her stood an old dwarf, his head bowed in grief, and a kender, his impish face ravaged by sorrow. The only rose upon the altar was a black one, found in Sturm's belt; the only ornament was a silver dragonlance, black with clotted blood.

The Guard carried the bodies to the front of the chamber and reverently laid them before the three friends.

On the right lay the body of Lord Alfred MarKenin, his mutilated, headless corpse mercifully shrouded in white linen. On the left lay Lord Derek Crownguard, his body covered with white cloth to hide the hideous grin death had frozen upon his face. In the center lay the body of Sturm Brightblade. He was not covered by a white sheet. He lay in the armor he had worn at his death: his father's armor. His father's antique sword was clasped in cold hands upon his breast. One other ornament lay upon his shattered breast, a token none of the knights recognized.

It was the Starjewel, which Laurana had found in a pool of the knight's own blood. The jewel was dark, its brilliance fading even as Laurana had held it in her hand. Many things became clear to her later, as she studied the Starjewel. This, then, was how they shared the dream in Silvanesti. Had Sturm realized its power? Did he know of the link that had been forged between himself and Alhana? No, Laurana thought sadly, he had probably not known. Nor could he realize the love it represented. No human could. Carefully she had placed it upon his breast as she thought with sorrow of the dark-haired elven woman, who must know the heart upon which the glittering Starjewel rested was stilled forever.

The Honor Guard stepped back, waiting. The assembled knights stood with heads bowed for a moment, then lifted them to face Laurana.

This should have been the time for proud speeches, for recitals of the dead knights' heroic deeds. But for a moment, all that could be heard was the wheezing sobs of the old dwarf and Tasslehoff's quiet snuffle. Laurana looked down into Sturm's peaceful face, and she could not speak.

For a moment she envied Sturm, envied him fiercely. He was beyond pain, beyond suffering, beyond loneliness. His war had been fought. He was victorious.

You left me! Laurana cried in agony. Left me to cope with this by myself! First Tanis, then Elistan, now you. I can't! I'm not strong enough! I can't let you go, Sturm. Your death was senseless, meaningless! A fraud and a sham! I won't let you go. Not quietly! Not without anger!

Laurana lifted her head, her eyes blazing in the torchlight.

"You expect a noble speech," she said, her voice cold as the air of the sepulcher. "A noble speech honoring the heroic deeds of these men who have died. Well, you won't get it. Not from me!"

The knights glanced at each other, faces dark.

"These men, who should have been united in a brotherhood forged when Krynn was young, died in bitter discord, brought about by pride, ambition, and greed. Your eyes turn to Derek Crownguard, but he was not totally to blame. You are. All of you! All of you who took sides in this reckless bid for power."

A few knights lowered their heads, some paled with shame and anger. Laurana choked with her tears. Then she felt Flint's hand slip into hers, squeezing it comfortingly. Swallowing, she drew a deep breath.

"Only one man was above this. Only one man here among you lived the Code every day of his life. And for most of those days, he was not a knight. Or rather, he was a knight where it meant the most—in spirit, in heart, not in some official list."

Reaching behind her, Laurana took the blood-stained dragonlance from the altar and raised it high over her head. And as she lifted the lance, her spirit was lifted. The wings of darkness that had hovered around her were banished. When she raised her voice, the knights stared at her in wonder. Her beauty blessed them like the beauty of a dawning spring day.

"Tomorrow I will leave this place," Laurana said softly, her luminous eyes on the dragonlance. "I will go to Palanthas. I will take with me the story of this day! I will take this lance and the head of a dragon. I will dump that sinister, bloody head upon the steps of their magnificent palace. I will stand upon the dragon's head and make them listen to me! And Palanthas will listen! They will see their danger! And then I will go to Sancrist and to Ergoth and to every other place in this world where people refuse to lay down their petty hatreds and join together. For until we conquer the evils within ourselves—as this man did—we can never conquer the great evil that threatens to engulf us!"

Laurana raised her hands and her eyes to heaven. "Paladine!" she called out, her voice ringing like the trumpet's call. "We come to you, Paladine, escorting the souls of these noble knights who died in the High Clerist's Tower. Give us who are left behind in this war-torn world the same nobility of spirit that graces this man's death!"

Laurana closed her eyes as tears spilled unheeded and unchecked down her cheeks. No longer did she grieve for Sturm. Her sorrow was for herself, for missing his presence, for having to tell Tanis of his friend's death, for having to live in this world without this noble friend by her side.

Slowly she laid the lance upon the altar. Then she knelt before it a moment, feeling Flint's arm around her shoulder and Tasslehoff's gentle touch on her hand.

As if in answer to her prayer, she heard the knights' voices rising behind her, carrying their own prayers to the great and ancient god, Paladine.

Return this man to Huma's breast:
Let him be lost in sunlight,
In the chorus of air where breath is translated;
At the sky's border receive him.

Beyond the wild, impartial skies
Have you set your lodgings,
In cantonments of stars, where the sword aspires
In an arc of yearning, where we join in singing.

Grant to him a warrior's rest.
Above our singing, above song itself,
May the ages of peace converge in a day,
May he dwell in the heart of Paladine.

And set the last spark of his eyes
In a fixed and holy place

Above words and the borrowed land too loved
As we recount the ages.

Free from the smothering clouds of war
As he once rose in infancy,
The long world possible and bright before him,
Lord Huma, deliver him.

Upon the torches of the stars
Was mapped the immaculate glory of childhood;
From that wronged and nestling country,
Lord Huma, deliver him.

Let the last surge of his breath
Perpetuate wine, the attar of flowers;
From the vanguard of love, the last to surrender,
Lord Huma, deliver him.

Take refuge in the cradling air
From the heart of the sword descending,
From the weight of battle on battle;
Lord Huma, deliver him.

Above the dreams of ravens where
His dreams first tried a rest beyond changing,
From the yearning for war and the war's ending,
Lord Huma, deliver him.

Only the hawk remembers death
In a late country; from the dusk,
From the fade of the senses, we are thankful that you,
Lord Huma, deliver him.

Then let his shade to Huma rise
Out of the body of death, of the husk unraveling;
From the lodging of mind upon nothing,
   we are thankful that you,
Lord Huma, deliver him.

Beyond the wild, impartial skies
Have you set your lodgings,
In cantonments of stars, where the sword aspires
In an arc of yearning, where we join in singing.

Return this man to Huma's breast
Beyond the wild, impartial skies;
Grant to him a warrior's rest
And set the last spark of his eyes
Free from the smothering clouds of wars
Upon the torches of the stars.
Let the last surge of his breath
Take refuge in the cradling air
Above the dreams of ravens where
Only the hawk remembers death.
Then let his shade to Huma rise
Beyond the wild, impartial skies.

The chant ended. Slowly, solemnly, the knights walked forward one by one to pay homage to the dead, each kneeling for a moment before the altar. Then the Knights of Solamnia left the Chamber of Paladine, returning to their cold beds to try and find some rest before the next day's dawning.

Laurana, Flint, and Tasslehoff stood alone beside their friend, their arms around each other, their hearts full. A chill wind whistled through the open door of the sepulcher where the Honor Guard stood, ready to seal the chamber.

"*Kharan bea Reorx*," said Flint in dwarven, wiping his gnarled and shaking hand across his eyes. "Friends meet in Reorx." Fumbling in his pouch, he took out a bit of wood, beautifully carved into the shape of a rose. Gently he laid it upon Sturm's breast, beside Alhana's Starjewel.

"Good-bye, Sturm," Tas said awkwardly. "I only have one gift that, that you would approve of. I—I don't think you'll understand. But then again, maybe you do now. Maybe you understand better than I do." Tasslehoff placed a small white feather in the knight's cold hand.

"*Quisalan elevas*," Laurana whispered in elven. "Our loves-bond eternal." She paused, unable to leave him in this darkness.

"Come, Laurana," Flint said gently. "We've said our good-byes. We must let him go. Reorx waits for him."

Laurana drew back. Silently, without looking back, the three friends climbed the narrow stairs leading from the sepulcher and walked steadfastly into the chill, stinging sleet of the bitter winter's night.

Far away from the frozen land of Solamnia, one other person said good-bye to Sturm Brightblade.

Silvanesti had not changed with the passing months. Though Lorac's nightmare was ended, and his body lay beneath the soil of his beloved country, the land still remembered Lorac's terrible dreams. The air smelled of death and decay. The trees bent and twisted in unending agony. Misshapen beasts roamed the woods, seeking an end to their tortured existence.

In vain Alhana watched from her room in the Tower of the Stars for some sign of change.

The griffons had come back—as she had known they would once the dragon was gone. She had fully intended to leave Silvanesti and return to her people on Ergoth. But the griffons carried disturbing news: war between the elves and humans.

It was a mark of the change in Alhana, a mark of her suffering these past months, that she found this news distressing. Before she met Tanis and the others, she would have accepted war between elves and humans, perhaps even welcomed it. But now she saw that this was only the work of the evil forces in the world.

She should return to her people, she knew. Perhaps she could end this insanity. But she told herself the weather was unsafe for traveling. In reality, she shrank from facing the shock and the disbelief of her people when she told them of the destruction of their land and her promise to her dying father that the elves would return and rebuild—after they had helped the humans fight the Dark Queen and her minions.

Oh, she would win. She had no doubt. But she dreaded leaving the solitude of her self-imposed exile to face the tumult of the world beyond Silvanesti.

And she dreaded—even as she longed—to see the human she loved. The knight, whose proud and noble face came to her in her dreams, whose very soul she shared through the Starjewel. Unknown to him, she stood beside him in his fight to save his honor. Unknown to him, she shared his agony and came to learn the depths of his noble spirit. Her love for him grew daily, as did her fear of loving him.

And so Alhana continually put off her departure. I will leave, she told herself, when I see some sign I may give my people, a sign of hope. Otherwise they will not come back. They will give up in despair. Day after day, she looked from her window.

But no sign came.

244

The winter nights grew longer. The darkness deepened. One evening Alhana walked upon the battlements of the Tower of the Stars. It was afternoon in Solamnia then, and— on another Tower—Sturm Brightblade faced a sky-blue dragon and a Dragon Highlord called the Dark Lady. Suddenly Alhana felt a strange and terrifying sensation—as though the world had ceased to turn. A shattering pain pierced her body, driving her to the stone below. Sobbing in fear and grief, she clutched the Starjewel she wore around her neck and watched in agony as its light flickered and died.

"So this is my sign!" she screamed bitterly, holding the darkened jewel in her hand and shaking it at the heavens. "There is no hope! There is nothing but death and despair!"

Holding the jewel so tightly that the sharp points bit into her flesh, Alhana stumbled unseeing through the darkness to her room in the Tower. From there she looked out once more upon her dying land. Then, with a shuddering sob, she closed and locked the wooden shutters of her window.

Let the world do what it will, she told herself bitterly. Let my people meet their end in their own way. Evil will prevail. There is nothing we can do to stop it. I will die here, with my father.

That night she made one final journey out into the land. Carelessly she threw a thin cape over her shoulders and headed for a grave lying beneath a twisted, tortured tree. In her hand, she held the Starjewel.

Throwing herself down upon the ground, Alhana began to dig frantically with her bare hands, scratching at the frozen ground of her father's grave with fingers that were soon raw and bleeding. She didn't care. She welcomed the pain that was so much easier to bear than the pain in her heart.

Finally, she had dug a small hole. The red moon, Lunitari, crept into the night sky, tinging the silver moon's light with

245

blood. Alhana stared at the Starjewel until she could no longer see it through her tears, then she cast it into the hole she had dug. She forced herself to quit crying. Wiping the tears from her face, she started to fill in the hole.

Then she stopped.

Her hands trembled. Hesitantly, she reached down and brushed the dirt from the Starjewel, wondering if her grief had driven her mad. No, from it came a tiny glimmer of light that grew even stronger as she watched. Alhana lifted the shimmering jewel from the grave.

"But he's dead," she said softly, staring at the jewel that sparkled in Solinari's silver light.

"I know death has claimed him. Nothing can change that. Yet, why this light—"

A sudden rustling sound startled her. Alhana fell back, fearing that the hideously deformed tree above Lorac's grave might be reaching to grasp her in its creaking branches. But as she watched she saw the limbs of the tree cease their tortured writhing. They hung motionless for an instant, then—with a sigh—turned toward the heavens. The trunk straightened and the bark became smooth and began to glisten in the silver moonlight. Blood ceased to drip from the tree. The leaves felt living sap flow once more through their veins.

Alhana gasped. Rising unsteadily to her feet, she looked around the land. But nothing else had changed. None of the other trees were different—only this one, above Lorac's grave.

I am going mad, she thought. Fearfully she turned back to look at the tree upon her father's grave. No, it was changed. Even as she watched, it grew more beautiful.

Carefully, Alhana hung the Starjewel back in its place over her heart. Then she turned and walked back toward the Tower. There was much to be done before she left for Ergoth.

The next morning, as the sun shed its pale light over the unhappy land of Silvanesti, Alhana looked out over the forest. Nothing had changed. A noxious green mist still hung low over the suffering trees. Nothing would change, she knew, until the elves came back and worked to make it change. Nothing had changed except the tree above Lorac's grave.

"Farewell, Lorac," Alhana called, "until we return."

Summoning her griffon, she climbed onto its strong back and spoke a firm word of command. The griffon spread its feathery wings and soared into the air, rising in swift spirals above the stricken land of Silvanesti. At a word from Alhana, it turned its head west and began the long flight to Ergoth.

Far below, in Silvanesti, one tree's beautiful green leaves stood out in splendid contrast to the black desolation of the forest around it. It swayed in the winter wind, singing soft music as it spread its limbs to shelter Lorac's grave from the winter's darkness, waiting for spring.

The story continues in

HOPE'S
FLAME

By Margaret Weis & Tracy Hickman

Available January 2004